HOSPITALLER

J. K. Swift

Hospitaller
Hospitaller Saga Book 3

Published by UE Publishing Co.
Vancouver, BC, Canada
Copyright© 2020 by J. K. Swift
All rights reserved.
Print Edition

Cover design by Chris Ryan, collecula
www.collecula.com

This is a work of fiction. Names, characters, places, and incidents are either products of the author's imagination or used fictitiously. Any resemblance to actual events, locales, or persons, living or dead, is entirely coincidental. No part of this publication may be reproduced or transmitted in any form or by any means, electronic or mechanical, without permission from the author.

www.jkswift.com
New Releases Mailing List
http://eepurl.com/hTAFA

BOOK DESCRIPTION

1291 A.D.

The Hospitaller Order is decimated. Acre is lost. The only home Foulques has ever known has been razed to the ground by the Mamluks. Only by the grace of God does Foulques and a handful of knights manage to escape to the island of Cyprus. Once there, Foulques learns that Najya has been taken captive by none other than Badru Hashim, the Northman. Foulques immediately attempts to organize a rescue force but his uncle has seized control of the Order of Saint John and considers the risks too high. Foulques is left with only two options: remain loyal to his uncle and the Order or forsake his oaths and strike out after Najya on his own.

For Brother Foulques de Villaret, there is but one path he can live with. Unfortunately, waiting at its end is Badru Hashim.

Hospitaller is the third book in J. K. Swift's ***Hospitaller Saga***.

*Better to walk without knowing where
than to sit doing nothing.*
—Tuareg saying

CHAPTER ONE

Najya stood on the deck of the English ship reflecting on how one's life can flip upside down faster than the single flap of a slave bee's wing. She had escaped the doomed city of Acre when most had not. The sun was warm on her skin, the sweet smell of salt water teeming with life filled her nostrils, and the gentle heaving of the planks beneath her feet lured her into a warm sense of security. She leaned forward and rested her hands on the railing, thanking God for her escape and in the same thought prayed for Foulques's welfare. In all honesty, she never expected to make it out of Acre before the Mamluks tore down its walls. Even though she offered her thanks to Allah, it was not God to whom she owed her deliverance. It was Foulques.

She had been one of hundreds, perhaps thousands, who had swarmed the docks pleading for refuge from the inevitable wrath of the city's besiegers. She, a lone Arab woman, neither rich nor clutching an infant like so many others, pleading for the masters of the last remaining ships to take on just two more souls, or at the very least one.

"Take the child! Please, take the child."

Najya heard the refrain again and again. The intensity of the cries and sheer mass of the crowd had her wondering why she had bothered to come to the docks in the first place. What right did she have to be here?

She turned back, forced against the seething wave of desperation all about her, but found her way blocked by the cold mail of a grim-faced man-at-arms. He reached out an arm as thick around as both of her legs put together and made to push her aside. But his eyes caught on something on her hand and he halted his motion in mid-air. His massive arm changed course and he seized her by her wrist, his eyes narrowing.

"Where did you get this?"

It took a moment for her mind to register his words, for they were English, a tongue she could understand better than she spoke. He gave her wrist a brisk shake, like a dog killing a rat.

"Where did you get this?" He pushed her own hand in front of her face and twisted it painfully until her eyes settled on the ring set loosely on her thumb. In the sunlight, the red stone overwhelming its center sparkled in a gaudy manner, demanding her attention. He gave her hand another shake and though she meant to speak in English, her words came out as, "Monsieur Grandison."

The English man-at-arms's grip on Najya's wrist tightened, if that were possible. He stepped past her into the crowd, pushing his way through those in front and pulled her along in his wake.

Long minutes later, she stood before a middle-aged

knight. Not squat and blocky like her escort, but lithe and lean with a weary face. Handsome due in large part to the bright eyes that peered at her with genuine curiosity.

"My name is Otto, Mademoiselle Malouf. We had almost given up on the honor of your company. Please forgive this rushed introduction but I will come find you once we are safely out of the harbor." He gave her a short bow and then whirled on his heel and began shouting orders to the sailors and soldiers around him. After he was gone, she realized he had addressed her not in English but in perfect French.

The ship was crowded to overflowing. Sir Otto de Grandison had taken on as many passengers as he dared, but Najya managed to find herself a spot on the main deck up against the railing. Her slender hands gripped the polished wood as she stared out over the water. Voices traded back and forth all around her in every language imaginable, and though she was constantly being jostled, she had never felt so alone.

As the burning city grew farther away it seemed to rob Najya's body of its heat and a chill came over her. There were a number of black dots on the water in every direction she looked. Some were easily identifiable as ships, others appeared no more than insects in the distance or debris void of any life. She stood there for a long time, watching Acre grow more and more distant. She became so cold she began to worry about the papyrus tube hanging from her neck, concealed beneath her linens. Every so often she could feel a vibration of the queen and her court and a short-lived peace would come over her. She closed her eyes to better picture the life carrying on in the tube oblivious to the madness consuming the outside world.

No one touched her, but all the same, Najya sensed a new presence at her side. She opened her eyes. They flitted from her own delicate but work-hardened hands to a much larger set which exuded grace and strength in equal measure.

"Ah, Mademoiselle Malouf. Will you not join me on the upper deck? Brother Foulques would never forgive me if I lost you after all he went through to get you on this ship." Sir Grandison stepped back and held out a hand indicating which direction to go. Najya stepped away from the railing and her position was instantly taken up by a young boy hardly tall enough to see over the ship's side. No mother stood anywhere near.

They weaved their way through clusters of people until they came to a soldier guarding the base of a short staircase leading up to the helmsman's deck. He moved aside when he saw Grandison approach. The leader of the English ascended the narrow stairs and Najya followed a step behind.

"Have you known Brother Foulques for a long time?" Grandison asked as he cleared the final step.

"Since we were children," Najya said.

They walked behind the helmsman and Grandison placed his hands on the sturdy railing there to look over the rear of the ship back toward the burning city.

"My father and his father were friends," Najya said. Then added, "of a sort."

"Ah. So you were playmates then."

Najya nodded. "His uncle took me in for a short time after my mother died. Foulques and I became very good friends." She thought she responded too quickly and had placed too much emphasis on the word "friends." The way Grandison raised an eyebrow confirmed her awkward fear. She focused on the coastline.

"I have not known him long," Grandison said. "But time is counted differently when you stand shoulder to shoulder with one in battle. I can imagine he would make a most loyal friend."

Najya considered saying more, even though the older knight was not at all pressing her further on the topic. There was an openness about Sir Grandison that invited her to unburden her thoughts. But what would she say? That she and Foulques had indeed been lovers for a brief period in their teens before he had taken up his black mantle? That they had explored an awkward and brief, but wonderful, few months together that neither one of them would ever dream of giving back? She held that thought. At least Najya knew she harbored no regrets of that time. How could she be sure Foulques felt the same?

"Was your father in the city?" Grandison asked quietly.

The coolness that took over her voice was instantaneous. "I doubt it. He is very good at avoiding situations that might be dangerous to his person."

"I am sorry. It was not my intention to pry."

Najya shook her head and let out a breath. "No, Sir Grandison. It is me who is sorry. When the topic of my father comes up I can be rude. He and I have not spoken in many years."

"I see. And the rest of your family?"

"I have a brother who is in Aleppo. He tried to get me to leave Acre earlier, but I would not listen. If not for Foulques, and you, I would still be somewhere in the middle of all that." Najya waved her arm toward the smoke spiraling up from the city. She closed her eyes to shut out the screams. She knew it was impossible to hear the suffering from this distance, but that did not stop the cries in her mind. "Or perhaps, if God willed it, I would be dead already."

"Sir Grandison," came a hoarse, gruff voice. It was the helmsman. His words were quiet, hesitant to intrude on his lord's conversation with the woman, but it carried with it an urgency that demanded both Grandison and Najya look to where he pointed. Far away, scattered among the various specks bobbing along in the sun-streaked water was one that seemed to stand a little prouder upon the horizon. It traveled on a parallel course and all of its sails were hoisted.

"They fly the sultan's colors," the helmsman said.

Grandison shielded his eyes and peered into the distance. "Are you sure it is us they want?"

"I have adjusted our bearing three times. As have they."

"The Mamluks have no warships. Who in their right mind would make an attempt on an English galley? They could not possibly know we only have a skeleton crew of soldiers on board," Grandison said.

Najya's mouth began to dry out and the sensation spread to her throat. She leaned forward and peered in the direction both men stared. The question repeated itself in her own mind. *Who would dare attack an English warship?*

There was one man who would not care how many soldiers stood against him.

"Can we outrun them?" Grandison asked, not taking his eyes from the faraway shape.

"If the winds were with us and we were not carrying triple the weight we were designed for, we would have a fair chance. But even so, that ship has some fine lines. She is fast."

Najya wanted to speak, to tell the men what she suspected. No. It was what she knew. But the dryness had turned into a poison that paralyzed her throat.

No one can outrun him, she thought.

She gripped the railing until she could no longer feel sensation in her hands. The queen in the tube hanging from her neck had been eerily quiet for some time now, and she prayed that she still lived.

For the next forty minutes, the English captain pulled out every trick in his repertoire to keep the Mamluk vessel from coming alongside, but he only succeeded in prolonging the inevitable. When the ship came close enough for Najya to make out warriors moving along its deck Grandison turned to her and said, "Perhaps it would be best if you found yourself a spot below deck."

Najya shook her head. "There are too many people in the hold already. I would much rather be in the open air when..." Her words trailed away as she sought a tactful way to express her lack of confidence in the English to hold off the Mamluks. After an uncomfortable pause, she settled for letting her sentence die as it stood.

"Then put yourself at the bottom of these steps with your back against the wall. It will afford you cover from any stray arrows."

A young man of average height with an elegantly hooked nose appeared at the stairs, where he stood and waited for Grandison to acknowledge him. He was narrow-waisted but his shoulders seemed to fill his mail and tunic well enough. In each hand he carried a longbow. The white of their sapwood backs contrasting with their amber bellies, the man-length weapons were bent with string and ready for use. One was noticeably thicker than the other.

"Are my archers in position, Gruffydd?" Grandison had reverted back to English and Najya's head hurt from the constant switching between languages. He seemed to always address his men in English, but it was obvious he took every opportunity he could to speak French.

"Aye. They await your orders, my lord." He spoke a strange form of English and Najya interpreted his words more than she really understood them.

Grandison turned back to Najya. "We may not have many archers here, but the ones I have will make those Mohammedan riffraff wish they had chosen an easier target."

"I hope so," Najya said. She looked at the man called Gruffydd. She kept thinking of him as young, but she was no older than he was and his eyes held a hardness that contrasted with his youthful appearance. Still, he was far too young to meet the Northman. They all were.

Najya was not sure why, or how, she knew it was Badru Hashim and his Mamluks that were coming for them. She had only heard stories of the Northman's ship and had never seen it firsthand. The Mamluks were not known for their sailing ability or ship build quality. But the way the galley in the distance cut through the water, her sails filled with wind and her nose unerringly turning to match the English helmsman's every attempt to leave them behind, told Najya this was no ordinary Mamluk vessel or crew.

"It is time for me to take my leave," Grandison said. "Brace yourself well when the two ships come together and I will see you soon enough." He gave a short bow and nimbly took the stairs to the main deck two at a time, holding one hand on his sword handle, tilting it to avoid making contact with the narrow stairway. He accepted the smaller of the bows from Gruffydd and the two men made their way to the rear of the ship where the other English soldiers waited.

Grandison had no more than a dozen archers at his disposal. Uncompromising, seasoned men, who had seen more than their share of battles long before their king had commanded them to accompany the Savoyard knight to the Holy Lands in a desperate attempt to relieve the Christian forces. They were a grim-looking bunch, leaning there on their long, elegant bows, the color of which reminded Najya of strong honey. All of them wore good mail, and swords or maces hung at their sides, as well.

Najya descended the stairs and linked her arm around one of the railing posts. From her vantage point she watched as the archers spread out along the aft of the ship. Beyond the English men, sitting slightly lower in the water, the Mamluk vessel gained on them steadily. Najya could now see forty or fifty men moving about on the deck. Before she could discern individual faces, she heard Grandison shout, "Loose at will!"

Whispers began to fill the air as the longbow-men heaved their strings back to their ears and released their long wooden shafts at the enemy. There was a pause before the Mamluks realized they were under attack from above, and then they scurried for cover under shields or against the sides of their vessel. After a moment of frantic motion, the Mamluks found their chosen sanctuaries. But the arrows continued to fall and men cried out as iron-tipped shafts found them behind cover. As the ships grew closer to one another, more and more men screamed as arrows found exposed legs or pierced shields to embed themselves in men's cheekbones.

Najya felt her breath catch in her chest with every Mamluk warrior who cried out. Her arm holding onto the railing began to ache. She watched Grandison loose another arrow. Beside him stood Gruffydd, and although both men bore the same weapon, there was a world of difference in their technique. The older knight was quick and efficient, demonstrating a skill with the weapon that had been achieved through long, hard hours of practice. Gruffydd, however, bent his bow and leaned into every shot with a grace one can only be born with, recognized, and nurtured. His body recreated the same fluid movement again and again. He nocked an arrow, pushed with his bow hand and pulled with the powerful muscles of his back while simultaneously lifting his bow until the bodkin point of his arrow was pointed at the sky. Then, just as he hit full draw, his bow arm would drop onto his target. The release was instant and so clean the string made hardly a sound as the arrow flew off the knuckles of his bow hand.

Though she fought it down hard, hope began to take hold of Najya. The young archer had gifts only God could imbue. Perhaps she had underestimated the English.

The enemy ship closed the remaining distance and her bow rammed into the English galley's aft hull. Instantly, grapples appeared and tied the ships together. Mamluks came swinging down from the riggings or streaming across boarding planks. The wide boards stood on small adjustable towers on the deck of the smaller ship, which allowed the planks to be raised level with the larger English galley.

The first of many conically helmeted heads began to appear on the English ship and the archers were forced to throw aside their bows and draw melee weapons. They organized around Grandison and charged the enemy as a group. Their war cries were furious and they drove into the enemy with such force Najya felt another great swell of hope. The English archers were strong and aggressive. The Mamluks began to give way to their assault, but numbers were not on the archers' side. Eventually, a small group of Mamluks formed on the English left flank and another on their right. They attacked with their curved swords and spears, and the archers, one by one, began to fall to the deck. She saw Gruffydd struck down and trampled. Only Grandison and two others remained standing, and then a spear caught the English knight in the chest. He went down on one knee, his mail pierced. The last two archers fought in place until they too were cut down.

There was a brief flurry of activity as the Mamluks forced everyone still alive on deck to their knees, sailors and passengers alike. Even children were cuffed across the head until they too got the message to take a knee or sit while the younger ones huddled in their mothers' arms and stared at the attackers with wide eyes. Two Mamluks ran chains through the hatches leading to the under-decks and secured them in place, locking in those below. Najya could hear fearful murmurs coming from the hold as the heavy chains were dragged across the exits.

All this took mere minutes, and then as suddenly as it began, it was all over. Najya was still frozen in place with her arm clutched around the railing. Somehow, she had been missed in all the action. She pressed closer against the wall, wishing she could disappear.

Movement caught her eye. Two men strode across the central boarding plank. The first was not a soldier. Set against the background of the cloudless sky, he was almost invisible with his pale blue tunic in the Turkmen style wrapped around his delicate frame. A step behind was the tallest man Najya had ever seen. He wore a short-sleeved coat of mail atop a crimson padded undercoat and a rounded helmet that bore no point. He held the smaller man's hand as he stepped off the makeshift bridge onto the deck of the English ship. The plank flexed under the giant's weight and creaked in protest when he hopped off to land lightly beside his companion. Every man within his view tipped his head to him and pressed his right fist to his heart. He walked in a slow circle and surveyed his surroundings.

His eyes came to rest on Najya and she felt the last of her strength drain from her body. Her grip around the railing with the crook of her elbow gave way and she found herself sliding down until she sat on the deck, staring over the first stair, between balusters, at the Northman.

Several years back, when a naive Foulques came to her and asked for her help in locating a man known simply as the Northman, she knew in her heart she should have refused. She had tried. In the end, the information she had obtained did nothing to help Foulques locate the elusive Mamluk slaver. But the mere act of searching for the man had somehow linked her fate to his. Even once Foulques had returned to Acre with the children, she could not help feeling that she would someday cross paths with the Northman. That feeling grew ever stronger during the long days and nights she spent at the gravely injured Foulques's bedside in the Palais des Malades. Years passed and she began to dismiss those premonitions as nothing more than a young girl's delusions during a trying time.

But now, here she was staring at the man himself. The man who had almost taken Foulques de Villaret from the world. From her.

Badru's lips parted to utter words she could not hear. He nodded his head once in her direction and two Mamluk warriors strode toward Najya. They pried her arm free of the railing and escorted her to where the other Mamluks had arranged all the survivors on their knees in front of Badru. There were perhaps a dozen sailors, another ten or fifteen refugees, mostly women and children, and only one English archer.

As the Mamluks deposited her roughly on the deck, she realized the archer was the man named Gruffydd. There were several people between Najya and the archer, so it took a moment for her to lean around them to get a good look. Gruffydd was bleeding from a scalp wound but he knelt up straight so did not seem to be too badly hurt. His attention was focused on something at deck level. Najya risked going up on one knee and saw that Gruffydd had his blood-soaked hand pressed tightly to the chest of Sir Grandison.

Najya let out a breath. The English knight lived. Thank the merciful God. But how hurt was he?

She craned her neck for a better view and saw Gruffydd do something strange. A young boy of maybe ten sat beside him. He carefully reached out and took his hand. He replaced his own bloody hand with the young boy's and pushed it firmly in place. He may have spoken a few quiet words. Then his head turned side-to-side taking in the whereabouts of the Mamluks.

Najya was sure he was going to try to overpower one and she begged him with her mind not to try such a foolish thing. Even if he managed to take a weapon from one and kill him, the retaliation of the others would be swift and violent. It was certain death. Wordlessly, Najya pleaded again with the young man.

He would have none of it.

Gruffydd eased himself to a standing position and had taken two measured strides before the first shout went up. The shout was met by another cry of alarm from another Mamluk. Gruffydd's pace picked up and after another few steps he was at the side of the ship. With no hesitation he hopped up on the railing and launched himself far off into the abyss.

Najya's breath caught in her throat as Gruffydd pushed himself as far away from the side of the ship as he could, his legs continuing to pump until he dropped out of view. The Mamluks went silent and seemed as stunned as Najya. After long seconds one of them ran to the edge of the ship and peered over its side.

"He lives! He lives!" His eyes were huge. No man of the steppes would ever dream of willingly throwing himself into the sea. That was the realm of devils and demons. The fact that this man had done so and lived spoke of an unnatural dealing with unholy forces. "Bring your bows, quickly!"

Two warriors appeared at the side of the ship. They leaned over and the first man pointed. "There!"

They nocked arrows to the strings of their wickedly curved weapons and drew them back.

"Let down."

The voice came from the left of Najya and it shook her at a primal level. Badru Hashim pushed into her field of vision and though she did not want to look at him, that was no longer her decision to make. He walked slowly toward his warriors and did not repeat nor elaborate on his command until he was at the side of the ship. However, unlike the other Mamluks already standing there, he did not peer over its side into the water.

"The English has had the courage to choose his own death. He is in Allah's world now, not ours. As God permits, he will live or he will die."

Deep in the folds of her clothing, Najya felt a frantic buzzing within the papyrus tube. And then nothing.

CHAPTER TWO

FOULQUES DE VILLARET slipped one leg over his mount's neck and slowly slid from the saddle. The ground received him with a softness that caused a stumble and reminded him he wore no mail, for he had left it back in Limassol to spare his horse. He wore sword and dagger though, for without them he felt unbalanced both in body and mind. It was a long ride to the king's palace from the Hospitaller hospice, and there were no destriers available at the stable. Foulques stroked the neck of the young gelding, his red hair darkened to almost black with sweat from the frantic pace of the trip. He had performed well and perhaps could have made the ride bearing the weight of a fully armored knight with no damage to his joints, Foulques realized. But what would have been the point? He would never be a destrier, like Donovan.

Foulques took a moment to wonder what happened to the horses in the stables of Acre. He told himself that the Mamluks would recognize their worth and take them for their own. Still, the city had been in flames when he last saw it. The Mamluk warriors would not harm the horses if they had any other choice, but Foulques had heard of imams barring the doors to stables and setting them to flame to rid the tainted animals of their unclean Christian teachings.

As a palace groom approached, Foulques pulled the horse's hair from around his eyes and gave him a last pat on the neck. "You have been born to the right stable my friend."

He surrendered the reins to the groom. "He will need water and a good rubdown."

"Of course, my lord," the groom said. He was a man of middle years and a crooked back, all of the younger stable hands having no doubt been pressed into the service of King Henry's army. Foulques thought to rebuke the man for calling him a "lord" but he simply did not have the energy. It had been a trying morning.

The grandmaster had undergone another surgery the night before. Foulques and Brother Alain had been standing outside a private room in the hospice since dawn awaiting entry to see their grandmaster. Brother Alain recited prayer after prayer, some in French, most in Latin, and a few Foulques was certain was a language of his own invention. Having studied to be a priest before joining the Hospitallers, Alain had a love of scripture that set him apart from the other Knights of Saint John, and some priests for that matter. The constant murmuring began to take its toll on Foulques. Finally, he could take it no more.

"Enough Alain. He will be fine. God will see to it and nothing you say will change things."

Alain let his hands drop to his side. "How can you possibly know?"

"I brought him back, remember? He was hurt badly, yes, but he is a strong man. Even as we carried him through Acre on a shield he was telling us to take him back to the walls. He still had more fight in him than most of us had left at that point."

"I pray you are right," Alain said. "But I spoke briefly to Rafi. There was something in his eyes that I did not like." He paused and looked at the door as though he could see right through it. "I should have been there, Foulques. Why did you not take me with you? I should have been there to fight for my city. To fight for Christendom."

Not this again, Foulques thought. He let out a breath. "I *was* there. As were most of our brethren. Our friends. And when I look at you now, I thank God you were not." His voice became almost inaudible. "No one should have been there, Alain. Not like that."

Alain nodded slowly, but said nothing. Instead, he turned back to stare through the door once again. But this time, it opened.

Hakim Rafi Baba stood there framed by the morning light from the room's single scraped-hide window. His black apron glistened like a butcher's. He put a contrastingly clean finger to his lips and nodded for the knights to enter.

Grandmaster Jean de Villiers lay on a physik's table. He was naked, save for a clean, white sheet that covered him from the waist down. His torso was wrapped in a thick bandage with not a trace of seepage from any wounds beneath. The grandmaster's skin on his arms and chest was pale but not gray and mottled like a man fighting for his life, and that fact gave Foulques hope. But then he looked at the grandmaster's face. His salt and pepper beard had turned to pure ash in a single day. His eyes, criss-crossed with red lines and moist like a drunkard's, flitted about the room and settled in the direction of the newcomers.

"Who is there?" His voice came out in a squawk and he attempted to roll toward Foulques and Alain but a firm hand from one of the nuns of the Order restrained him.

"Someone has come!"

Foulques was caught off guard by the grandmaster's strange demeanor and when he said nothing, Rafi walked to the grandmaster's side to put a reassuring hand on his arm. "Brother Foulques and Brother Alain have come to see you, master. Would you like to speak with them?"

"No! Send them away. We have no time. We must get away from this place."

Foulques finally found his voice. "We are on Cyprus, Grandmaster Villiers. We are safe here."

The grandmaster's hand shot out from his side and fumbled about until it latched onto Foulques's wrist. He pulled Foulques in and used the leverage to lift himself up on one elbow, much to the dismay of the nun trying to hold him down.

"But the city has fallen?"

"Acre, yes. Acre has fallen to the Mamluks. But we are in Cyprus, Grandmaster. We are quite safe."

"No, no, you do not understand." His strength gave out and he fell onto his back once again with a grimace. "We are not safe. How can we be?"

Foulques looked at those around him. First at Alain and then Rafi. They avoided his eyes.

Foulques put his hand on the grandmaster's and tried to disengage his grip from his wrist, but it would not give.

"Sir. A group of Templars are still in Acre. They have barricaded themselves up in their fortress and are protecting a large number of civilians. I would like your permission to use the Order's resources to mount a rescue."

"Order? The Order is finished! We cannot see to our own safety; how can we protect pilgrims? We deserve our fate. Our sins have become too heavy to bear." He continued spewing nonsense about retribution and fate, before a series of coughs racked his body.

Foulques no longer recognized the red-faced man before him. He felt a hand on his shoulder.

"Come Foulques," Rafi said. "We should let him rest."

"Yes, of course. He needs rest," Foulques said. He directed his next words to Grandmaster Villiers. "I will come and see you again soon, sir."

Foulques tried once again to untangle the older man's grip from his wrist but he summoned a sudden burst of strength and pulled Foulques close. "No, wait. I must tell you something."

Foulques leaned down until he could smell the sour breath of a man who had gone without food or water for too long. The grandmaster's bloodshot eyes caught his own and drew him in even closer. His voice became steady, but little more than a whisper.

"God has forsaken us," he said.

His hand opened from around Foulques's wrist and he fell back upon the table to stare at the ceiling. Foulques stumbled back and Alain had to put a hand in the center of his back to steady him as he made the sign of the cross with his other.

"Enough," Rafi said, stepping between Foulques and the grandmaster. "He must rest. All of you, out."

Captured and held in place by those recent memories, Foulques stood in the street in front of the palace for a long time after the groom had led his horse away. People passed by on all sides, jostling him, but he hardly noticed until someone tugged at his left hand. He looked down to see an old woman before him on her knees. White, wild hair poked out from every side of her head covering.

"Please, lord. A moment of your time."

The desperate need with which she clutched his hand reminded him of the way Grandmaster Villiers had held onto him. Foulques fought down the urge to shake the old woman away, but he was a Knight of the Order of Saint John.

"What can I do for you, grandmother?"

She pointed at the white cross on his chest. "You came from the city?"

Foulques felt his mouth set in a hard line. "If you mean Acre, then yes, I did."

Emboldened by the fact that Foulques had acknowledged her and not pulled his hand from her own, words began to flow from her like a grassland spring oozing up around a horse's hoof.

"I came across days ago on an early ship, but my boy was held back for the wall. City watch came and led him away. Said he would meet me here when the fighting was over. The ships have stopped coming in and still I have not found him. Have you seen him, good lord? Are there still more ships to come? The man at the harbor said no more will come. How can that be?"

Foulques recognized that glimmer in her eyes. A dancing madness threatening to take over. He squeezed her hand back.

"I am sorry. I do not know what fate befell your son. The man at the harbor was right. There will be no more ships."

The spark of madness lit a bundle of something within. "But you are here. A soldier of the cross. You have God's favor, perhaps you can bring him back for me? Can you do that, sir? He is tall with hair the color of cinnamon."

"I would like nothing more," Foulques said shaking his head. "But what you ask is beyond me. It is beyond anyone now. Seek solace in your faith and in God. That is what we must all do."

She threw his hand away from her own. "You call yourself a man of God? Why are you here and my boy is not? This was your fight, not ours. You were supposed to protect him!"

Foulques forced himself to hold her gaze. As mad as it was, there was still a mother grieving the loss of a son in there somewhere. "God forgive me, I tried. We all tried."

She jabbed him in the chest with her bony fingers. "What use are you and your kind? You bring nothing but misery." She poked him again and spit near his feet. Then she spun and thrashed her way through the crowd. He watched her go until the last of her spiky hair disappeared in the crowd.

Eventually, he uprooted his feet and pressed on toward the palace.

FOULQUES WAS ONE of a dozen people standing in the high-ceilinged antechamber. The tapestries on the walls and the carpets underfoot gave the small room a muted feeling, so different than the clamoring streets outside. Spoken words, which were few, died out soon after they were uttered. Everyone who had made it into this room had convinced the king's secretary that they had legitimate business with his majesty, and their minds were preoccupied with what they would say to the monarch when their few moments came. Those words must count. With the fall of Acre, the demands on the king's time had never been so great. It was unlikely that one would ever secure a second audience with the ruler of the Kingdom of Jerusalem.

At what point did a kingdom cease to exist? Foulques scanned the nervous faces around him. Most were too preoccupied with their own thoughts to notice him. Every person there was a refugee from Acre. Most were high-ranking nobles, a few were tradesmen or merchants. Martin Mason, the builder, was there, as was Kas the Jew, the master baker. Henry's kingdom, whatever it was to be called in the future, would have need of men such as these. Unlike a knight of an order sworn to protect Christians venturing along the path to Jerusalem. At what point would the need for such a man cease to exist?

A hand on his arm pulled him from his thoughts. "Brother Foulques de Villaret. Your king will see you now."

He followed the king's secretary into the same room where he had first met King Henry not even a year ago. The world was a different place then, as was the man who stood before him.

King Henry had aged ten years in that time, but for all the troubles carved into his young face, he exuded an unyielding strength that Foulques had not noticed in their previous encounter.

"Brother Foulques. I am relieved you are well."

Foulques did his best to perform what he hoped was a courtly bow. "Thank you, Your Majesty. I too am glad to see you looking so healthful despite the trying times."

"Yes, it is a strange thing. The falling sickness has left me alone for months now. I am not sure if it is due to the ridiculous foods the hakim of your order has me eating or if it is simply due to the stresses of ruling a kingdom perched on the threshold of annihilation."

"As long as the disease is held at bay, I suppose it does not matter," Foulques said.

"Perhaps. But I would gladly trade one for the other."

He turned from Foulques and walked behind his plain, very non-regal desk. He dropped into his chair, pushed a scattering of parchments into a pile on one side opening up a spot immediately in front of him. He interlaced his fingers and fixed his eyes on Foulques. "Still, Hakim Baba is a good man and I am grateful that you have made him available to me. Now, my time is short, I am sorry. What would you have of the crown? I warn you, though. It is strained to near breaking."

Foulques cleared his throat. "There is a contingent of Templars barricaded in their fortress in Acre. I have been told they have many citizens taking refuge with them as well."

King Henry gave one curt nod. "I know this."

"It is only a matter of time before the Mamluks break through their defenses. I wish to lead a rescue mission. The fortress has its own harbor. If we approach by sea we can use it to ferry most of those trapped to safety."

"You do not require my permission to attempt this."

"I need soldiers. Fifty men should suffice."

King Henry sat back in his chair and raised an eyebrow. "What of your own Hospitallers?"

"Grandmaster Villiers will not give me permission to use any Hospitaller sergeants. As you may have heard, he was wounded in Acre and even now fights for his life. I am afraid he is not thinking clearly."

King Henry wasted no time in shaking his head. "Impossible. I simply do not have the men to spare. Have you not looked to the streets? Cyprus is teeming with starving refugees and mercenaries who are used to taking what they need. Cyprus is threatening to throw me and I am holding on to her with a rotten bridle. Fifty soldiers? I dare not give you one."

"If we could rescue those in the Templar fortress, our ranks would be bolstered," Foulques said.

"As would the mouths we have to feed."

Foulques knew he should hold his tongue. The king had rendered his decision. But his thoughts became words too quickly. "There are innocents trapped there with the Templars. They thought it a fortress protected by God, a refuge. Not a crypt."

King Henry's mouth hardened into a grim line. "You think I do not know that? Brother Foulques, you see the world with blinders shielding you from everything except what your morality has set its eyes upon. A king cannot do this. What if the Mamluks chose to attack us here? Or God forbid, the Mongols should set their sights on our island? We are in no position to offer even a bread crumb of aid."

"The Mamluks have no fleet," Foulques said. "With some time to regroup, and reinforcements from the Christian world, we could—"

King Henry slammed his palm on the desk and stood. He came around its side until he was face-to-face with the Hospitaller. Foulques watched him rein in the fire in his eyes. When he spoke he seemed to have regained control, but there still remained a dangerous simmer just below the surface.

"What do you think is happening here, Brother Foulques? Do you see the loss of Acre as a mere setback to Frankish holdings in the Levant? Could you be so naive? How many Hospitaller Knights survived the siege?"

"We have almost a hundred soldiers at the barracks near

Limassol."

"I said knights, Brother Foulques. Those boys you call soldiers will be nothing more than a drain on your finances. Like the Templars, it is the knights who fund your order. You surrendered your holdings to the Order when you joined, if you had any. Perhaps your parents donated a pittance to the cause as well. Other than that, your funding comes from grateful nobles who died in your hospices. Perhaps the odd one who managed to survive, as well, but in my experience the living tend to be much less generous than the dead."

"My parents contributed nothing," Foulques said. *Nothing but me.*

Foulques had but one memory of his mother and it came unbidden whenever anyone mentioned her. It was not even a true memory. It was one that had been planted within his mind by his uncle years after her death. When Foulques was nine or ten, he had asked his uncle how his mother had died: "Desert raiders killed your father and mother for drinking their water and for refusing to renounce Jesus. But you survived because, with her last bit of God-given strength, your mother crawled under a bush and sheltered you from the sun and the pagans with her own body."

"How many, Brother Foulques?"

"Your Grace?"

"How many Hospitaller knights yet live?"

With a hard edge to his voice, Foulques answered the king. "Seven."

He had arrived at that number earlier that morning. He

had tried to ban his mind from working on that question but as of late his thoughts were often uncontrollable. In truth, that was not exactly the question his mind wrestled with. It was the faces of the dead that he could not stop seeing. The real question was: how many of his brethren had perished?

King Henry blinked. He took a step back. "I am sorry. I was insensitive. Even a Hospitaller Knight, especially a Hospitaller Knight, should be granted the right to grieve. You have earned that much."

"There will be a proper time to grieve, Your Grace."

King Henry crossed his arms. "I have news to relay. Your uncle is expected to arrive tomorrow."

"My uncle?" Foulques's dead heart began beating once again. "Does he bring reinforcements?"

"Not enough to make a difference."

"Even a single man can sway a battle."

King Henry's eyes softened and even though Foulques was at least ten years his senior, the king looked at him like he was a young man caught up in the idealism of youth. He placed a slender hand on Foulques's shoulder and the Hospitaller flinched like it was a hot steel freshly removed from glowing coals. When the king spoke his voice was quiet and calm.

"I know it is early, but have you given any thought to what you will do next?"

"Next?"

"My source says that your uncle has come to restructure the Order of Saint John and refocus its energies on its hospitals in France. I suspect that once that happens, it will have little need of men with your talents."

Those words shook Foulques like he had just been hit in the chest by Brother Jimmy's hammer. "I... I have heard nothing of the sort."

"A king has more ears than most. Outremer is lost. Your hospitals and all your holdings in the holy land are lost. Knights and sergeants are not needed to protect something that no longer exists."

Foulques shook his head. "We will take them back. We will rebuild our forces and petition the pope for a new crusade. In time, others will take up the cross."

The king lowered his eyes and removed his hand from Foulques's shoulder. He walked back to his desk and lowered himself into his chair. His movements were not those of a young man.

"I like you Foulques, and this is why I want to be as honest with you as I can. Mark my words. The era of the Templars and Hospitallers is coming to an end. The Holy Orders will receive little support, if any, from Frankish lands. Without financial support and fresh recruits, your order will shrivel and die. You may limp along for a few more years on coffers and reputation, but eventually, even the Jewish moneylenders will turn their backs on you."

Foulques shifted his weight from foot to foot and then forced himself to stand erect. His hand fumbled at his side to find comfort on the pommel of his sword, but he remembered that he had been relieved of his weapons by the Cypriot knights outside. Instead, he clasped his hands together behind his back and stared straight ahead at a point far above the king's head.

"You have served your order faithfully, Brother Foulques, but it may be time to consider relinquishing your vows. No one will hold you to them now. There is still a way you can make use of your God-given talents. Join my knights. I will start you out as a captain of my guard and how far you go beyond that will be up to you, and God of course."

It took some time for the king's words to sink in. The holy land without the holy military orders was impossible to imagine. But why? There was certainly a time when they did not exist. Albeit, that was almost two hundred years ago.

"I did not imagine my offer would still your tongue so completely. Take some time to think about it. You will always be welcome in my service."

"Thank you, Your Grace. That is a generous offer and I will consider it carefully."

"I expect nothing less from you. Now, the day is short and my tasks are many. If you will excuse me?" From his chair he reached beside him for a long tasseled rope of linen that hung from the ceiling and gave it a brisk tug.

"Your Grace, there is one other thing if I may?"

The door opened and Henry's secretary started to come through. The king held up his hand and the man froze, silhouetted in the frame.

"Go on."

"Is Sir Grandison in the palace somewhere? I would like to have a word with him."

Henry shook his head. "He is not. Two of his ships are

here, I am told, but Grandison has not yet arrived on Cyprus. If you find him, ask him to come see me immediately. We have matters to discuss."

A chill went through Foulques. Grandison should have been here two days ago, along with Najya. He knew they escaped the city before the worst of the fighting, so what could have happened? His imagination began to run wild.

Foulques felt a hand on his arm. The king's secretary gestured toward the door. The next thing he knew, Foulques found himself outside the palace grounds, standing on the street. He could not remember if he had bowed to the king before he had left or not.

CHAPTER THREE

NAJYA WAS ALMOST the last to come out of the hold and when she emerged onto the deck of the Wyvern she did so on unsteady legs, like a chick breaking free from its shell. She paused to let her eyes adjust to the mid-afternoon sun, but a firm hand on her shoulder spun her around and pushed her in the direction of where the rest of the captives were lined up, waiting their turn to cross the gangway leading to the docks of Acre. She had traveled far, but in the end had gotten nowhere.

She took a few steps forward and stopped. She watched as two Mamluks carried the inert form of Sir Grandison out of the hold roped to a plank. He was the only wounded man on board, for the leader of the English forces had value. The other archers that had been fortunate enough to survive the attack only lived long enough to have their throats methodically slit by the Mamluks and were then tossed overboard like night soil.

The two men exited the hold and deposited Grandison on the deck. Though unconscious, he let out a groan and Najya saw fresh blood on the makeshift bandage she had wrapped around his chest. She threaded through the Mamluks and knelt at Grandison's side. A hand immediately grabbed her shoulder but she twisted away, fixing the man with a venomous glare.

"His bandage needs replacing," she said.

"We will take him to our hakim once we are in the city. Get back in line."

"And will your surgeon understand him when he wakes? This man only speaks the language of the English Isles. Do you?" She caught the eyes of each man around her. "Do any of you? I did not think so. I speak it fluently so you would be wise to let me stay at his side and tend to him." She had gambled that neither one of the Mamluks knew Grandison was actually a native French speaker, a language much more common within the ruling class of the Mamluks.

Two of the men looked toward one. He nodded. "Get the woman some fresh cloth and let her check his dressing. When she is done, bring them both to the emir."

"As you say, Safir." Each man put his hand over the left side of his chest and gave a short bow, which he held until the higher ranking Mamluk left.

Najya wasted no time in checking on Grandison. His breathing was strong but he had lost a lot of blood. She loosened the bandage and peeked beneath it. The wound did not look good. When the Mamluk returned with a clean wad of cloth, she did the best she could.

When she was done, the two men picked up Grandison and told her to follow. They headed toward the bow of the ship and as they came around the main mast, Najya saw two men standing over at least a dozen bodies arranged in two straight lines and covered with cloaks or blankets. Though he had his back to her, even from this distance she recognized the imposing form of Badru Hashim. Facing her and Grandison's porters was the Mamluk from earlier, Safir. The Northman did not turn around even as his men dropped Grandison in front of Safir. Badru continued to look out over the smoldering city as everyone stood in silence. The wind shifted direction, ash began to fall all around them, and still no one moved.

When Badru Hashim finally turned, Najya had to fight back a gasp. He looked nothing like the man she had seen only a day before. Her first thought was that he too had been wounded and was dying from poisoned blood. His face had taken on a tinge as gray as his eyes, which now were dull and rimmed in red, completely devoid of the sharp and ruthless intelligence she had seen when he had spotted her hiding behind the staircase in that moment of terror not so long ago. Something had happened.

"This is the woman. She claims to speak the English tongue," Safir said.

Badru gave Grandison a glance and then his eyes slowly traveled upward until they settled on Najya. She felt him looking through her, rather than at her, and the feeling made her want to shift her weight so she was not in his direct line of sight.

"Send them both to the red tent," Badru said. His words were slow and uninterested. He started to turn away.

"Do you not even want to know how he is?" Najya said.

Badru's head snapped around and he looked at her like he was seeing her for the first time. His eyes narrowed.

"Who are you?" he asked.

Najya was suddenly frightened and wished she had resisted the urge to speak. She shook her head. "No one," she said.

"You are Muslim?"

"Yes."

"Are you his slave? Do you let him use you?"

Najya's heart began to pound in her chest. She shook her head. "No. No, I am a free woman."

"Not anymore," Badru said.

"What will you do with us?"

Badru shrugged. "You are the sultan's property now, not mine. I imagine he will be sold back to his people, if he lives." He continued to stare at her. "Will he live?"

"I need honey," Najya said.

"Honey." That one word seemed to reach out and hit Badru like a thick, unseen tree branch.

"For his wound. Even with it I am not sure if he will live or die."

Badru turned away. "Safir."

"Yes, my emir?"

"Get the woman some honey."

Safir looked at Najya and the timing was unfortunate, for at that exact moment, the papyrus tube she had kept concealed beneath her robes shifted. Reflexively, she reached for it and Safir's perceptive eyes caught her intention. With Badru's back to Najya, the Mamluk must have thought she was reaching for a weapon.

Safir let out a howl and pounced on Najya. He threw her to the ground and pinned her there with his shin across her neck. She gasped for breath as he reached inside her robe and pulled out the papyrus tube, holding it high in the air.

"Hashishi!"

Najya was close to blacking out but Safir knew his trade well. He applied just enough pressure to control her but not so much that she would lose consciousness.

Badru plucked the tube from Safir's outstretched hand. He gave it a shake and then popped out its cork. Keeping it a safe distance away he looked inside. A frown crossed his face as he bent down and dumped its contents onto the deck in front of Najya. The queen lay there motionless on its back. Then, with a great sense of relief, Najya saw life fill the bee's little body and she flipped over onto her legs.

"What is this?" Badru motioned for Safir to let the pressure off Najya's neck so she could speak. He removed his shin but kept her pinned with his knee in the center of her chest. She could barely speak.

"I am a chandler," Najya said. "I keep bees."

It was Safir's turn to frown now. He was probably trying to decide if he had just saved his emir from certain death or made a fool of himself. Badru, however, no longer looked confused. His face was calm and composed.

He stretched out his hand, coaxed the bee to climb onto his finger, and held her up to his face. He then used his thumbnail to carefully separate her head from her body and then flicked the head away. He turned his hand upside down and let the queen's body float to the deck.

"Not anymore," he said.

"No!" Najya pushed Safir's knee to the side and slipped out from under him. She rolled onto her hands and knees and swept the bee's body toward her with one hand. Maybe he had not done what she thought he had. She invoked God's name again and again in her mind. But there was the headless queen. She closed her eyes. "Why would you do such a thing?" But she knew why. He was the Northman and all the stories were true. He was a monster.

Faster than a cobra, Badru reached down and grabbed Najya's jaw between his thumb and fingers and jerked her to her feet. She cried out in pain and surprise. He released her with a shove once she was standing, but if not for Safir catching her from behind, she would surely have fallen back to the deck.

Badru leveled his fingers down at her face. "Life is a fleeting gift. A gift that can be taken away by God, but more often than not, it is man who will steal it. You would do well to remember this."

He turned his back on her. "You will have your honey. Make sure the English does not die."

Then the Northman walked away, leaving a dying knight on the ground and Najya in the arms of one of his Mamluks. And all the while, black ash continued to fall from a clear blue sky.

CHAPTER FOUR

THE MOMENT GUILLAUME de Villaret stepped off the dock and put his foot on bare soil, he lowered himself to his knees one leg at a time. As he crossed himself and bent his forehead to kiss the ground, two men almost collided with one another behind him on the narrow gangway. Unconcerned with those who followed, Guillaume kissed a cross he had hanging around his neck and prostrated himself once more, and then, with his hands clasped in front of his face, he began to pray. All the while, porters and other men began to accumulate on the dock behind him. When he was done, Guillaume raised himself to his feet and let his eyes settle on Foulques standing only ten yards in front of him.

He crossed the distance with long strides, his heavy, black mantle flowing behind him. New crosses, flashing brilliant white in the sun, stood out on one shoulder of his mantle and on the chest of his black tunic beneath. He wore no armor but had a curved blade strapped to his side. Rumor had it he had almost been killed in a duel with a Saracen as a young man and he had then thrown himself into learning everything he could about swords of Turk and Mongol origin. Eventually, he abandoned straight swords forever going so far as to give his own knightly blade, and family heirloom, to Foulques on the day he was knighted.

The lines that had always creased his forehead had grown in number and his beard was much grayer than the last time Foulques saw him. But that was to be expected, for it was almost eight years ago.

"Foulques." Guillaume put his hand on Foulques's shoulder. "You look good, my boy." He kissed him on either cheek.

"You too, Uncle. Your arrival is most timely." As he said it, a sense of relief flooded through him. Guillaume had never been the warmest man but there was no one who would ever argue against his efficiency. Years ago he had given up his life in the east to go back to France and fight a campaign of another kind. He kept the Hospitaller estates in Europe in line, and made sure they kept contributing to the war efforts in Outremer. In terms of procuring resources, no man had contributed more to the Hospitaller cause in the Kingdom of Jerusalem than Guillaume de Villaret. If anyone could find a way out of their current predicament, it was him.

"How does Jean fare?"

Foulques chose his words carefully. "The grandmaster is doing as well as can be expected."

His uncle patted Foulques on the shoulder. "I will go see him soon. But first I would like to get settled." He turned and beckoned to two men who stood behind him.

"Gentlemen, come meet my nephew. Sir Laurens and Sir Beauvais, may I present to you Admiral Foulques de Villaret."

Both men bowed and Sir Laurens, a tall man with a wide jaw and hooded eyes, said, "Admiral? I was not aware the Hospitallers had a naval force."

"Oh, but we do, Sir Laurens," Guillaume said. "Unfortunately, it is comprised of a few orphans from the alps who have never seen an ocean and led by a man more ferocious than any other on land, but who cannot take a bath without losing three days of food in the process. Or have you finally grown out of your sickness of the seas, Foulques?"

Foulques forced a smile at the jest. "It has lessened, somewhat."

"Do not let it bother you, Brother Foulques," Sir Laurens said. "Not everyone can have the constitution of a peasant fisherman. I suppose that is why God did not make you one."

"Come, lords. We still have a short ride to endure before we can rest. Will you escort us to our lodgings, Foulques?"

"Of course, Uncle." He glanced over Guillaume's shoulder at the men unloading cargo from the ship. "I do not see many soldiers," he said.

"Soldiers? The time for soldiers has passed, Foulques." He gestured to the knights beside him. "Our future lies with men such as Sir Laurens and Sir Beauvais and the other great families of France. Ones who still believe in what the Order has to offer. But enough. I will explain all in good time. Although my voyage was not as difficult as it may have been for you, it was still tiring, as you can imagine. Take us home."

Foulques bowed and did as he was bid.

✠

MUCH LATER THAT same day, three hours after the sun had dropped from the sky, Foulques and Vignolo picked their way through the labyrinthine streets leading to the main docks of Cyprus. The flood of refugees made their task easier and more difficult at the same time. Small cooking fires at every turn lit their way well, but many of the footpaths were blocked by the huddled forms of men, women, and children who had carved themselves out some semblance of a shelter right there in the middle of the street.

"Do you know where you are going?" Foulques asked. He followed Vignolo as he stepped around a woman sitting on the cobbled street holding a young child. They huddled together under a ratty cloak suspended above their heads on two forked sticks.

"Not a drinking establishment in the Levant that I cannot find."

"I am sure you cannot remember the location of many," Foulques said, "but I doubt there are any you have not patronized."

"Not entirely true. I can think of several that have barred my entry, for one reason or another."

They continued on in silence for a time until Vignolo asked, "And… how did it go?"

"How did what go?"

"The joyous reunion with your uncle, of course. And you damn well knew what I meant."

"No reason to blaspheme."

"Life itself is a reason to blaspheme."

After a pause, Foulques said, "It went well enough, I suppose. Once he accepted the manor house was nothing of the sort he was accustomed to. 'We have fallen far,' were his exact words. Thankfully, I had the foresight to prepare my own room for him. That appeased him somewhat."

"You did? Where will you sleep?"

"I prepared a pallet for myself in the Schwyzers' barracks."

"No offense, Foulques, but what does your uncle expect? He walked these streets when he got off his ship. He probably saw that same toothless hag with the burned child we saw minutes ago. These are trying times and he should be thankful for whatever he gets."

"It pleases me you should think so," Foulques said.

Vignolo stopped walking. "Nothing pleases you. What do you truly mean?"

"I gave your room in the manor to the two knights who accompanied my uncle."

"What?"

"They are French nobles. I could not put them in soldier barracks."

"Unlike me, for I assume that is where I will be spending my restless nights? Amongst the rats, and worse, the Schwyzer sergeants?

"I set you up with a pallet right next to mine. Not quite

as high up off the ground, mind you. We must all maintain appearances."

"What about all my possessions?"

"I had Thomas and Pirmin remove them to the stables. They were dismayed at how many sets of clothing you possess."

Vignolo groaned. "The stables, Foulques? Really?"

Foulques stretched out his arm, motioning for Vignolo to carry on and lead the way. The Genoan shook his head and trudged on, continuing to mumble something about how German speakers were the worst snorers. They pressed on through the fire-lit streets.

Foulques could not stop thinking about how old his uncle had looked. Vignolo was right about one thing. These were trying times for them all. He could not imagine the pressure his uncle must be under. But he was a resourceful man and there was no one more capable in the Order of Saint John to see them all through these dark days. Foulques was thankful he was here. But who were the knights that followed his every step? They were fighting men, strong of build and sharp-eyed, and their clothing and arms confirmed they had come from well-to-do families.

"Ah! Here we are," Vignolo said. He pointed through the darkness at a squat building so old the dust and grime of the city had begun to accumulate around its edges, making it look like its stone walls had been dug two feet into the earth. A rectangular sign, unreadable in the near darkness, hung above the open doorway from which light and the sound of raucous voices spilled into the street.

Foulques was mildly surprised when Vignolo unhesitatingly ducked into the doorway first without deferring to the Hospitaller knight. Vignolo had an uncanny ability to sense dangerous situations, so apparently, this was a place he had no qualms about entering. It was all Foulques could do, however, to push through the sour stench of sweat and poor quality ale that accosted him at the threshold. The room was dimly lit with lanterns that hung from the low ceiling. The light they gave off would have been much brighter save for their filthy glass covers and the clouds of tiny fruit flies swirling around them. No one gave the newcomers a second glance even though Foulques wore his black Hospitaller tunic over full armor. The smoky room seemed to hold more whores than men, but that may have been because no sooner had Foulques stopped moving than a woman ran her hand along his mantle at the shoulder and pretended to admire the weave.

"Sorry sister," Vignolo said, grabbing Foulques by his other arm. Your charms will not work on my eunuch friend."

"I cater to Venetians as well," she said, fixing Vignolo with a lecherous smile. "In fact, I prefer them."

"Oh, I bet you do," Vignolo said. "I will be sure to send the next one I see your way."

He pulled Foulques deeper into the room and pointed at six men leaning against a wall. They were Franks, but their fair skin and lack of facial hair on five of the six marked them as English. All were armed with daggers or swords, but no one wore the English king's livery.

"Hello mates," Vignolo said. He took a second to look them over while they eyed him with suspicion.

"We know you?" a short, thick-chested man with a scraggly beard said, his hand straying to rest easily on his dagger.

When Foulques joined Vignolo at his side, the looks turned less hostile but remained wary.

"Any man that spent twelve hours bobbing around in salt water on a hot day before getting fished out would look like that," Vignolo said. He stuck his finger in the face of a young man immediately in front of him. The man's face and head were completely red with sunburn, except for the flaky patches on his forehead and nose where the skin had peeled away to reveal new growth. His hand flew to his sword but Foulques stepped in.

"He is not accusing you of anything. We have questions only," he said in the best English he could muster, which was not saying much.

"I recognize you," the bearded man said. "You were on the walls."

"You are Sir Grandison's men?" Foulques asked.

"Aye. We were," the sunburned man said. "Not sure whose men we are now."

The bearded man turned to him. "We are Longshanks's men! Always been!" He gave the red man a casual shove on the shoulder causing him to grimace in pain. "Oh, sorry mate."

Foulques waited until the man's face beat back the discomfort. "You are the man called Gruffydd Blood, then?"

"Aye. Famous, I suppose I am now."

"Is Sir Grandison dead, then?" Foulques asked.

"As good as, the last I saw him."

"Did you see an Arab woman on board?"

"Saw lots of them. That was our problem, we had nothing but women and children on board. Not enough soldiers."

"This one was different. Maybe you saw her talking to Sir Grandison. He would have looked after her for she had his ring."

Gruffydd's eyes flickered.

"You saw her?" Foulques asked.

Gruffydd nodded. "I think I did. He was talking to her just before that giant camel herder rammed into us."

"Giant." Foulques's voice came out in a whisper.

The man kept talking. "None of us were too worried. Sure we were outnumbered, but that is nothing new. And we had an endless supply of arrows. We figured we would set up and pick them off one by one as they tried to board. But I have never seen a ship that quick, and when they hit, those camel monkeys were on us so fast I thought they were stowaways. I was told the Mamluks did not know how to fight at sea. They are supposed to be afraid of water."

Foulques turned slowly to look at Vignolo. The Genoan avoided his stare. Apparently he could understand English just as well as Foulques.

"Their captain. You said he was a big man."

"No, Hospitaller. I said giant."

Foulques did his best to keep his voice from cracking.

"And the Arab woman? What happened to her?"

"She was alive when I decided it was time to leave. I saw them drag her from her hiding spot. Was she somebody important?"

Foulques washed his hands over his face and down his beard. They shook. *Was she somebody important.* He felt bile rise to the back of his throat.

Foulques beckoned to a woman with a large jug walking by. "Mademoiselle."

She stopped. "You serious?"

"Fill these men's drinks. Vignolo here will see you with payment."

"And bring two more cups," the Genoan said.

CHAPTER FIVE

"Do you think it can be done?"

Guillaume de Villaret stood next to one corner of the desk in Foulques's old room in the Hospitaller manor house. Dressed in his nightshirt, and with the room lit by only a single oil lamp sputtering away on the opposite corner of the desk, the man still managed to give off an impressive aura of spirit, if not physicality. He was formed from sharp angles and lacked the thick, sturdy build that Foulques possessed, but for a man of sixty-some years he was extremely fit. Like Foulques, he had piercing blue eyes, but his dark hair was now shot through with an abundance of gray. The last time Foulques had seen him in the Levant, that gray had not existed.

"I do," Foulques said, nodding. "We take my galley and the merchantman. We leave the galley anchored in deep water and use the merchantman to ferry the Templars and those who have sought refuge with them to the galley. All told, there cannot be more than seventy or eighty people holed up in the fortress. We will be in and out before the Mamluks are any the wiser." Foulques took a deep breath and watched his uncle's mind work over the problem. Guillaume leaned back against the desk and ran his hand through his long beard.

"And what of Sir Grandison?"

"Once the Templars are rescued, my men will use the galley to bring them back here. Myself and a small contingent of men, volunteers of course, will continue on with the merchantman. We will make landfall in the morning and send an emissary to the sultan to negotiate Sir Grandison's release."

"And if they take him to Cairo?"

"We will follow. A small group of men should be able to go unnoticed trailing behind an army."

Guillaume de Villaret rubbed at his eyes with the thumb and fingers of one hand. "And how does the Malouf girl work into your plans?"

Foulques let out the half-breath he had been holding the entire time he had been explaining his plan. "I do not have the details worked out yet, but I am confident we can find out which markets will be dealing in Muslim slaves."

Guillaume shook his head. "And you will go to those markets in hope of buying her back? That is your plan?"

Foulques looked down at the beaten wood planks at his feet. It was not much of a strategy. He knew that well enough. He also knew he did not have much time. The Mamluks would glut the local slave markets with Christians immediately. But since the Quran forbade a Muslim from owning another Muslim as a slave, the Muslim prisoners would have to be handled with more tact. They would have to "willingly" sign contracts of servitude, or be discreetly sold to Christian slavers, or even married off. There were as many ways to make a free person a slave as there were stars in the midnight sky.

"I do not have all the details sorted," Foulques said. "But you know I cannot let Najya be condemned to a life of slavery. Or worse."

His uncle stared at him for a long moment, like when Foulques was a child and he was trying to discern the true nature of his thoughts. "You have kept in contact with Najya for all these years?"

The question caught Foulques off guard. "Of course, Uncle."

Guillaume pushed himself off the desk and without taking his eyes from Foulques's own, he stepped forward and put a hand on his shoulder.

"My boy, you need to be honest with me or I cannot help you. You understand that, do you not?"

"I… do," Foulques said.

"Have you transgressed the boundaries of your vows?"

Foulques said nothing as he tried to interpret exactly what his uncle was getting at.

"Know this, Foulques. I will always be there to help you. Like when you were a young boy. Was I not the one who was there to pick you up when you fell? Who looked after you when your father died?"

"Yes. Yes, of course Uncle. But what—"

"A transgression is not the same as a sin. It is not easy for us to keep to all our vows all of the time. That is why the

Order has a strict set of rules for how to discipline a brother who has strayed down the wrong path."

Understanding dawned on Foulques like a blind man's sight returning after fifty years. "Are you accusing Najya of…"

Guillaume nodded. "Women are the source of the ultimate sin, Foulques. You cannot—"

Foulques jerked his shoulder, throwing his uncle's hand away. "Stop it! You have no right to speak of her that way. And no, I have not broken my vows. Do not ever ask me this again."

His uncle backed away, back to his perch on the corner of the desk. He kept looking at Foulques with that same, cold stare, burrowing into his mind and sorting through his innermost thoughts.

"Do not ever ask me that again," Foulques repeated.

"Very well, Foulques. I believe you. I just wanted you to know that there is nothing you cannot tell me. The future of the Order balances on the edge of a cliff and it is you and I who are holding onto it with a frayed rope. We must stand together to get through this."

Foulques willed the beating of his heart to slow back to an almost normal pace. "Of course, Uncle. I understand. Then back to the matter at hand."

"It is late Foulques. Decisions like this are best not made in the dead of night after being roused from a warm bed. We will discuss it first thing in the morning."

"But time is of the essence. We must—"

"We must do nothing. Being men of faith means accepting patience in all our tasks. We will chose our actions carefully after considerable thought. Now go get some rest. You are going to need it in the days to come. We all are."

✠

FOULQUES STEPPED OUT of the chapel into the early morning light. He had suffered a fitful sleep after leaving his uncle the night before. The prayers of prime had done little to clear his head and he was having a difficult time exercising patience as his uncle had suggested. The chapel was only large enough to accommodate thirty or forty people at a time, so there was a group of sergeants waiting to enter as he and his group exited. Brother Alain was at his side.

"What is this?" Alain asked, pointing ahead. Four Cypriot knights sat atop destriers. One of them held the reins of another smaller horse. It was saddled and ready to go.

"Brother Foulques?" one of the knights asked the two Hospitallers as they approached.

"I am. What brings the king's guard here?"

"His Majesty has requested a meeting with you in all due haste."

"Has something happened? Is the king unwell?"

The Cypriot knight held out the reins of the spare horse. "I presume nothing, for that is not for me to say."

"Shall I go with you?" Alain asked Foulques.

"King Henry sent only the one horse. We cannot wait," the knight said.

Foulques bent to retrieve the sword he had put in the weapon rack outside the chapel and wrapped it around himself. He wore only his black robe with a small white cross stitched on one shoulder.

"No, Alain. Stay here and prepare for tonight's meeting. I will be back before then. Perhaps check in on my uncle and see if he needs anything."

"Of course, Foulques. Godspeed."

On the ride to the palace Foulques did not press the knights any further on what they knew or did not know about the king's request. They were soldiers sent to do a task. They were fulfilling the role God had chosen for them in this life. Nothing more, nothing less.

They entered the palace grounds through the lesser used east gate, the guard there waving them through without question. But instead of continuing on to the palace itself, the knights led Foulques around the inner grounds to the Tower of Jonas. That was not its name in any official capacity, but simply one that commoners and guards alike had come to know it as. For the tower housed the gaols of Cyprus, its executioners, its torturers. Like the belly of the whale, few who entered ever came out.

"The king is here?" Foulques asked as he and the knights dismounted.

"Yes. He is waiting with someone he wants you to meet."

"Oh?" Had he captured someone who knew something about Grandison or Najya?

One of the knights pointed at Foulques's sword. He unbuckled his weapon and relinquished it, then he and the others gave the same knight the leads of their horses. Foulques and his three escorts entered the guard room on the ground floor of the tower.

The gloom was immediate and barely held at bay with several wall-mounted lanterns. A rush of air from outside pushed past Foulques to his right and stirred the dust on a winding stairway leading to the upper floors. To the left was another set of stairs leading down and that was where the Cypriot knights led Foulques.

They descended past two landings, each giving Foulques a glimpse of a low-ceilinged hallway with a series of cells stretching along its length. The sounds of human movement and misery could be heard clearly at each intersection. As they climbed down farther into the belly of the beast, the sounds from its denizens grew softer, more subdued, but the smells did not. When they left the stairs and stepped into the hallway at the third landing, the acrid stench of lantern tallow mixed with the odor of human excrement was overpowering. Foulques gagged and covered his mouth and nose with his hand. He was thankful he had not had time to break his fast that morning.

They went to the end of the hallway, passing cell after cell with heavy timber doors and grated peepholes. Sounds came from some of them, but many were empty, or the poor souls they housed simply had nothing left to say. They stopped in front of the last door and one of the knights fumbled with its latch.

Foulques, still holding his hand over his face, looked around. *Where were all the guards?* He had not seen a single one since they entered the tower. Something was not right.

"Where is the king?" Foulques asked.

"He is with a special prisoner," one of the guards said.

"And who might that be?"

"You," the knight said, his mouth twitching.

Foulques punched him in the face before his insidious grin was fully realized. Caught unawares, he went down hard.

Foulques whirled searching out the other two and at the same time reached to his belt for his rondel. Of course it was not there. In his haste, he had left it on the weapons rack outside of the Hospitaller chapel. The knight, or whoever he was, closest to Foulques had almost cleared his sword from his scabbard. He was a short bear of a man and over his shoulder Foulques caught a glimpse of the exit to the stairs. He leapt forward and seized his wrist with both hands to stop him from freeing his blade. Even using both hands it was a struggle to hold his wrist because the man's full-length mail made it even thicker than it already was. Foulques leaned in close and used his head. Twice to the bridge of the man's nose. Blood sprayed freely on the second hit and Foulques jammed his hand down, sheathing his sword in its entirety.

He contemplated trying to take the knight's sword and using it against him, but he quickly thought better of it. He was strong and although half blinded by his own blood it would be a wrestling match Foulques was not sure he could win. Especially since there was another man coming on strong with the glint of steel leading the way. Foulques threw an elbow across the stocky man's face for good measure, released him completely, and dove at the ground. He tucked into a roll in the direction of the door, not entirely sure where the swordsman was, but trusting his instincts which told him he had to be very near. Foulques rolled to his feet and kept his momentum going to help him break into a dead run. He did not bother checking over his shoulder, for he was confident, unarmored as he was, he would be able to outrun the knight chasing him.

A nasally voice erupted behind him. "Get that shit—he broke my nose!"

If I get my hands on a blade that will be the least of your worries, Foulques thought. He had no idea who these men were, or what they wanted, but now was not the time to find out.

He rounded the corner of the stairwell ready to take them two at a time, but a blinding flash erupted in his field of vision. He had been hit in the head enough times to know what had happened, but it was the details of the matter he lacked. A splitting pain in the center of his forehead and cold stone beneath his fingers began to paint a picture in his mind. He was on the ground. A hand grabbed him by the hair from behind and hauled him to his feet. He struggled, fighting against the darkness more than his attackers. His vision cleared around the edges, enough to reveal the fourth knight, the one who had been left holding the horses, standing before him. The point of his sword was leveled at Foulques's chest. A thick arm wrapped around his neck and tightened. Foulques thrashed and tried to get his chin down into the crook of his attacker's elbow, but the man hauled back on his hair once again and tightened his grip.

"You shit bucket," came the nasally voice again.

"Do not kill him!" the fourth man said.

"Pox on that."

Those were the last words Foulques heard before the darkness dragged him down and enveloped him completely.

CHAPTER SIX

Foulques came to with his heart beating like the wings of a humming bird and a burning need to gulp down long deep breaths. He raised his hand to his throbbing forehead only to be rewarded with a heavy, metallic rattle. His right hand was cuffed with iron and tethered to a long chain.

He opened and closed his eyes several times to try and clear the blackness. It hardly helped for he realized he was in a darkened room, the only relief for which was a rectangle of reddish-orange light broken up by bars along the top of a stout door.

He tested the cuff around his wrist, the cold iron digging into his skin, and followed the chain for a few feet to where it terminated in a large metal hoop embedded in the stone wall. He moved as far away as he could and pulled on the chain with both hands until his head pounded. On the cold stone floor at his feet, several open cuffs attached to more chains, splayed out toward the walls like the legs of a spider. At the bases of the opposite walls, two dark shapes lay crumpled on the ground. One of them stirred and began to sit upright slowly, ever so slowly, like a wraith rising from a crypt.

"No sense struggling." His voice was clear, cheery even. "Those chains are pinned good. I should know. Was an iron tradesman out there at one time. Even linked a few chains just like these." He paused, and his next thought was spoken to himself more than Foulques. "Though… if I had known then what I do now, I would not have done my work so well."

Foulques could not make out the subtleties of the man's features in the low light, but his voice was that of a younger man. Either the room's natural acoustic properties were very good or else Foulques's hearing was enhanced and had stepped up to help out with tasks his eyes could no longer perform.

"Who are you?" Foulques asked.

"Hermes. You?"

"My name is Foulques. How long have you been here?"

He perceived the man's shrug more than saw it. "Hard to know for certain. Forty-seven meals of bread and water, well forty-nine if you count the two of his I have eaten." His chain sang out as he raised his arm to point at the prone form still lying on the other side of the room.

"Is he dead?" Foulques asked.

Hermes said nothing. He may or may not have nodded. "Did you kill him?" Foulques asked.

The man laughed. It was a forced, humorless sound that echoed around the room.

"No, not him."

"Why have the guards not removed him?"

"Because I have not told them he is dead. And you better not either. I can suffer sleeping next to a dead man easier than I can my stomach gnawing my backbone."

"It is not right," Foulques said. "He needs to be buried. I do not suppose anyone heard his confession?"

The man made that robust, forced laugh of his again. "His kind do not get buried. He will get thrown onto a pile with the others and lit afire at week's end."

"What did he do?"

A shrug in the darkness. "He came in here with no tongue. I kept asking him and he kept waving his hands around like he was trying to tell me something, but as you might have guessed, hand-talking does not work so good in here."

"I suppose not. How often do they bring food?"

"Like I said, hard to tell. If I had to guess, I would say once a day. But some days seem pretty damn long."

Foulques slid backward until his back was up against a wall. He was tired and the welt on his forehead was throbbing. He wanted to be as far away from the man as he could be in case he passed out or drifted off to sleep. The chains were long enough that they could reach one another in the middle of the room, but he reasoned he was safe enough up against the wall. Besides, the noise of the dragging chains was overwhelming in the small room so Foulques was confident he would wake if the man came for him.

"I saw a cross on your robe when they dragged you in here. You a friar, or a priest or something?"

"I am a Hospitaller Knight."

"A man of the hospital?" Genuine surprise registered in his voice. "I thought your lot was not subject to the king's justice. What are you doing here?"

"I wish I knew."

What was he doing here? Were the men who ambushed him really Cypriot knights? He very much doubted it. One thing was for certain, the answers he sought would not be found in here. He had to get out. Perhaps Hermes knew something that could help him.

"And what is your story?" Foulques asked.

Hermes kept quiet for a while, but Foulques suspected he would speak soon enough. It would be hard to resist an opportunity for conversation. Especially when you never knew when your current cell mate might just drop dead.

"It is a common enough story I suppose. Got pulled into Prince Amalric's army and was supposed to fight at Acre, but there was no way in hell I was going to fight for that little piss-ant. Luckily, I missed my ship. Unluckily, I killed a man missing that ship."

"You are a deserter," Foulques said.

"And proud of it. I never even been to Acre. Why the hell should I die for it?"

"It is larger than that," Foulques said. "Acre is—was—part of the Kingdom of Jerusalem. We are at war."

"That was Amalric's problem. Not mine."

"Are you fine with the Infidel controlling the birth place of our lord and savior? Are you fine with good Christians being murdered on the road and being denied entry to the

Holy Sepulcher? Does that not even bother you a little?"

"The Musselmen can have Jerusalem. It was theirs anyway before we came to take it away. We got it once and now they got it back. Seems fair enough to me."

"Are you so uneducated that you do not even know the Muslims took the Holy Land from good Christians in the first place?"

"How do you know they were good Christians? I seen plenty of bad ones. I bet you have too. One or two of them might have even tossed you in here."

"Our war on Islam is a just war. We seek only that which was taken away from us in the first place."

"Keep telling yourself that, Hospitaller. But it seems to me, without your war, you are nothing more than a friar after all."

Foulques took a breath. He was debating a mad man in the dark. Who knows what he had been through? "You speak like a man who does not have God in his life," Foulques said.

"Of course God is with me. Who do you think gave me all this?" There was a rattle of chain as Hermes swept his arm around all four corners of the room.

"You cannot blame God for your sins."

"Never said I committed any of those."

"You said you killed a man."

"So? You never killed a man, Hospitaller? Or are you just one of them bandage-changing black knights? The ones that never hack up a Musselman before breaking his fast every day? God put me in here all right, same as he did you."

Foulques leaned the back of his head against the rough stone wall. "God did not put me in here. Men did."

He closed his eyes and the pain between them lessened.

✣

"YOU WILL SAVE me," Najya said.

"Why would I do that?"

"Because that is what knights do, Foulques. You know that. They help people. It is right there in your oaths you are trying so hard to memorize."

"God has forsaken us."

He saw the Grandmaster's face mouth the words, but it was his own voice he heard them in.

Foulques jerked awake. His head had drooped between his knees and as he threw his head back it made a thudding contact with the wall. A flash of light split through his head once again, and he could not stifle a groan.

"Ah. You are back. Was it a good dream?"

Hermes spoke quietly, like someone might if it were the middle of the night, and he wanted to avoid waking others. Which it could very well be. Foulques had no idea how long he had slept, if it could be called that.

"Who is Najya?" Hermes asked.

"No one I want to talk about with you," Foulques said.

"You are a dream-talker. I will find out eventually. Some men come in here and when they sleep… nothing. Complete silence. Like they die for a bit every day and then get brought back to life. But not you. You got some dreams, Friar

Foulques."

Hermes's chain vibrated as he stirred in the darkness. "I thought so, I thought so! You hear that?"

Foulques craned his neck and held his breath. After a long wait he began breathing normally again.

"I hear nothing," he said.

"You will. You will, I tell you… there!"

This time Foulques did perceive something. He was not exactly sure what it was he heard, just that something was different. A presence more than a sound. Then, unmistakably, footfalls sliding across stone far away in the distance. They grew nearer. He could picture them clearly now. Three, maybe four distinct sets. They grew in volume and once they had become so loud Foulques thought his ears would bleed, they stopped.

Metal grated against metal as someone worked a key in the latch. The timber-slab door swung outward on well-oiled hinges and blinding light blasted them from the doorway. Foulques snapped his head away and brought his hand to his eyes. For the first time, he caught a brief but clear image of his cellmate. He noted two things about Hermes before the sudden influx of light forced him to clench his eyes shut in pain. First, Hermes was incredibly thin, with long filthy hair oiled tightly against his skull. Secondly, he had a long line of drool streaming from one corner of his mouth.

A voice came from within the penetrating glare of light. "Oh, heaven above."

That voice. Foulques knew that voice. He split his fingers apart and opened one eye.

"Uncle Guillaume?"

He could hear the caution in his own voice. He had not been here long, but already he had learned it best not to trust his own senses in the belly of the whale.

"Yes Foulques, it is me." He crossed himself. "Get that lantern out of his eyes."

Foulques let out a shuddering breath of relief, but it took another long moment before he was able to summon words. "Praise God. It is you, Uncle. I am beyond words."

"It is all right now, my boy. Take another deep breath." He turned to the man beside him, the gaol-keeper Foulques decided, for he had a ring of keys on his belt. In one hand he held a lantern and in the other a short club worn black with age and use.

"Who are these other men fouling my nephew's space?"

The gaol-keeper flinched under Guillaume de Villaret's incriminating tone. "I am sorry, my lord. I did the best I could. The cells are all full and getting fuller by the day, what with all the refugees on the streets and all the comings and goings in the port."

Foulques stifled a groan as he pushed himself to his feet. Guillaume's eyes took him in from head to foot. His face soured but he said nothing before moving on to the squinting Hermes. Finally, his gaze settled on the third form in the cell.

"Is that man dead?" Guillaume asked the gaoler, who promptly walked over and whacked the man's leg with his club.

"He was groaning only minutes ago!" Hermes offered

up. "Just needs a good meal, I think."

"You are either lying or you have never seen a dead man before," Guillaume said.

Foulques shambled toward his uncle but was stopped short with a jerk from the chain around his wrist. "Gaoler. Get this manacle off me." His voice was already hoarse from speaking at normal levels.

The gaoler kept his eyes on Foulques and skirted along one wall, staying well outside of Foulques's reach. When he was back at the doorway, he leaned out into the hall and shouted, "Boy! Get in here!"

Foulques gave his chain another shake and glared at the gaoler. Perhaps this boy was the one with the key for his cuff.

The boy was so small, Foulques did not notice him until he was three steps inside the room. He was no more than ten and almost as dirty as Hermes. He threw an armload of straw to the ground in the center of the room and then, with the same practiced ease, he retraced the gaoler's steps, staying out of reach of the chained men. Then he darted toward Hermes and grabbed the bucket that passed for the communal chamber pot. There was a sloshing sound but the boy was deft and lost nothing of the bucket's contents. Just as quickly as he had appeared, the urchin passed between Guillaume and the gaoler, leaning to one side with the weight of his treasure in hand, and was gone.

Guillaume and the gaoler, who had both been forced to step aside to give the boy room to pass, closed the gap at the doorway once again. But before they did so, Foulques caught a glimpse of another man beyond them.

Foulques did not understand. Why was he still chained in place? He looked at his uncle, who returned his stare with a pitying, complacent expression on his face.

"Uncle?"

"I am sorry, Foulques. It will only be for a few days. I promise you that. Do not fall into despair."

"I... I do not..."

Guillaume turned to the gaoler. "You are to bring these men food twice every day. I will send someone to check on you so do not even think of disobeying me."

"Of course my lord. I would never—"

"With meat, and wine included for at least one of those."

The gaoler made a sucking sound between clenched teeth. "Meat is not easy to come by these days, my lord."

"I will see that you are supplied," Guillaume said. "And you," he pointed at Hermes. "As long as Brother Foulques is here, and remains fit and healthy, you will enjoy his same benefits. But if anything should happen to him, while in your care, I will bring the devil's will down upon you, I swear by all that is mighty."

Hermes nodded, and kept nodding so hard it looked like his head was about to roll off his shoulders and drop to the straw-covered floor.

"Stop this!" Foulques yelled. "What are you playing at, Uncle? You cannot leave me here."

"I play at nothing, Foulques. I am trying to both save you from yourself and preserve the Order. These are not games! Do you think I want to do this?" He gritted his teeth and gave the fire in his eyes time to subside. "Patience, my boy. A few days, one week at most and I will have things sorted. Now, I will see to your food."

Guillaume whirled and stepped through the door. The boy was coming through at the same time and he had to make a swift dodge to avoid crashing into Guillaume, but he managed it easily. He took the circuitous route along one wall into the cell, dropped the bucket halfway between Foulques and Hermes, and then sprinted back through the door. The gaoler followed after him, backing out of the cell, his club tapping out a disjointed rhythm into the meaty palm of one hand.

"Do not leave me here. Uncle. Uncle!"

The door began to move, choking off the light from the lantern in the hallway.

"Uncle!"

The door stopped moving and Foulques caught his breath.

A man in the black robe of a Hospitaller Knight stepped into the doorway. He was stocky, with thick wrists and both his eyes were blackened. His nose was flattened across his face and grotesquely swollen. He nodded at Foulques and smiled even though Foulques could tell the action caused him more than a little discomfort. He stepped back and slammed the heavy timber door closed.

Footfalls receded into the distance and soon Foulques began to wonder if anyone had ever been there in the first place.

CHAPTER SEVEN

THE SULTAN'S RED pavilion was still on the same low hill outside the walls of Acre that it had occupied for the entire siege. It was near enough to the water that the favorable winds kept the stench of the burning city blowing away from it.

When Badru Hashim answered the sultan's summons, Khalil was seated outside the tent at a low table drinking tea. The thin and scholarly Baydara sat nearby at another table. He had quill in hand and a stack of parchments and scrolls scattered about his feet. He was the vice-sultan, his next in command, not his clerk, Badru thought. He should not be busying himself with such mundane duties. But Baydara was a Mamluk of a different order and was more comfortable with quill and ink than sword and shield. Far more comfortable. In fact, the thought of the man even holding a sword made Badru's lip curl in disdain.

Badru had spent the last few days in his cabin on the Wyvern. Normally, he did not spend any more time on the water than he had to, but recently it seemed to be the only place where he was guaranteed to be alone. He relived

Yusuf's last moments on this earth constantly in his mind, whether he was alone, or in the company of others. But he preferred to face his demons when alone.

The sultan's guards let him pass without challenge. They knew who he was. Everyone knew who he was now. He stood a respectful distance from Khalil and his vice-sultan.

"And the harbor?" Baydara asked, his quill scratching furiously on parchment.

"Have it filled in," Khalil said. "Throw the dead in there. That should make it unusable."

"The dead often float, My Sultan. The currents may carry them to our own cities."

"Ah. Then fill it in with stone. Tear down the city's walls or churches. I do not really care where the debris comes from. The important thing is that the Franks can never use that city again."

"Very wise."

Khalil noticed Badru standing there. He stood up immediately. "Ah! Emir. There you are. I was expecting you hours ago."

"I am sorry, My Sultan. I was detained."

Khalil pulled out a chair across from him. "That is not important now. Here. Sit. Sit. We have much to discuss."

Badru looked at the chair and hesitated but the sultan had already sat back down and poured himself another cup of tea. Badru squatted down but the chair was so low his knees were thrust up in front of his face at an uncomfortable angle.

"You have served me well in this campaign, Badru. I

want to reward you and though I have asked your men what you desire most above all else, they have been extremely unhelpful."

"I do nothing for rewards in this life," Badru said.

"There must be something. A new boy, perhaps?"

Badru caught himself glaring at the sultan. He realized what he was doing and turned his eyes on the hapless Baydara instead.

"Oh. Perhaps that was insensitive," Khalil said. "You were quite fond of him, were you not? That is what Baydara here has told me. Said he went everywhere with you."

Badru longed for the darkness of his cabin, once again. "Allah has called Yusuf to his side. I see no sense in talking about the dead."

"Good. Good. You are right. There is enough to do in this life without also dwelling on those that have gone before us."

"My Sultan, I have much to do with my ship. If that is all I would—"

"Absolutely not, Badru. We have yet to decide upon a reward. It must be something... unique. Something—"

An idea struck Badru and became words before he could stop them. "A price on the heads of two men, then."

"A bounty? Is that what you ask?"

Badru nodded. "Yes."

The sultan smiled. "Done! Baydara, make a note to place a bounty for the heads of..."

"Alive," Badru said. "I would have them brought to me, and only me. But they must be alive."

"Even better. The names of these men?"

"A Hospitaller, Foulques de Villaret and his accomplice Vignolo dei Vignoli."

"Excellent. Did you get that?"

"I will make the arrangements immediately," Baydara said.

"How long will it take?" Badru asked.

"I do not know. It depends on the price of course, and—"

"Ten thousand denarii," Badru said.

Khalil's eyes lit up. "Make it twenty thousand," he said.

Badru could feel the sultan looking at him, feeding off his need to find the Hospitaller and the Genoan and make them pay for what they had taken. Foulques de Villaret was an unshakable parasite, hanging off Badru and at some level rejoicing at his misery.

"How long will it take?" Badru repeated.

It was the sultan who replied this time. "Just long enough for you to complete a simple task for me, Emir. I have decided to gift the English king's commander to the Mali Empire. There has been bad blood between Mansa Sakoura and King Edward for many years, I am told."

Badru did not like the sound of this. "That is in western Africa," he said.

"Yes. And I am told you know the route to Timbuktu well."

"I have traveled it more than I cared to."

"In your slaving days, correct? Well, I am going to give you the opportunity to revisit those times. The eastern markets are glutted with Christian slaves. But the west is crying out for fair-skinned ones. You will take a hundred of the finest and trade at every market between Cairo and Timbuktu."

"That could take months, My Sultan."

"It will take what it takes. But I suggest you make good use of that time. Spend it dreaming of what you will do to the two Franks I will have in chains awaiting your return."

That is something I already know, Badru thought.

※

A GROAN ESCAPED Sir Grandison's lips and Najya lifted her head from her arms. She was not sure if she had actually heard him or if she had been dreaming.

They were housed in a room on the lower floor of the palace in Acre. Only a ten minute walk from her humble chandler's workshop in Montmusart, the northern district of the city. The march from the harbor had been heartbreaking, for Acre was no longer a city she recognized. Fires burned everywhere and she wondered if her workshop still stood, if any of her hives had survived. She doubted she would ever know, for the small room they had put her and Grandison in was barred from the outside. There were no windows but sunlight streamed in from slits along the upper length of two walls, providing not only light but fresh air as well. The room had probably served as a larder for the palace's foodstuffs, nothing of which remained, of course. She had always wanted to see the inside of the palace, but she had come to realize some wishes were better left unfulfilled.

On the ground, Grandison lay on a pallet she had cobbled together by breaking down some old boxes. It was nothing more than a few flat boards, but she hoped it was enough to separate him from the cold, stone floor.

He groaned again and his eyes flickered. She had not imagined it. She turned over the wet cloth on his forehead and was rewarded with both eyes cracking open.

"Sir Grandison? Can you hear me?" She kept her voice low. The less the guards outside the door knew about Grandison's condition the better.

His eyes went from slits to fully open. They traveled the room in a slow circle before settling on her face.

"It is me, Najya. Do not move too quickly."

No sooner had she said it than he grimaced and sucked in a mouthful of air between clenched teeth.

"That… was not quick," he said in French with a hoarse voice.

She held a water gourd up to his lips with one hand and supported his head with the other.

"Shh… we must speak only in English," She said. "If they know you speak French, or anything else for that matter, they will separate us."

He gulped down a good amount of water and leaned back, exhausted. "Who would want that?" he asked in English.

"How do you feel?"

"Did any of my men survive?"

Najya shook her head, short rapid movements side to side.

"What about everyone else? Did they take prisoners?

Or…"

"The Northman spared everyone who did not fight against him. And they forced your crew to sail the ship back here, to Acre."

"Thank God. We were heavily loaded. I should have never taken so many on." The water had washed some of the weariness from his voice. "Who is this Northman? Why does he fight for the Mohammedans?"

"He is a mixed blood, not a true north man but a Mamluk. His real name is Badru Hashim."

Grandison closed his eyes. "Whoever he is, his men can fight."

He rested for a moment and when he reopened his eyes they were clear and full of life. For the first time in days, Najya felt that he was going to live after all.

"So you told them I only speak English and you are my interpreter? Good thinking. I can imagine things were a little hectic for a bit there. You did well to come up with that one."

Najya could not help but smile at how the Savoyard knight had a way of understating everything. A little hectic, all right. She had never been so terrified in all her life.

She heard something. "Someone is coming. Remember, Sir Grandison, no French."

"Only if you promise to call me Otto from now on. I am not feeling too knightly at this moment."

The sound of a heavy timber sliding on the other side of the door made Najya jump. A few seconds later the door swung open.

The room erupted with light and Najya shielded her eyes. Just as quickly, it returned to darkness as a figure stepped into the doorway.

Badru Hashim moved into the small room, followed by another Mamluk who had his hand on his sword. His name was Safir. Najya remembered him as the man who had thrown her down on the ship and nearly choked her unconscious.

"How is he?" Badru asked in Arabic.

"Faring poorly," Najya said, standing up. "What did you expect? You ran a spear through his chest."

Badru brought the back of his hand across her face, spinning her in place. She was back on her knees but did not remember falling. She recalled Grandison shouting something a fraction of a second before the blow landed, but now her mind was consumed by a white hot pain pulsating up and down the entire length of her face.

"Emir…" Safir said.

Badru glared at him and then turned back to Najya. "If I had stuck this man with a spear he would be dead, and I would have none of the troubles he brings me."

Najya flinched at his words and said nothing, afraid she might somehow bring out his wrath again. But Grandison was muttering a litany of foul words in English. Most of which she could not understand, but they were accompanied by a fair amount of spitting so she assumed they were not cordial.

"He seems good enough to travel," Badru said. "Make sure that he is, for we depart tomorrow."

"Travel? Look at him! He cannot possibly walk or ride." He looked like he might hit her again, but Najya would not be cowed. "How far do you mean to take us?"

"Prepare him for a long journey. I will drag him all the way to the Mali Empire if need be. And if he dies somewhere along the way, know that I will leave you there beside him in the dirt." He raised his hand again, but only pointed at her to drive home his next words. "Tomorrow. Make ready."

Badru turned and left the room, ducking his head on the way out. Najya looked up at Safir, but he had trouble meeting her eyes. He backed out of the room and the door closed behind him. No sooner had the locking timber slid back into place, than Grandison reached out and grabbed Najya's wrist. The sudden movement brought pain to his face, but he wasted no time in speaking.

"Najya, listen to me, carefully," he said.

"English," she said. "Only English!"

"Of course, I am sorry. Now listen. You must do everything within your power to escape. But if you cannot do that, you must, at any cost, not be with me when I am delivered to the Emperor of Mali."

"Do you think I can simply walk away when the Northman's back is turned? It is not that simple."

"How do you know? Have you tried? I think you have done everything within your power to stay here, by my side. I would bet my life on it, and in a way I have. But you have done enough. It is no longer safe for you to be near me."

"Why? What are you afraid of?"

"My king and I had some dealings with Sakoura twenty

years ago, and the recklessness of youth had us do some things I am not proud of. Suffice it to say, he will not be happy to see me, and knowing the type of man he is, he will gladly sate his anger on anything, or anyone, I hold dear."

"But if he would do me harm, what would he do to you?"

Grandison shook his head, "Nothing much, I am sure. He will most likely just hold me and squeeze King Edward for a sizable ransom."

"I see," Najya said. But perhaps not the way Grandison wished her to. For she too knew of Mansa Sakoura. He had grown fat and rich off of copper, salt, and the African slave trade. In addition to that he controlled all the gold mines in the west. His city Timbuktu was a trading doorway through which all paths led.

What use did a man with all these riches have for one paltry ransom?

CHAPTER EIGHT

THE FIRST MEAL Foulques received was a wedge of crusty bread submerged in a bowl of water, with a stringy, half-raw piece of mutton thrown on top. He did not eat it. Nor did he eat his second or third meals, much to Hermes's delight. He gleefully accepted the bowl when Foulques pushed it toward him, squealing in delight as he sucked down its contents in seconds. While Hermes had never been happier, Foulques sunk into a half-conscious state of despair. What had he done to make his uncle leave him here in this hell?

He was overwhelmed in turn, by a predictable string of emotions. First came anger, which quite quickly was replaced by confusion. By the time fear sought him out, all he could think of was that every passing moment he spent in the darkness increased the chances he would never see Najya again. Perhaps she was already dead.

"You should eat, Friar Foulques." Hermes pointed at the cold bowl of food in front of him. Foulques had no memory of how it had gotten there. "At least drink the broth."

Footsteps sounded in the darkness. Hermes's head

snapped up to point at Foulques, his expression unreadable in the low, almost nonexistent light. Hermes spidered his way on hands and knees to the end of his chain, then with uncanny dexterity he flipped to his back and stretched out his long leg toward Foulques. He gripped his bony toes on the edge of the bowl of mutton-water and, ever so carefully, dragged the bowl bumping recklessly toward him across the flagstone floor. Once it was within reach he flipped onto his stomach and slurped and smacked the contents away, employing both hands and a good portion of his face in the process.

Perhaps emboldened by his recent meal, Hermes made the mistake of not holding his tongue when the gaoler and his boy entered the cell. As usual, the man stood in the doorway with club in hand.

Tap, tap, tap...

The boy performed his laps of the cell, emptying the waste bucket and dropping off bowls of food. When he came close to Foulques he noted the boy smelled more of mutton than his bowl actually did. Perhaps that was something Hermes also noticed, leaving him a little reckless.

"The fancy monk said we was to get wine. Have not seen any of that yet," Hermes said.

The tapping stopped.

"No? Not seen any wine, have you? Must be too dark in here. Boy, fetch the lantern."

Hermes began to go back on himself. "I did not mean nothing by it. You can have my wine. And his. I swear I will not say a word. I swear it on the virgin."

"Get in your corner."

"No, please. I swear, I did not mean anything by it."

"Get in your corner!"

The dirty urchin had not yet moved. He grinned so wide his teeth flashed and seemed to set the room alight. He took a step to the door, turned back like he was afraid to miss something, took another step, then turned back again.

"Get the bloody lantern!"

He ran to do as he was told. He returned with the light and placed it in one corner near the door, then sat down on the ground beside it. He pulled his knees up to his chest and rocked back and forth like he had front row for a puppet show.

The gaoler gave Hermes a slow and deliberate beating that dragged on until he was winded and breathing so heavily he could hardly raise his glistening club. All the while, Foulques screamed at the gaoler and rattled his chain. He tried again and again to reach the two men but succeeded only in making his wrist slick with blood. The events unfolded just outside of his little world and, like the boy, Foulques could only look on from afar.

Foulques ate every meal after that. Hermes skipped the next four, but by the fifth he was able to open his mouth far enough to suck on a tiny piece of fatty mutton, groaning in ecstasy as he did so. The crusty bread proved too challenging, but he squirreled it away somewhere under his filthy robe for the future. When Foulques saw that, he knew it was just a matter of time before Hermes was back to his usual deplorable self.

With the first meal Foulques ate, he made a mark on the wall with the sharp edge of his wrist manacle. He did the same for every meal thereafter. It was not the most accurate measurement of time, for he was sure the gaoler was none too diligent where meal times were concerned. However, it gave Foulques some way to mark the passing of the days. Every mark was one mark closer to when he would get out of here. And it was a much more acceptable system than counting one's nightmares.

✠

FOOTSTEPS IN THE dark. It was too soon for food. Foulques cocked his head. Three sets of footsteps: one heavy, one light, and a third that shuffled. This was the new one.

The door opened. "Get in your corners. Do not look at me. Do not even breathe."

The gaoler pushed a man before him into the cell. From light into darkness. His hands were tied behind his back with rope. His ankles were likewise hobbled. The moment he set foot in the cell, Foulques was struck with the scent of manure. Not human waste, but a great combination of all kinds of animal excrement at different stages of decomposition, from fresh to soil. It was overwhelming, even for a man in Foulques's foul situation.

Foulques took advantage of the lantern light to look at the newcomer. The hobble was unnecessary, for he was old and limped from a twist at his hip that pained him with every step. His days of running away were long behind him. His gray hair may have had a bit of its original black preserved, but it was as plastered to his head and face in filth as that of Hermes so it was hard to tell for sure. As old as he was, he looked like he had been in captivity for much of his life.

After chaining him to the wall and removing his ropes, the gaoler hauled off and hit him once in the stomach with his club. Both he and the boy looked disappointed when the old man folded in half and slid silently to the ground, without so much as an exhalation of air. He lay there unmoving, curled up in a ball, like a man waiting to die. Dejected, the gaoler and his boy walked to the door.

"I do not think your new friend will be here long, so do not get attached."

The door slid back into place, though not as silently as Foulques remembered it to be. Perhaps his hearing had improved again. He focused on the receding sound of footfalls. One set heavy, one light. They seemed to go on forever.

"Do you think he will get mutton?" Hermes asked.

It was a good question. Foulques stared at the new lump in the cell. It shifted, then moved again. It pulled itself up into a sitting position against the wall.

"Peace be upon you, Foulques."

Foulques squinted into the gloom and contemplated how much further his mind could go to deceive him. To what depths would it stoop? It was playing an awful trick on him at this moment. But admittedly, one that he deserved.

"Monsieur Malouf," Foulques said, thinking that the act of saying the name aloud would somehow banish the illusion this place taunted him with.

"Yes. It is me, Foulques. I know you doubt it, but it is me."

Perhaps silence could succeed in warding it away.

"Say something, Foulques. Are you injured?"

"You know the friar?" Hermes asked.

He had been unusually quiet up until this point. A hard-learned survival strategy, no doubt.

"Monsieur Malouf. Truly?"

"Yes."

"Have you come to kill me?"

"No, not directly. But I may yet have a hand in your death."

"I think you are going to get mutton," Hermes said.

"Still your tongue!" Foulques said. He took a moment to gather himself. "How did you get in here?"

"Getting inside a place such as this is not as difficult as you might think. Getting out is another matter entirely."

"Can you? Can you get us out?"

"What would you do if I could? Would you take revenge on those who put you here?"

"You mean my uncle?"

"Yes," Malouf said. "Among others."

"I do not pretend to know what my uncle is playing at, and to be honest, I am not sure I care. I have more important things on my mind. When I get out of here, I intend to see those tasks to completion."

"What are these important things?"

"I think you know. Why else would you be here?"

Malouf said nothing and Foulques answered him with a silence of his own, a skill that he had recently mastered. Eventually, Malouf's silence gave in. The chains at his wrist rattled and his silhouette began to move. The wall lifted him to his feet, no longer bent and withered, but his usual graceful, yet average in all ways, self. Foulques wondered how he had failed to recognize Najya's father under the light of lanterns when now, draped in almost utter darkness, he stood before Foulques clear as day.

Malouf lifted one knee up to his chest and used his hands to remove something from between his toes. He returned his bare foot to the ground and less than a minute later his manacles hit that same ground with a shuddering clang.

"Did... did your chain fall off?" Hermes broke the silence and both men ignored him.

Malouf walked swiftly to the door and pressed his ear against it.

"Give me a moment."

He twisted the handle and lifted the door in an awkward motion and it popped open. He walked the door open slowly and disappeared. Very little light spilled into the room, for there was no one with a lantern standing outside. The sputtering oil lamps spaced at regular intervals along the hallway drove away the darkness to a degree, but their warmth was soon taken away when Malouf closed the door.

Silence. Not even the sound of footfalls.

Foulques felt his heart twist in his chest. Was this the latest nightmare? Had he imagined everything? He cast his eyes around the cell, looking for the man he had imagined to be Najya's father. Nothing was there. Nothing had changed.

"He is coming back," Hermes said, causing Foulques to jump. Once he caught his breath and his heart adopted its normal rhythm, he focused on listening.

One man. Dragging something heavy.

The sound stopped near the door. Then rapid footfalls receded into the distance. Minutes passed and Foulques heard nothing but his heart. Then, the hallway came back to life once again with the sounds of someone approaching.

One man. Dragging something light.

The cell door was pulled open. It swung wide on its hinges until it banged on the wall. An arm reached into the cell and set down a lantern. Then came Malouf, dragging the gaoler by one arm. Foulques felt his stomach twist when Malouf ducked back outside and returned towing the boy by one leg. He dumped the body near the door with the gaoler, then picked up the lantern and proceeded to where Foulques leaned against the wall.

"Hold out your hands."

Malouf produced a ring of keys and began to methodically try each one. Foulques's cuffs surrendered on the third try and Foulques thought his hands were going to fly away.

"God is glorious," Malouf said. He held up the lantern to shed light on Hermes's corner and looked at Foulques with questioning eyes. Foulques nodded and Malouf set about freeing him as well. Foulques helped Hermes to his feet and the exertion left him breathing hard. They were a sorry pair.

"Stay close to me unless I tell you otherwise," Malouf

said. "If God permits, we should encounter not a single guard, but we must leave now."

They passed by the gaoler and the boy at the door. A smear of blood traced their beginning to somewhere down the hall. But it was not the only blood trail in the corridor. Far from it. It was just the freshest. Foulques cringed when he considered how much blood that floor had tasted over the years.

"You did not have to take their lives," Foulques said to Malouf as he closed the door and locked it.

"If I had not, your uncle would have."

Before coming to this place, Foulques would have responded with outrage. But today, or tonight, Foulques had nothing to say.

Holding the lantern before him, Malouf set off down the hall. Foulques and Hermes struggled to keep up and they had to rest at every landing on the stairs, but Malouf proved to be true to his word. The gaol was eerily absent of any guards. However, the way Malouf kept urging them on suggested to Foulques that the arrangements Malouf had made were time sensitive. Foulques wondered how many scratches on a cell wall they had left exactly.

Foulques and Hermes were both breathing through open mouths and were beyond talking when they finally stepped over the last threshold and their feet hit bare earth. The fresh air hit Foulques in the face and he fell to his knees. Hermes remained standing but leaned on his fellow prisoner's shoulder like it was a walking stick. Malouf gave them a moment and Foulques was thankful for it. He clenched great wads of moist soil and grass between his fingers as he sucked in mouthfuls of cool air, laced with moisture. It was night and Malouf had given up his lantern at some point in their flight from the belly of the beast.

"We can wait no longer," Malouf said.

Hermes helped Foulques to his feet. He gave his shoulder a last pat with his bony hand.

"Thanks for the mutton, Friar Foulques, and I do not want to sound ungrateful, but I do prefer game birds." He gave a low cackle, bowed his head to Malouf once, and set off in an awkward lope toward the north exit of the palace grounds.

Malouf led Foulques away toward the harbor. Anyone who saw them gave them a wide berth. Foulques knew they must look terrible, but Malouf stunk so badly even Foulques was close to vomiting if they stopped moving for too long.

Eventually, with his legs aching and his lungs burnt raw from his labored breaths, Foulques found himself swaying with a familiar sensation. He was on a ship.

"I would bet even my crass Genoan accent sounds like the voice of an angel this night, eh Foulques?"

Vignolo. Good old Vignolo. Foulques was at the end of his reserves, so he could not even pretend to keep the smile from his face.

"A lesser one, perhaps," Foulques managed.

"Good God, Malouf. What is that smell?" Vignolo asked, holding a hand over his mouth and nose.

"All things great, and some that are not. As much as I appreciate how it guarantees quick processing by city officials, I think I would like to take a swim. Do we have time before departure?"

"Yes, yes. By all means. Just do not do it in front of the ship. I do not want to sail through anything you leave behind. And do not look at me that way, Foulques. You are no country maiden fresh out of a babbling brook yourself."

Someone else greeted Foulques, but by the time he saw him his eyelids had given out. He could not recall if he had found a bed, a floor, or if he had collapsed right there on his feet. All he knew was that it was the sleep of a lifetime.

CHAPTER NINE

Foulques slept the entire next day and through the night as well, but at mid-morning he awoke with a start. He had a rumbling belly and a host of questions on his mind.

First of all, whose ship was this? It was not as large as even the smallest in the Hospitaller fleet, such as it was. He was below deck, in a cabin of sorts. There were three other hammocks hanging in the cramped room besides his own. He swung his legs over, put his feet on the floor, then tentatively stood up. He swayed like a thin tree in a gale and his stomach lurched. Foulques was thankful there was no food in it.

He cannot take a bath without losing three days of food in the process.

Why did his uncle do it? Foulques had no answer.

His arrival on deck was greeted with enthusiasm, though everyone maintained a greater than usual distance. There were thirteen men on board, including Foulques: nine sailors, Vignolo, Malouf, and to Foulques's surprise, Gruffydd, the archer who served Sir Grandison. He was also the only man Foulques knew of to come away from an encounter with the Northman physically intact, if Foulques did not count himself. Whether or not Gruffydd had fared so well spiritually was yet to be seen.

Malouf, freshly bathed and clothed in a pure white robe and matching turban, rolled out a multi-hued carpet on the rear deck, away from the main workings of the ship. Foulques, Vignolo, and Gruffydd joined him there. They sat around the carpet and a sailor brought bread, cheese, olives, and wine before returning to his duties.

Foulques watched the man as he walked away. He thought he recognized him as someone Vignolo had used in the past.

"Can we trust them?" Foulques asked.

Vignolo and Malouf answered at the same time.

"Yes."

"No."

The two men looked at each other. Malouf popped an olive into his mouth.

"Of course we can trust them," Vignolo said. "They are Rhodians. You will not find a better crew on the Mid-Earth Sea. Or any body of water that I know of, for that matter."

"That does not mean we can trust them," Malouf said. "It is often easier to buy a skilled man than it is a simpleton."

Foulques had to side with Malouf. Vignolo had a blind spot for the men, and women, of Rhodes. Which was ironic because they had virtually thrown him out of an estate he owned on the island. But that did not stop him from employing their services. Rhodes was surrounded by dozens of tiny islands and dangerous reefs. That, coupled with the unpredictable squalls known to frequent the area, bred a population of tenacious seafarers.

"Where exactly are we?" Foulques asked, reaching for another piece of bread. He had swallowed his first piece of cheese and it had ignited a fierce appetite within him.

Vignolo pointed across the deck at a shoreline far off on the horizon. "See that patch of brown sky away over there? That's Acre, and she is still burning."

That struck Foulques as odd, for the place Vignolo pointed to was behind them. "Why are we headed south then? Acre, or as near as we can get, should be our starting point. We could sneak into the city and see where the slaves are being held, what markets they are being sent to. And maybe some of us could sail into the Templar harbor and start getting people out of there."

Vignolo grimaced.

"What is it?" Foulques asked.

"There is no one there to save," Vignolo said.

"King Henry saw to it?"

Vignolo said nothing. "My uncle?"

"The Templar fortress collapsed six days ago. Everyone inside was killed. Saracens, Templars, women, children, everyone."

The men sitting around the carpet observed a long moment of silence and no one looked directly at Foulques while he took in this new information.

"How long have I been gone?"

"Two weeks," Malouf said.

Two weeks! Foulques had thought no more than six or seven days. But that would mean...

Foulques looked at Malouf. "And Najya? Any survivors would have been taken from the city and sold by now. How can we know where they will have taken her? She could be in Spain for all we know!"

"Calm down, Foulques. We have not been idle. My son was amongst the Mamluk army for days. He gets word to me when he can."

"She is alive, then?" Foulques grabbed Malouf's white sleeve.

"Malouf nodded. "He saw her from a distance. In Acre."

"Then why are we here? You speak in circles, and we travel opposite the direction we should."

"There have been complications," Malouf said, detaching Foulques's hand from his arm, leaving behind black finger marks.

"What do you mean?"

Malouf was slow to respond so Vignolo took over. "Well, it seems our friend was discovered and had to run for his life. So he lost track of her."

Foulques realized he still held a piece of bread in one hand. He put it on the carpet in front of him for he had suddenly lost his appetite and could no longer think of food.

"But you know where they are taking her, or we would not be on this ship."

"She is somewhere along the Thirty-Day Road," Malouf said. He looked at Foulques and for the briefest of instances, Foulques caught a glimpse of the old man from the Tower of

Jonas.

"And so is Sir Grandison," Gruffydd said. The young man did not speak much, and when he did Foulques could hardly understand his English.

"What is this road?" Foulques asked.

"A trade route that runs all the way from Cairo to Timbuktu, with only a few stops in between," Vignolo said. "Some of these places are nothing more than watering holes, but two or three are good-sized towns, trading hubs grown up around the slave and salt trades. Our plan is to be at the markets of these places before they arrive, and if they are selling something we want, we buy it. Or them. Simple as that."

"Except that it is the Thirty-Day Road," Malouf said.

Vignolo rolled his eyes. "You keep saying that."

"And you do not know what you make light of," Malouf said.

"Then tell me what you hint at," Foulques asked.

Malouf looked at him. "The route crosses the northern edge of the Great Waterless Sea, the Sahara. It is said that the desert exacts a toll from amongst those who would enter. One life per day is what she demands. That life may come from your caravan, or one from another party on the other side of the desert. The desert does not care, as long as she is paid."

"How long must we be on this road before the first slave market?" Foulques asked.

"Maybe ten days."

"Well, I suppose we will just have to hope the Mamluks

pay the desert lady's toll for us, then," Vignolo said.

"So long as that debt is not paid with the life of my daughter or Gruffydd's lord," Malouf said.

Foulques approved of the plan. At least what he had heard so far. "Excellent. We lay in wait at one of these towns, then? When will they leave Acre?"

Vignolo and Malouf looked at each other. "There is more you should know," Malouf said.

"A lot more," Vignolo added.

"They took ship three days ago and landed in Barqa, on the north coast of Africa directly south of where we are now. They had camels and guides waiting for them and set out immediately."

"That makes sense," Foulques said. "It would be ridiculous to attempt the journey overland from Acre. But... are we behind them, then? Are we to go to this Barqa as well?"

Vignolo shook his head. "No. That is Mamluk territory and we cannot risk being spotted. Besides, we want to be ahead of them to get to the slave market in Zuwila and set up before they get there. We will dock in a small town farther west controlled by the Hafsid Berbers, where Malouf has already arranged for guides to take us on to Zuwila. This route will cut many days off our journey."

This all sounded good to Foulques, but Vignolo was rambling. He always did that when he was nervous. "What is our concern, then?"

"Our concern," Vignolo said, "is the ship that docked in Barqa."

"Why should that bother us? You said we are not even

going to Barqa."

"It was the Wyvern, Foulques."

The Wyvern. He should have known. Still, it made sense. Foulques shrugged. "He has provided ship transport for the slaves. I doubt he will be escorting them himself."

It was Malouf's turn to respond. "The Northman is there. The sultan himself has tasked Badru Hashim with delivering the English general to Timbuktu."

Foulques's head was spinning and he had almost forgotten about Grandison. "Why would Khalil send Grandison away? He could easily ransom him to King Edward himself."

No one had an answer to that, so the conversation turned to the practical considerations of the journey. The more he heard the better Foulques felt about the plan. At least they were doing something, and although he was not particularly fond of the desert, it would be good to be back on hard ground once again.

Malouf's son was already en route to the west, to Timbuktu. He would set out with his own group from there and head east in case his father's group was unsuccessful. They discussed the supplies they already had and those they still needed to acquire. As Vignolo mentioned, Malouf had already hired guides. Apparently, the Thirty-Day Road was not really a road in any sense of the word, and if you did not know where you were going, you could wander around the desert for the rest of your life. Which, in that case, would be considerably shortened.

At that point, Foulques had to excuse himself. In the excitement, he had begun eating again and his stomach was not at its best. He went away from the group as quickly and as far as his innards would permit and then leaned over the side. The sight of the swells lapping against the side of the ship brought on a series of heaves that left him emptied and pale. When he opened his eyes someone was beside him.

"That is about the poorest use of wine I have ever seen," Vignolo said as he used his long knife to peel the skin off a stubby root of ginger. He sliced off a small piece and said, "Chew it but do not swallow it down." He tucked the rest of the root into the pocket of Foulques's robe and then leaned out into the wind.

Vignolo moved with the wood beneath his feet, like he was privy to the sea's intents and its effect on the ship seconds before every lurch and sway. Nothing seemed unpredictable for the Genoan when he was at sea. Foulques envied him at that moment. He would have made a formidable admiral. If he could curb his drinking, whoring, gambling, blaspheming…

"Give me the news," Foulques said. "You have avoided it long enough."

Vignolo let out a low whistle. "Are you sure you are ready for it?"

Foulques nodded but had to turn away and focus on the horizon.

"Where should I begin?"

"Grandmaster Villiers."

"Alive, but still recovering. And he is Brother Villiers now."

Foulques suspected as much. "My uncle is grandmaster

then? How did he manage it?"

"You remember those two French knights he brought with him?"

"I do."

"Well, Guillaume swore them in at the rank of Knight Justice and the next day appointed them to the Grand Cross."

Foulques did some figuring in his mind. "But that would still leave him one vote short for becoming grandmaster."

"Blame yourself. You voted for him."

"Me? I was in the bowels of hell!"

Vignolo closed his eyes and shook his head. "Oh, Foulques. The path around the world is not always as straight and smooth as you like to see it. Think on it. You gave the man your room, your bed, your desk."

Even with his head half in his stomach, Foulques was beginning to understand. "My seal. He has my seal."

"And you, my friend, are on a diplomatic mission to the Mongols. You may be gone for months. How long do you think he intended to keep you in that hole anyway?"

"He said only a few days. But I imagine as long as it took to convince me to back him as grandmaster." He reflected on that for a few moments. What exactly would Foulques have been willing to do to get out of that place?

"There is more, Foulques."

What more could there be?

"He, along with your help, disbanded the Hospitaller navy and retired the position of Admiral."

"Ah. That is perhaps the only thing thus far that makes

sense." But if he disbanded the navy... "What of the Schwyzers?"

"They are gone Foulques. Guillaume made some kind of deal with King Henry. They serve him now."

Of all the things he had heard, this one tore at his soul the most. He did not know exactly why, for he had often thought of the Schwyzers as a burden, but one he was destined to bear. For it was Foulques who had taken them away from their homes, their people. And most of them had paid the ultimate price. Less than a hundred of them still survived. How many had there been? Four hundred? Five hundred? The number was not important. What was a hundred, give or take, when compared to the thousands that had fallen in the last few years.

"How does that sit with you, Foulques?"

"What of Alain?"

"Alain is just Alain. But he has been stripped of his Knight Justice title. I do not know exactly what happened there, but apparently he is part of the clergy now. Does not even carry a sword."

Foulques shook his head. "Tell me Vignolo. What kind of path has God set us upon?"

"A twisty, rutted, horse shit covered one, I would say." He patted Foulques on the shoulder. "Might be a good time for you to go wash up. You are not too easy to be around right now, my friend."

Foulques nodded. A wash would feel good, but what he really needed was a fresh start. An entire new baptism.

Foulques walked with one hand on the railing as he left

Vignolo to seek out a bucket. He was ten steps away when Vignolo called out.

"Did I mention that I have not been paid for over a month now?"

Foulques wanted to throw him a base gesture any Genoan would readily recognize, but it would have been a two-handed ordeal, and he was afraid to take his hand off the railing.

CHAPTER TEN

THEY DOCKED IN a small fishing settlement called Yamina, the most southerly point on the north coast of Africa. No sooner had Foulques and his company set foot on dry land with their supplies, than the Rhodes men were already pushing away. They had instructions to return in twelve days and remain in the town for another week, keeping the ship ready to sail at a moment's notice. If no one showed after that week, they were to sail for home.

Malouf called over a boy who was watching them unload their things into a pile at the end of the dock. He spoke a few words and pressed something into his hand. The boy disappeared down a dusty, well-used road that led to a gathering of huts. Forty minutes later two men clad turban to foot in black scampered back on that same road. They led a string of horses, tacked out and ready for the road, complete with saddlebags filled with food, water, and a few other necessities for the trip. Along with the riding horses, there were two unburdened pack horses ready to accommodate the party's belongings. Malouf exchanged words with one of them, handed over a large purse, and they dropped the reins of their horses. Without another word, they turned their backs on Foulques and his companions and walked swiftly away.

"I thought we were getting guides," Foulques said.

"Not here," Malouf said, rummaging through a large saddlebag on one of the horses. He pulled out three black robes and three tagelmust, the preferred head wraps of desert travelers, and draped them all over his saddle. "Here. Put this on. Keep the scarf over your face. You are all Arabs from this point on." He tossed another one each to Vignolo and Gruffydd, who was sitting on a boulder waxing his bowstring. "You will need to hide that for the time being," Malouf said, pointing at the longbow. "It will only invite questions."

"I was going to put it in a greased sleeve anyway," Gruffydd said. "This air is far too dry for it."

"Why are you the only one who gets to wear white?" Vignolo asked.

Malouf spread his hands before him. "It is God's will. And if He permits, eyes will be drawn to me rather than you. We humans have a tendency to seek out that which is different from ourselves and others."

"That is God's way to stop inbreeding," Vignolo said. "Though I have known a lot of—"

"And, I find it cooler," Malouf added, not letting Vignolo finish. He led a packhorse over to their pile of supplies taken from the ship and began to go through them.

Foulques saw a chest that seemed very familiar. He looked at Vignolo. "Is that…?"

"It is," Vignolo said. "I threw your armor and an extra sword in there as well. I must say, you are an easy man to pack for."

Foulques went to the chest and untied the ropes keeping it closed. He threw back the lid and looked at everything in this world that he owned. A sword belt, complete with his old rondel dagger attached, was on top of his hauberk. He pulled these out and set them on the ground. Next, was his padded gambeson, then two pairs of breeches, one linen, one cotton, and two shirts. He dug deeper to see his extra summer weight black mantle and his one fur-lined winter mantle. There was a red war tunic and an extra pair of boots. He kept digging until his hand closed on what he had been seeking. A breath of relief washed through him. He pulled out the looking glass Najya had given him on the day he was knighted. It had been a princely gift then, but today it was simply irreplaceable. He wrapped it carefully in his winter mantle and put everything back inside his trunk. He eased the lid shut and cinched up its ties. The only thing he kept out was the sword and dagger.

Foulques and his companions rode south along a meandering trail for two hours, until it abruptly merged with a wide, well-traveled road. At this point Malouf motioned for everyone to check their tagelmust, as he adjusted his own to cover his face. With only his eyes visible, Foulques was surprised at how twenty years seemed to drop from Malouf's features. With the hard lines and angular jawline concealed, his face seemed to take on a new identity. Even the way he sat in his saddle changed ever so subtly.

"From this point on, you are no longer Franks," Malouf began, looking first at Foulques and then at each man in turn. "Though this fact will be impossible to hide for long, if you do as I say, it should suffice. The moment we enter the town, dismount and lead your horse. Look at your feet, or stare at the back of the man in front of you. I do not care. But look no one in the eye. When we get to the bazaar, sit in a circle and stare at the ground until I come back and tell you to move."

Juma was not a town so much as a cluster of long-term tents battered from the northern winds and caked with the dust kicked up from the many caravans that passed through the village every week. Likewise, the bazaar was not a place where villagers would go to purchase everyday items. There were no stalls with vendors hawking fresh meat or colorful silks. This was not where trade goods began nor ended their journey. It was a meeting point, a hub where caravan masters passed their wares along to other caravan masters. Most of these caravans had set up camps on the outskirts of the small town where they would wait for their masters or merchant delegates to conduct their business.

The four men gave these camps a wide berth and pushed on to the center of town. Eventually, they found themselves in a large square with two wells, one at either end. People stood in line with their beasts of burden waiting to fill all manner of skins and gourds with the precious liquid. Surrounding the square, small groups of men sat on the ground smoking, eating, arguing, or talking in hushed voices.

Malouf brought their band to a halt far away from any other group and motioned for them to tie their horses and sit. Then he set off across the square. He approached two Arabs sitting beside a camel. They exchanged words and one of the men lifted an arm and pointed toward a hut on the edge of the square.

"What is he doing?" Gruffydd asked.

"Looking for his contact," Foulques said. "This is where we will get our guides."

Ten minutes later the door to the small hut opened and Malouf stepped out into the sunlight. He held a tiny tea cup, which he graciously surrendered with both hands to someone inside. He shielded his eyes for a moment from the sun, and then set out at a brisk pace toward Foulques and his men. He had crossed half the distance before Foulques noticed a man two strides behind him. He was dressed all in black and wore no face scarf, though that was not readily apparent for his skin was the color of onyx. It was difficult to tell where his clothing began and where it ended.

"Mount up," Malouf said in Arabic. "This man will lead us to our caravan."

Foulques stood, and for the benefit of Gruffydd, motioned for him to get on his horse. The whites of their guide's eyes grew as he watched Gruffydd. His pale skin and wide shoulders had already attracted attention. Foulques turned with one hand wrapped in his horse's mane and caught Malouf's eye. He nodded, acknowledging he had seen the same thing Foulques had. He shrugged as though to say it was God's will. He did not seem too bothered so Foulques told himself to relax. Malouf seemed to have an answer for everything thus far.

The black sleeves of the man fluttered as he raised his arm and blew a sound from between his pursed lips that was half whistle, half screech. It cut through the low murmurs of the marketplace and pierced Foulques's skull with the subtlety of a blacksmith's white-hot pincers. He closed his eyes at its suddenness. When he opened them again he saw a small, lithe horse weaving unerringly toward them from the far side of the square. The mare was unsaddled and wore no bridle or bit. She had only a loose loop of rope hanging around her neck. None of these seemed to deter the man from hopping into the air and settling on her back with the erratic, yet gentle windswept motion of an autumn leaf falling from a tree. With one hand in the ring of rope he nudged the mare into a walk and did not look back to see who was following.

The man led them past clumps of hastily erected structures, patched together with scraps of wood and animal skins faded by the sun to the same tawny shade of the sand and rock surrounding them. As the ramshackle huts gave away to open ground, temporary camps of man and beast began to appear. They passed by several different groups of Arab and Turk merchants. The men leaned against their kneeling camels, talking with one another in hushed voices, which trailed away to nothing when Foulques's small group approached. Their guide gave the camps a wide berth but even so, Foulques could feel eyes boring into his back from afar.

"Suspicious lot, these traders," Gruffydd said under his breath. Their guide was several horse lengths ahead of the four of them.

"That is why they are still alive," Vignolo said. "Out here there is always some bastard hiding behind the next dune ready to take you and yours."

Malouf turned in his saddle and gave them a stern look that said enough talk. Vignolo grunted and raised a wineskin to his lips. He swirled the liquid around in his mouth for a good while before swallowing.

Vignolo put on a good show, but Foulques could tell he was not himself. He was out of his element here and not for the first time, Foulques wondered why he had decided to come. What was Najya to him? He could understand Gruffydd wanting to help rescue his lord, but there was nothing in this for Vignolo and Foulques had no doubt Vignolo's discomfort would only escalate the farther they got from the Mid-Earth Sea.

They skirted around the last Arab encampment and never returned to the main road, such that it was. Foulques began to acknowledge a sense of dread growing in his guts.

They continued south for another ten minutes and then climbed a short rise. Spread below them was another camp. But this was no group of merchants and pack animals. Varying shades of blue were everywhere, from the lightest sky blue to the deep indigo of dusk. From his high vantage point Foulques counted at least fifty warriors. That was how many he could see. There were always more. Their blue robes stood out in dark contrast to the rocky, scrub brush land, but Foulques knew from experience that on the flats, set against the skyline, it would be impossible to tell their number as they charged toward you.

Their guide wheeled his horse around to face the men. "This is as far as I go," he said. "Outsiders are not welcome here." It came out as part-warning, part-question. *What are you doing here?*

Malouf threw the man a coin. His horse was already trotting back toward the town as he caught it.

"Who are they?" Gruffydd asked.

"The Blue People," Vignolo said, shaking his head. "These are the ones I was talking about earlier. The ones hiding behind every dune."

Foulques spurred his horse forward a step until he could grab Malouf's arm.

"What is this?" he said, spinning the older man in his saddle. Malouf's eyes showed no trace of surprise. He shrugged the one shoulder that was not pinned by Foulques's grip.

"We have our guides. Their route will pass by every major slave market from here to Timbuktu. And more importantly, they have agreed to take us with them."

"Tuaregs? They are desert dwellers. The worst of them all. They are not just thieves. They will take us to the middle of the desert, slit our throats and watch us die before taking everything we own."

"I understand your misgivings, Foulques. The Tuareg are the lords of the Waterless Sea. Who better to guide us on our quest?"

"I will not be indebted to people such as these," Foulques said.

They were interrupted by a loud, roaring bellow. All four of them looked up to see a lone, riderless camel enter the open ground between the men and the camp. It broke into a run and headed straight toward them. Its head rocked forward and back on its long neck, seeming to carry its massive, awkward shape forward faster with every lunge. It was twenty yards away, on a straight collision course for them.

"Sweet Mary!" Gruffydd said. He had his longbow half out of its sheath.

At the last second, it veered to the left. As it passed it looked down on the four men from its great height, opened its maw, revealing yellow teeth and half-chewed cud, and let out an extended garbled cry that set the hair on Foulques's neck standing on end. The horses pranced and Gruffydd fell off to the ground in a scramble of dust and curses. The second the camel passed them the horses quieted right back down. Gruffydd, however, had his bow out and was fumbling with the string trying to brace it.

"Where do you suppose he is going?" Vignolo said, looking over the barren land.

"Where we should be," Foulques said. He hated camels but he would have given anything to be riding that beast away from here.

Out of nowhere, not ten steps away, a blue-robed man appeared. The wind whipped his layers about him and threatened to tear off the matching tagelmust shrouding his head and face. He walked slowly, muttering words under his breath in a language Foulques did not understand. He did not once glance at the four men even though he passed only a few strides away. He had a straight sword belted at his waist and a thin walking stick in one hand. On the horizon the camel was still running. The Tuareg kept walking in that direction and did not give the four men a moment's notice.

Looking back toward the camp Foulques could see three men riding toward them on horses of questionable stock.

"Remember your roles," Malouf said. "And more importantly," he fixed his eyes on Foulques, "remember that we need these people's help."

Their horses may not have been bred for war, but that was not the case of the men who rode them. Two had swords hanging from shoulder-slung baldrics and one was armed with a short spear. Two of the warriors came to a halt immediately in front of the party, while the third, the spearman, walked his horse behind them. He kept his mount moving, pacing side-to-side. Foulques eyed him warily. It was much easier to commence a charge if your horse was never brought to a standstill.

Malouf greeted the men in front and ignored the one behind. After exchanging the customary pleasantries, the smaller of the two warriors introduced himself as Zola.

"I take you," he said simply and pointed at the camp.

The two Tuaregs led the four outsiders down into the tent village with the ever-wary spear-man following close behind. Blue-robed men stopped what they were doing and openly watched the small procession pass. Every single one of them had their faces covered with blue scarves but the shades were innumerable. The women, on the other hand, did not appear often in blue and not one of them covered their face with a veil or a scarf. They gawked at the newcomers with just as much unbridled curiosity as the men did.

They came to a tent larger than all the others with several people sitting outside. A man wearing a midnight-blue robe that almost could have been called black, sat on a stool while two women washed his feet in a large wooden bowl. His face was uncovered and if he had been a woman, Foulques would have called him beautiful. Perhaps ten years older than Foulques, he was beardless and his light brown skin was unmarred by both sun and time. He had a thick mustache and dark, full eyelashes that his wife and sisters must have coveted.

He eyed the men as they passed. Their three guards touched their fingers to their foreheads and tipped them in his direction. The man did not acknowledge the guards for he was too busy taking in all he could about Foulques and his companions. Foulques decided he was not so beautiful after all. His stare had a penetrating presence to it and Foulques found himself choosing to look away rather than be measured.

Foulques directed his gaze to one of the women washing the man's feet. She too openly stared at them, but unlike the man, he found he could not take his eyes off her. Like all the other women he had seen, she had no veil covering her modesty, but she wore a detailed head covering that fit tightly with a train that fell over the back of her neck. It was largely red with black and white accents intricately woven in, and the whole thing was ringed with tiny hanging ornaments of polished shells and silver. Her hair was bunched at the back except for one long braid that emerged from under her head covering, draped across one eye, and then disappeared again under her head piece.

She caught him staring and returned it with a radiant smile. Once again Foulques looked away.

They threaded their way through a half-dozen more tents, a herd of goats, and then stopped. Zola pointed at a weather-beaten tent that had lived through more than one trans-Saharan journey.

"This be your home. Do not take your horses inside. I will send someone for them."

He turned his horse away and he and his companion trotted off. The third warrior rode his horse completely around the tent once and then spurred his mount to catch up to the others.

"What did he say?" Gruffydd asked no one in particular.

"No horses allowed in the tent, no matter how much you love them," Vignolo said.

Gruffydd spit on the ground. He looked confused. "What do these people think we are?"

"Barbarians," Malouf said. "But it is not what you think." He dismounted and worked at removing his saddle. His horse glistened with sweat. "The desert tribes often bring their animals into their tents during bad sandstorms."

"Ah. Well that makes sense, then," Gruffydd said. A sheepish grin crept onto his face. "I suppose we do the same back home. Except not with horses, and not in tents. Maybe sheep. And there are definitely no sandstorms to worry about. Mud is our great fear."

"So, you do nothing of the sort then," Vignolo said.

"I can tell you for damn sure we do not have any of those beastly, spindly-legged camels terrorizing the countryside!"

"Speaking of which," Foulques said, "I wonder what they would have thought had you put an arrow through their camel?"

"Killing another man's camel is an instant death penalty," Malouf said.

"And so it should be," Vignolo said. "They are such beautiful, godly creatures."

Foulques was surprised at how well Vignolo spoke English. Besides his mother tongue of Italian, it was perhaps the only language Vignolo spoke better than Foulques. Of course, you never knew with the Genoan. He often liked to make himself out to be the dimmest man in the room, right before he took you for everything you had.

"Where is home?" Foulques asked Gruffydd. He realized he knew next to nothing about the young archer.

"Wales. A small place called Llantrisant."

"I do not know it," Foulques said.

"I would choke to death on my own spit if you did. Like I said. Small place."

"I have never been to the English Isles, but I have known a lot of good men from there."

"Sorry to say, Brother Foulques, but you may be the first tolerable French man I have ever known." Gruffydd had a penchant for saying what was on his mind. Foulques liked that in a man, and a woman. Najya never had qualms about saying what she thought, either.

"I have difficulties with many of them myself," Foulques said. "And now may be a good time to request that you do not call me Brother Foulques. Foulques will do." It suddenly dawned on him that Brother Foulques of the Order of Saint John may very well no longer exist. That thought hit him hard, so instead of dwelling on it he chose to go and finish unloading one of the pack horses.

After the unloading, everyone entered their assigned tent, not sure what they would find. From outside it looked like it had fallen off a camel and been trampled by several more. But inside was a different story. Clean carpets covered the ground and four sleeping areas had been made up complete with blankets for lying on and under.

"Well look at this!" Vignolo said.

In the center of the tent was a large clay pot, a jug, and four cups. Vignolo pulled the lid off the pot to reveal a meat stew of some sort with several pieces of flatbread stacked on top.

"Still warm too. I think I may come to this inn again someday." He poured himself a cup of wine from the jug. The others joined him and soon they were all seated around the pot with wine in hand. Malouf said a short prayer for himself and Foulques said grace for everyone else. Vignolo, Malouf, and Gruffydd tore up pieces of flatbread and used them to coax bits of stew out of the pot. They laughed and joked and became hungrier with every mouthful.

Foulques sipped at his wine but did not eat a single bite of the food.

CHAPTER ELEVEN

When Foulques sensed the shadow falling on him from above, the first thing that went through his mind was why did he not post a guard? He knew the Tuareg could not be trusted.

Ever since his rescue from the gaol, he had felt out of sorts, not himself. He had frequent headaches and often found himself alone with the blackest thoughts. When he closed his eyes his dreams were filled with murder, deceit, and lechery. Was this his true nature? Something he had come to discover during those long hours in the Tower of Jonas with nothing but a madman and his own thoughts for company?

The figure's weight landed on his chest and took the air from his body. Firelight filtered in through a slash at the side of the tent where there should not have been an opening. It was not much light, but it was enough to distinguish more than one moving form in the darkness. His attacker straddled his chest and raised his arms overhead. They came down in an arc, smashing something hard and dense, but not sharp, across the side of Foulques's head. He raised his arms to strike again, but a new shadow came hurtling in from the side. It merged with the one straddling Foulques's chest and the suffocating weight was lifted.

Foulques drew in a breath and with it his senses began to assemble information. The sounds of fighting were all around him. Someone lengthened the burning wick in a lamp and Foulques could see like it was midday. Beside him he heard a grunt and a string of complex curses that could only have been Welsh.

Gruffydd grappled with the man who had seconds before been about to cave in Foulques's skull. The masked man had a long knife and he was trying to push it through Gruffydd's chest. But the archer had gotten both his hands around the man's wrist and although he was on the bottom, he pushed the man's entire body weight up and turned the dagger on his attacker. There was a moment of panic in the man's eyes as he realized just how strong Gruffydd was. He fought with all his strength to turn the knife away, but Gruffydd pushed it forward relentlessly as though he wrestled a child. There was a popping sound and a soft hissing of air as the knife entered the man's throat.

"There we go, you bastard," Gruffydd said. He gave the knife a twist, withdrew it, and rolled to another area of the tent.

Foulques was up on his feet now. There must have been a dozen men in the tent. There was no time to tell who needed aid the most, so he grabbed the turban, along with a fistful of the hair beneath it, of the first black-robed man he could reach.

Foulques spun him around and down, slamming his face into the carpets. He let out a muffled groan but was still blindly flailing around a club. With one hand still wrapped up in the man's hair, Foulques squatted down and brought his knee into the man's temple, again and again, until he stopped moving and collapsed on his side. Foulques grabbed the club and was seeking out a new assailant when the tent became even brighter and more bodies entered the fray, but from the proper doorway this time.

It was Zola and his two fellow guards. The spear-man took three strides into the room and skewered a man wrestling with Vignolo. Zola hopped forward and cut a man open with three quick slices from his straight-bladed sword, while his fellow guard thrust his own sword into the back of a man confronting Malouf. Within seconds the tide had turned.

Only one black-robed man was still standing. He threw down his dagger and yelled for mercy, putting his hands together. The spear-man leveled his spear at his chest. "On your knees!" The man readily complied.

Zola sheathed his sword and walked over, looking like he intended to question the man or take him prisoner. But he did not get the chance to do either. For Malouf appeared behind the man and drew a small dagger across his throat. Zola looked at Malouf and frowned as the man toppled over.

Malouf spit on the man and shouted, "For Allah!"

Zola spewed off orders to his fellow guards and they rushed out of the tent, while he remained inside with Foulques and his companions.

"Who were these men?" Zola asked.

"You tell us," Foulques said. He bent over and ripped the head scarf off a dead man. "Recognize him? Was it you who paid him to slit our throats or are you just here to clean things up?"

"I do not clean things up," Zola said. With perfect timing, spear-man threw open the tent flaps and ushered in a half-dozen men. They were in sleeping attire and did not look happy to be there, but they bowed deferentially and began to set the room right.

"They clean things up," Zola said. He began shouting orders in his own language, pointing at certain things to emphasize his points. It was obvious he was telling the men to get the bodies out, clean up the blood, and repair that hole in the tent.

Zola turned back to Foulques. "If you wait outside while the slaves do their work it will go much faster."

Foulques felt a hand on his shoulder and Malouf steered him out to wait under the stars.

✠

SHORTLY AFTER FIRST light, before anyone was awake save Foulques, a voice called out from beyond the tent's opening. It was Zola but his voice was loud and formal.

"Guests. Guests. Are you awake? Peace be with you. Are you awake?"

"Yes!" Vignolo said.

"Peace be upon you," Malouf added, sitting up from his blankets.

"Pleased if you would come outside as soon as you are ready."

"Of course," Malouf said. He gave Foulques a puzzled look.

They rose and dressed quickly. Upon emerging from the tent into the morning, the first thing Foulques saw was a large circle formed by about twenty blue-robed warriors. Foulques shook his head. First, he had been foolish enough to not post a guard last night, now all these warriors had assembled a stone's throw away while the others slept and he had not heard a thing. He swore to God that he would be more alert from this moment on. The second thing he noticed, just beyond the circle, were the birds pecking at the naked bodies of their attackers from last night tied to posts dug into the ground.

Zola gestured toward a carpet upon which food and drink were carefully arranged.

"Our chieftain provides refreshment and entertainment. Please sit."

Once they were seated, Zola removed his robe and breeches until he stood in the full sun with nothing on save his undergarment wrap and tagelmust. The sunlight played and pranced along a mass of welts and scars on his light brown skin. He picked a stick up off the ground and stepped into the circle. Three men stood up, each armed with a similar stick. A man sitting outside the circle started tapping out a slow rhythm on a drum.

Zola let out a deep-throated grunt and the three men came for him all at once. He blocked most of the strikes with lightning fast parries but one man's stick slapped across his naked back with a resounding echo. Zola grimaced in pain and danced away. They charged him again and he defended and countered, striking one man in the leg and another across the head. The man who was struck in the head sat back down only to be replaced by someone else.

Foulques watched with interest. It was obviously a training method to teach their warriors the use of the sword. But the movements were quick and strange to his eyes. Their stances and techniques were similar to the ones used when fighting with a curved sword, but the Tuareg favored a straight blade called a takouba. This stick dance was almost a hybrid of two different sword fighting styles.

Every time Zola landed what would amount to a killing blow, the receiving man sat down and another stood up from the circle to take his place. But Zola was granted no such reprieve. After only ten minutes, he was battered and bloody, and had lost all the bounce to his step. Foulques was finding the beating hard to watch, but the warriors kept coming and they did not hold back. Zola started to fall to the ground. He got back to his feet a half dozen times, but finally he could rise no more. The three men inside the circle with him started screeching in the shrill manner of desert dwellers everywhere and danced around their fallen foe. The drummer's leathery hands picked up their pace and he began chanting, the warriors danced faster. Finally, the drumming abruptly stopped. Each man, in turn, bent over and struck Zola once more with his stick, then turned his back on him and walked out of the circle. Zola lay there unmoving, unable to get up. Two men entered and dragged him out of the circle on his knees.

Foulques looked to Malouf, Gruffydd, and Vignolo. The others were as disgusted as he was. Even Vignolo had sampled neither food nor drink.

"The chieftain will meet you now," said a little man with a dirty face and a neck clanging with a number of gaudy metal necklaces. He stepped back, which sent his necklaces warring with one another. "This way."

As Foulques and his group followed the man toward the large tent, he saw another man disrobe and step into the circle. It was the spear-man. As they carried on toward the chieftain's tent, Foulques heard the drums start up again.

Two warriors flanked the entrance to the chieftain's tent. They held the tent flaps aside and motioned the foreigners forward. When the man with the necklaces tried to follow, they stopped him with a hand to his chest and a few harsh words, followed by a cuff to the head. He scurried away without any argument.

The interior was clean but its furnishings were certainly not extravagant by Arab standards. The right half of the tent was partitioned off with brightly colored linen curtains, making the interior look much smaller than it did from the outside. At the far end the man Foulques had seen the day before stood on a slightly raised platform, wearing the same midnight-blue robe with a slightly lighter colored tagelmust. The lower portion was pulled down, so once again his entire face was revealed. The one new addition to his wardrobe was a sword attached to a wide, multi-colored baldric that hung over his shoulder. His hand rested on the back of a low, wide chair. And to Foulques's surprise, in the chair was the young woman with the braid hanging over one eye. He assumed now that she was his wife.

"God be with you," Malouf said bowing deeply.

The man stepped down from the platform, his hand on the pommel of his sword, and returned the bow.

The sword was not for show, Foulques noted. The way he slid his feet and maintained an easy balance with every step was a sure giveaway. Even an untrained eye could tell he was a warrior.

He cleared his throat. "My name is Faraji Mensah. It is my honor to relay the words of my chieftain, the Exalted Rashida, daughter of Maroun, daughter of Iras."

Foulques blinked, and his eyes went to the girl seated on the dais. She was chieftain? Then this Faraji must be her regent or vizier. She caught him staring and like yesterday she met his eyes. Although Foulques thought them warm enough, she did not grace him with a smile today.

Malouf touched his fingertips to his forehead and bowed. "God grant the Exalted Rashida His favor. I am Karim Hakimi, the speaker for myself and my companions. May I present to you the traders Valentino Bonello and Elvezio Testani, and their manservant Gruffydd Blood."

Faraji did not look at each man as his name was mentioned but kept his eyes locked entirely on Malouf. Malouf had barely finished his introductions when the Tuareg launched into his next address, like he was reading it from a scroll.

"First of all, the Exalted Rashida would like to express her sincere regret for what happened last evening. As well as her relief that none of you were harmed."

"It is of no consequence," Malouf said, waving the chieftain's concern away with one hand. "We thank you for allowing your brave warriors to intervene."

"You are our guests. To do otherwise would invoke the wrath of Allah." His substantial brow furrowed and he spoke the words forcefully. Foulques got the impression he did not think much of Allah's rule.

"Regardless, it is to men, and women," Malouf bowed to the chieftain, "to whom we owe our lives. We are in your debt."

The chieftain leaned forward and spoke a torrent of words. Her voice was soft, musical, but Foulques did not understand a single thing. He did not speak any more than a few words of the Tuareg language, but he had heard enough to know that this was not that. Looking at Malouf and Vignolo he could tell they were bewildered as well.

Faraji nodded. "The Exalted Rashida is sorry to say that it is no longer permissible for you to travel with us. You may stay one more night, then you will leave."

At first Foulques thought he had heard the man wrong. But this was Arabic, his second tongue. There was no mistake. It even took Malouf a long time before he could speak.

"I do not understand. As I have said, last night was of no consequence to us—"

"She feels after last night's events, we cannot guarantee

your safety. It would be an affront to Allah to promise otherwise."

"It is our belief that we have paid you well for your services already, but let me talk with my partners. I am sure we could come up with a few more denarii to sweeten the purse."

"The matter has been decided. We will return your payment."

The chieftain chirped a few words and Faraji turned to her and listened as she said something else. He frowned, clearly shocked, and spoke back to her in that strange language of theirs. Whatever she had said, he did not approve. They had a couple more exchanges and then she cut him off with a chopping motion of her hand and he went silent.

Faraji turned slowly around. "The Exalted Rashida says there is perhaps a way for you to stay and accompany us on our journey. But you must agree to her condition."

"Of course, if it is within our means," Malouf said.

"The Exalted Rashida is a student of language. She would like one of the Venetians to teach her their tongue."

Malouf glanced first at Foulques, then Vignolo, while Gruffydd looked from man to man trying to get even an inkling of what was transpiring.

"I would be honored to share my language with the chieftain," Vignolo said.

"Not you. Him." Faraji pointed at Foulques and his eyes were not at all kind as they fixed him with a penetrating glare.

Foulques looked at Vignolo then Malouf. He did not move his lips, but Foulques could hear Malouf repeating his earlier words in his head. *We need these people's help.*

"Please tell the Exalted Rashida I would like nothing more," Foulques said.

"Very well. You will report here to me every night after the evening meal. We begin tonight. Are we in agreement?"

"A question, if I may. Why did the chieftain choose me over my companion?"

Faraji forced his response from between half-clenched teeth. "She said you have a gentle face."

His tone and demeanor suggested he saw something else entirely within Elvezio Testani.

CHAPTER TWELVE

THE SMALL MAN with the necklaces once again showed up to escort Foulques to the chieftain's tent. Outside the tent were the usual two guards flanking the entrance, but tonight Faraji was also there. He had pulled his stool off to one side of the entrance and as close as he could get it to the tent itself. His scabbarded sword was balanced across a small table to his right. His eyes watched Foulques approach while his hands busied themselves by carving the bark off a long, weathered piece of wood with a small knife, leaving a collection of finely curled shavings on the ground at his feet.

"Peace be upon you," Foulques said.

Faraji said nothing. He reached over with his branch and tapped the nearest guard's spear three times. The guard stepped forward and drew Foulques's sword from his scabbard. He set it aside, then used his rough, calloused hands to give Foulques and his clothing a thorough search. When he was satisfied, he stepped back leaving Foulques to rearrange his disheveled robe and tagelmust on his own. Once they deemed him presentable, the guards pulled the tent flaps aside. Foulques took a step forward only to find his way blocked by Faraji's stick.

"What is that?" he asked. He tapped Foulques's empty scabbard. Attached to his scabbard was a tiny leather sleeve that housed a knife that Foulques used only for eating.

"This? It is only an eating utensil."

"Do you intend to eat something in this tent?"

Faraji nodded at one of the guards, who promptly pulled the miniature knife out of its sleeve and set it with Foulques's sword. He slowly raised his stick and made a sideways gesture with his head, which Foulques took as a sign to enter even though it appeared more of a "no" than a "yes."

The tent was brightly lit with a number of lamps arranged within the circumference of the room. Like earlier, the curtains to what Foulques surmised to be the chieftain's private quarters, were drawn closed and no lights burned within. A small brazier near the door kept out the coolness of the night and the familiar smell of frankincense was heavy in the air. The Exalted Rashida sat in the middle of the room on the carpets, her legs folded to one side and hidden beneath a red robe embroidered with white and gold patterns. There was a small table in front of her just large enough to hold the teapot and two cups set upon it.

"Buona sera," she said and gestured for Foulques to join her at the table. The movement set off a pleasant tinkling as her many hoop earrings and charms dangling from her headpiece played off one another. That radiant smile from the first time he had seen her was back and it made Foulques nervous on many levels.

He returned the greeting and lowered himself to the

floor. He went over in his mind what he was going to teach her for tonight's lesson. Greetings and introductions were a good place to start. Perhaps he could build on the teapot and introduce some table pleasantries.

Continuing in Italian, she said, "I am pleased to make your acquaintance. My name is Rashida." In her case, jewelry was not just something to be admired with the eyes, but also served as a subtle accompaniment to her voice.

Foulques was about to state his own name, but she beat him to it. "Elvezio Testani, was it not? I should like to keep these sessions as informal as possible. If it suits you, please use only Rashida when addressing me. May I simply call you Elvy?"

Foulques was speechless. Her Italian was better than his would ever be. And although her words were soft and musical, there was a force behind them. She was used to setting the tone for any conversation she participated in.

"Of course," he said. "It would please me immensely."

"Excellent!"

"I must say... Rashida, you speak Italian very well."

Color rose to her cheeks and she smiled. "Do you really think so? I am happy to hear that."

"So well in fact, I think there is very little I can teach you. For I am not from Venezia proper, but rather a small town in the countryside." Foulques said. He was concentrating hard.

"I thought you sounded different than others I have spoken with," she said. "But I was not sure, for it has been some time since I have seen a merchant from your country."

"I honestly do not think there is much I can teach you," Foulques said.

"Can anyone truly give a language to another? I think it is something you must take for yourself. And the only way to do that is to spend time with someone skilled in its use."

"That is true with most things," Foulques said. "But perhaps my partner would be more suitable for your language studies. He was born in Venezia and is much more educated than I, coming from the country, as I have."

"You are so thoughtful, Elvy! But, no. I want you."

Foulques forced a smile. He thought he felt the corner of his mouth twitch.

"No one needs to teach anyone anything in these sessions. You can ask me any questions you have and I will do the same. We will simply come together and have tea." She lifted up the teapot and filled both their cups. "We will spend time together, that is all. Does that sound so bad?"

✣

IT WAS DARK when Foulques got back to his tent. The others sat up from their blankets and demanded an update.

"Did she seem happy with her lesson?" Malouf asked.

"Did you get to colors? I hope she did not ask you how to say 'indigo'," Vignolo said.

When the four men were together the bulk of the conversation took place in French, for Gruffydd had demonstrated a passable understanding of it. However, whenever Gruffydd had something to add, he always spoke in English, which Malouf detested.

"As much as I hate to say it, Vignolo was right," Foulques said. "We should have fought harder for him to be her teacher. She has a better understanding of Italian than I ever will."

Malouf's eyes clouded over.

Vignolo groaned. "I knew it! She is a clever one, our little desert fox. She played us from the beginning with all that 'we cannot take you now, it is for your own good' crap. Do you think she knows you are not Italian?"

"I cannot be sure," Foulques said. "But if she knew I was lying, why would she play me along? Why agree to take us anywhere?"

Malouf, who up to this point had been uncharacteristically uninvolved in the conversation, spoke up. "I am troubled to say, we may have a problem." When he had everyone's attention, he continued. "The men who attacked us last night were no random thieves."

"You think the chieftain sent them after us?" Gruffydd asked.

Malouf visibly cringed when Gruffydd spoke. "No. They were bounty hunters."

"Oh. Well that makes sense. Those scum always show up at the worst possible times," Vignolo said.

"These ones were not sent by some jealous husband, Vignolo dei Vignoli. They were commissioned by the Sultan of Cairo."

"Khalil put out a bounty on you?" Foulques was going to say more but cut himself off. No one else knew Malouf was responsible for the poisoning of Khalil's father. But even if he knew it had been Malouf, why would he want him dead? Malouf had made Khalil a sultan.

"Not me, Foulques. The bounty is for one particular Hospitaller knight and his accomplice, a certain Genoan pirate."

"Well, Khalil has got his horses crossed, then. Because Foulques here is no longer a Hospitaller and I have certainly never been a pirate."

Being just told he had a price on his head did not seem to faze Vignolo in the least. Foulques, however, could not understand why the Mamluk Sultanate even knew who he was, never mind was willing to pay to have him killed.

"What possible danger are men like us to the sultan?" Foulques asked.

Malouf looked first at Vignolo and then Foulques and then shook his head. "How are you both still alive? Do you not live in the same world I do? Are you so sure it is the sultan that wants your head and not, perhaps, a man who has come to be his most trusted emir?"

Understanding dawned on Foulques like a spring rain. "Badru Hashim," he said.

"Oh," Vignolo said.

"But anyone who brings your head to him gets nothing. Apparently, Badru Hashim has his own plans for your death."

CHAPTER THIRTEEN

THE SECOND LESSON began as the first. Even though Foulques was quite capable of making it the short distance to the chieftain's tent by himself, the necklace man showed up after the evening meal to escort him. He made a grand procession out of it too, going out of the way to pass by as many people as possible. The coolness he was greeted with by the chieftain's guards made Foulques wonder if he had been ordered to bring him or if he had simply taken it upon himself as some kind of a status boost among the other tribe members. Tuaregs were a confusing people, with their Exalted Rashida perhaps one of the most puzzling.

Foulques had learned in their last conversation that Faraji was not her regent, as he had thought, but her uncle. As per last time, he sat on his stool outside the tent scraping on a piece of wood, his scabbarded sword on a table next to him. Foulques did not bother to greet the man this time. Malouf would have been aghast, but Foulques did not care. He was tired of Faraji always looking at him like some kind of miscreant. The guards searched him thoroughly once again, being careful to make a show of ridding him of his dangerous eating knife, and he was ushered into the private domain of the Exalted Rashida.

As before, Rashida was seated at her table in the center of the room. "Good Evening, Elvy. I am so glad you could come."

Foulques exchanged pleasantries and took his seat across from her.

"What shall be our topic of discussion, tonight?" Rashida asked, pouring them both tea.

"If you would permit, I thought I might ask you questions about the Tuareg. I know very little about your people."

Rashida clapped her hands. "Excellent," she said and her eyes lit up like a little girl. "We *Kel Tamasheq* love to talk about ourselves."

As do most people, Foulques thought. This topic had actually been Malouf's idea as a way for Foulques to direct the conversation to areas that would not stress his vocabulary.

"Tamasheq? Is that what you call yourselves?"

"Yes. Tuareg is an outsider's name for us."

"I understand there are several clans, or tribes, of the Tamasheq. Are any of the others ruled by women?"

Her brow crinkled, as did the top of her fine nose, and she looked at him from under her braid. "Some of the others may have a man as a chieftain, but they are all ruled by women."

This caught Foulques by surprise. He had wrongly surmised that Rashida's position was a rarity.

"Have women always held a prominent place amongst the Tamasheq?"

"Always. Women own the tents and all of the animals, which are passed down from mother to daughter. Oh, sometimes a man will own his own camel, for he needs that when traveling with the caravans. But it is the women who decide what business matters to pursue. This is why I must learn your tongue."

"I see."

"Men have their talents, but business and ruling a tribe is certainly not one of them."

"Why do the men always cover their faces?"

"Because there are things in the desert, spirits of great power, that will enter a man's nose or mouth if he does not take the proper precautions."

Foulques waited for her to laugh, or smile even, but she did not. "And the women? Why do they not cover their faces?"

"Because we are beautiful, and our men like to look at us." This at least brought with it a smile. "Do these things trouble you, Elvy?"

"Of course not. I… just find it different. It goes against my understanding of the Quran."

She nodded and laughed. "Do you think the Tamasheq were born the day the Prophet Mohammad arrived? We are an old people, Elvy. We were here when there were no others, when only the ifrit of the djinn ruled the desert. We accept the Quran as the great truth here, amongst the younger people of the world. But out there," she waved her hand to the west, to the Sahara, "we follow the old ways."

"And yet you speak perfect Italian. You do not shy away from the new either, it would seem."

"We are survivors. I do what I must for my people. And to be honest, I do it a little because I enjoy speaking to people from other lands."

"Have you done this before?"

Rashida smiled. "Yes! But do not be upset, Elvy. You are one of my favorites."

"Are you never concerned for your safety? I mean being alone in your tent with a man you do not know."

"Did you not see my uncle sitting outside? He can hear every word we say. Though he cannot understand a one." Her eyes lit up again with that mischievous smile and this time, Foulques could not help grinning a little himself at the thought of Faraji straining to understand them. But what she said next tore that grin from his face and trampled it underfoot.

"Now, enough of my people. Tell me about your home. Do you have roads of water in your city as well?"

✹

THE TUAREGS BROKE camp the following day. At dawn Foulques was awakened by, as Gruffydd called it, the "terrible bleating" of camels. The Tuareg let their camels range free and live off the land while they were in camp. But now that they were ready to move on, animal handlers had set out while it was still dark to round them up. Some would stray for miles, so all morning men were bringing more and more of the beasts back from the wild. The tent village swelled with man and beast and the camels' large, flat feet kicked up clouds of dust that choked Foulques and his companions the moment they ducked their heads out of their tent. Not seconds after they had all their possessions out than a dozen men descended upon them. The tent was torn down, rolled up into manageable sections and, along with all their possessions, tied onto camels with an efficiency that left Foulques slack-jawed under the safety of his scarf. Dust was caked around the slits of his eyes and he now understood why the Tuareg men were always masked.

Gruffydd stood silently by and watched the organized chaos.

"Do not worry, Gruffydd," Foulques said. "They are not as comfortable as a horse by any means, but it will not take you long to get used to their sway." He talked a brave fight, but Foulques himself dreaded climbing up onto the lumpy back of one of the smelly, inelegant beasts.

"My mates back home would never believe this," Gruffydd said shaking his head.

Foulques looked at the caravan line as it began to form and stretch out. He estimated it was going to be seventy or eighty camels in total.

"I suppose we will all have some stories to tell after this journey," Foulques said.

Apparently, the Tuaregs had been dismantling parts of the camp for days, for it was only three hours past dawn when Zola came leading four camels. He limped a little and he had a new stripe across one side of his face that had blackened both eyes, but other than that he was his usual blunt self. He forced the animals into a kneel, which they loudly protested with throaty roars. He called Foulques and his companions forward and instructed them on how to climb aboard and sit.

Once everyone was in place, Zola made a clucking sound and all four beasts began the ponderous rocking back and forth motion required for them to rise to their full height. A span of time through which Gruffydd squawked continually.

Zola whistled and another camel walked to him and dropped only its front legs down to the ground. Zola grabbed onto some saddle ties, clambered his way up, and bid the camel to rise. His two faithful companions appeared on the ground next to him. Apparently, they would walk to Timbuktu. And they were not alone. As the line of camels stretched out people followed suit on foot until two or three people flanked every camel. Then, everyone simply stopped moving. The line was formed and Foulques had difficulty counting exactly how many warriors were present for it seemed that almost all the men wore a blue robe and turban of some shade or another. The women were dressed mostly in the colors of the earth, but each one of them had a bright accent of some kind, such as a piece of jewelry or a finely woven head covering. Unlike the men, whose faces were almost always covered, not one of the women wore a veil or attempted to hide their face.

A solitary drum began to sound and Foulques saw Rashida emerge from her tent. Hers was one of the few tents still standing, for not everyone would desert the camp. This was a full-time camp for the Tuareg, one that swelled and receded with the trading season.

The chieftain climbed onto a huge camel covered in multi-colored tassels and a headdress with as many tiny, sparkling ornaments as her own. The single drum kept beating. Rashida's camel rose with her in its saddle and then she stood up on the beast's back like it was the most natural thing in the world. She raised her arms and let a long, loud cry of the desert people pour forth from her lungs and it was answered by a hundred voices. She jumped into her saddle and urged her camel into a run. She raced to the head of the caravan, urged on by the deafening trills of the Kel Tamasheq.

✥

"You got in late last night," Vignolo said. He had urged his camel forward to ride next to Foulques. "Should I be concerned for your honor?"

Foulques gave him what he hoped was a dark look. "Have you never spent an evening with a woman and not succumbed to your base desires?"

"Many times. But those occasions usually involved a husband or brother driving me from a warm bed."

"It was not the bed they drove you from."

"You are evading me, Fou—er, Elvezio."

"Please. Call me Elvy."

Vignolo's mouth fell open. "Foulques... tell me the truth. Have you and our Exalted Rashida been putting out the lantern *before* you leave her tent?"

"Vignolo!"

"What? Would it be against your vows? What vows? You have to belong to something to have vows. You do not owe the Order a damn thing. Not your respect, not your loyalty, and damn well no vows of whatever."

It seemed that his and Foulques's treatment at the hands of his uncle, and then the Order, had left a sour taste in Vignolo's mouth. This had obviously been building up inside him for some time now and he had finally let it out. It was understandable. Without his stipend from the Hospitallers it was just a matter of time before Vignolo was broke, if he was not already. Perhaps he had some creditors Foulques did not know about. Ones that were making him nervous. Or, could it simply be Foulques's disappearance for those two weeks had been harder on Vignolo than he let on? He had admitted that if it had not been for Malouf contacting him, he never would have known what had happened to Foulques.

"I am sorry," Vignolo said. "All I meant to say was if I were you, I would be making up for all those lost years."

Lost years. Is that what they were? Had he been mistaken about his calling? Had he spent all those years walking a path God had not meant him to take? It was, after all, his uncle who had brought him into the Order of Saint John, not God.

"I enjoy talking with her. She is an interesting woman. That is all," Foulques said, more to break the silence between them than anything.

"And beautiful?" Vignolo asked, raising an eyebrow.

And beautiful, Foulques said only to himself.

"You know it is just a matter of time before she steers the topic of conversation toward men and women and—"

"How do you make these wild speculations out of nothing?" Foulques said.

Vignolo laughed. "She calls you Elvy! For the love of Mary, what else is a man to think?"

Foulques left it at that and used his switch to rap either side of his camel's neck sending her trotting ahead. He had had enough of Vignolo's rants for one day. He had wanted to ask his advice on something that had been troubling him, but he did not have the energy now. His thoughts were too scattered.

He was tired of pretending to be someone he was not, of lying to Rashida. Now that they were on the road, what would be the harm in her knowing the truth of who they were? The Tuaregs were loyal only to themselves. Yes, they were Muslim, though perhaps they flirted with some pagan beliefs as Rashida herself admitted, but they were no friends to the Mamluks.

He looked back over his shoulder. The bulk of the line of camels stretched off into the distance, shimmering in the afternoon haze. Looking ahead, if he squinted, he could just make out Rashida's camel plodding along, leading them all to God only knew where.

CHAPTER FOURTEEN

THEY WERE NEARING the end of their first day of overland travel and Badru had already come to an understanding with his three Hausa guides. Firstly, they were not to talk to him or any of his men unless absolutely necessary. Secondly, if they touched any one of the sixty-seven women or twenty-two children in their retinue, they would die a slow and miserable death by his hand, and his hand alone. In his youth, he had learned to never trust the nomads, no matter what tribe, and when he first saw who Vice-Sultan Baydara had arranged to be his guides to Timbuktu, he immediately disliked them. He reverted to his old mindset, deciding his instincts had served him well back then so there was no reason to change his ways. That was what he had missed about the desert. Neither it nor its people ever changed.

The three guides rode at the front of their column while Badru and Safir followed on their own camels a short distance behind. The rest of his men, twenty-three Mamluks who had been with him since time immemorial, were mounted on camels and rode spread out amongst the slaves.

At the very rear were another dozen mercenaries he had recruited in Barqa, where they had left the ship. He could have gotten more, for the sultan's purse had no bottom and everyone sensed it, but Badru trusted no one except his own Mamluks. He felt twelve additional men were enough should they run into trouble with nomads, but not enough that he would have to fear their betrayal. It was a healthy balance, but he knew it was only a matter of time before he had to make an example of one of their number. Too many of them wore hungry grins on their faces when they looked at the slaves.

Once again, Badru reflected on how much he had missed the desert.

"We will be stopping to make camp for the night soon," Safir said. "What do you wish done with them?" Safir nodded over his shoulder at the camel behind them. A litter constructed of two long poles tied to the camel's saddle dragged the English king's commander through the dirt. His servant, the Arab woman with a penchant for honey, rode the same beast.

There was one camel for every two slaves. If they could not both fit on the camel, one had to take turns walking. Baydara had organized only one camel for every five slaves but Badru did not want this journey to take any longer than need be. He had used the sultan's purse to purchase every additional camel he could find in Barqa. Never before had Badru had so many camels for a slave run. Baydara would be furious, but Badru did not care. What he cared about was getting this task over and done with.

"Put a four-man guard on them and another four-man guard on the Barqa mercenaries. Keep it discreet, but Allah as my witness, they will be up to no good before long."

"Very well, Emir."

※

NAJYA SAT IN the dark next to Grandison's litter while in the distance a single fire burned, which most of the Mamluks and their men-for-hire sat around. The Frankish women and children, in their flea-ridden desert garb that the Northman had supplied them with, were on the other side of the warriors. For whatever reason, the Northman was keeping Grandison and herself separated from the other captives.

The darkness brought with it a welcome relief from the scorching day's sun, and although it had been hot, they were not yet in a true desert. The ground was full of broken rock and the landscape was dotted with boulders, some as big as the camel she rode. They had stopped several times during the day for the camels to graze on the short clumps of grass carving out an existence in the shadows of the larger rocks.

Najya put her hand to Grandison's forehead. He was not feverish and seemed to be in a deep sleep. She took it as a good sign. She stood and began walking into the darkness. She had gotten ten or twelve paces when a Mamluk sitting on the ground with his back up against his saddle, asked her where she was going.

"I must tend to myself," she said and kept walking. He must not have been too concerned for he did not even bother to stand. He just waved her away. And why not? In his eyes, it was Grandison who held all value. She was nothing to them, not even a slave they could sell in this land, for she was Muslim. And anyway, where would she go? Alone and on foot, only a nomad could survive out here.

She had walked farther than she had intended but it felt good to be away from the dust and grime of humans. She stared at the stars, wondering how God decided who went where in this world. Did it matter to Him who became a slave and who was destined to be a sultan? How did He decide who to make a Jew, a Christian, or a Muslim? She could accept that everyone lived and died by His will, but how did He arrive at His choices?

Not far away, a large shadow moved, and then another. Najya realized they were camels searching for forage.

"You should not be out here."

She turned to see one of the Barqa men sitting on a rock. His black robes blotted out the stars behind him, but did little else to hint at his presence. Still, the night was not so dark that Najya did not recognize him. He wore a sword at his side, but he was no warrior. In fact, he was little more than a boy. He was the one Badru had hired to look after the camels.

"I did not see you there," Najya said.

He nodded. "That is why I knew you were not one of them."

"Who?"

"The demons that roam. The ifrit."

Najya laughed. "I assure you I am no demon. If I were, and I had their powers, I definitely would not be here."

The young man's brow furrowed and Najya regretted laughing at his superstitious beliefs.

"You should not mock them," he said. "What if one of them should hear?"

"I am sorry. You surprised me is all."

"Are you a princess?"

Najya really had to fight back the urge to laugh this time. "No, I am not."

"Why do the Mamluks keep you apart from the others? Why do they make you tend to the white man?"

The innocence in his voice was refreshing. "They do not make me look after that man," Najya said. "They hurt him and I am doing my best to heal his wounds."

He took this in and turned it over in his mind for a moment. "You are Muslim?"

"Yes."

"Then if you kill the white man they will no longer need you to care for him." He shrugged his shoulders. "Perhaps they will let you go then."

"No," Najya said. "I will not do that."

"Why?"

She could see him wrestling with her predicament. "Because he is a great man and very important to his people. I must do everything I can to keep him alive."

This seemed to make sense to him and his face relaxed. He was a couple of years away from being what Najya would call a man, but he would be handsome when he was.

"What is your name?" Najya asked.

"Are you a sorceress? If you are, I cannot tell you my

name."

Najya shook her head. "My name is Najya."

After a moment of watching her closely, he said, "I am Akari. You should not be out here. The night is early and the demons may yet come."

She thought of the fires in Acre, the sounds of children crying for their mothers, of the grunts and screams of men as they hacked each other to death.

"The demons are already here," she said, deciding then and there that there had been entirely too much randomness to God's decisions of late. "The Mamluks do the demons' bidding by keeping the white man from his people. I must get him away." She pulled off a bracelet from around her wrist. "Take this. It is yours if you help me."

He looked at her, and then at the silver bracelet. As if in a trance, he pushed himself forward off his rock and gently took it from her hand.

"I will give it to my mother," he said. He looked at Najya. "We can take two camels and go now. Come."

"It is not that simple," Najya said.

At that point Najya had some misgivings about her plan, but what was done was done. It was time she helped God decide her fate.

CHAPTER FIFTEEN

"WHY ARE WE stopping?" Foulques asked Malouf. The caravan train was in open country, the sun still not yet directly overhead and they had come to a full stop.

"It looks like the chieftain is sending a couple of scouts up ahead."

"To where?" Foulques could see nothing but hard rocks and the same dusty, beige landscape in every direction. Up ahead, Rashida consulted with her uncle and a couple of other men.

Minutes later, Foulques could make out the camels of the two scouts returning. His curiosity got the better of him and he urged his own camel on to the front of the line. Zola, who was taking his turn walking, trotted along wordlessly beside him.

He arrived at Rashida's side just as the scouts returned. They gave a brief report, of which Foulques understood nothing. He had to resort to watching Rashida's face for hints. It was not difficult, for she was not one to hide her emotions. Her uncle was even more transparent. His thick eyebrows and heavy lashes cast a raptorial shadow over the rest of his face as he put two fingers in his mouth and let out a shrill whistle. Within seconds a dozen warriors pushed their way to the front of the caravan.

"What is happening?" Foulques asked Rashida.

"It is nothing to concern yourself with, Elvy," she said. "My uncle will look after it."

From his current position, Foulques could now see the tops of a few trees in the distance. A small oasis, he realized.

"Are there enemies up ahead? At the oasis?"

"It is nothing. Just some Hausa who were here when we passed through two weeks ago. Do not concern yourself."

The dozen warriors had fully gathered around them now. Rashida's uncle drew his sword and whipped his camel into a dead run, with his warriors only a second or two behind him. The air filled with the high pitched cries of desert raiders and the hair on Foulques's neck stood on end. He kicked his own camel and was rewarded with only a disappointing trot. Rashida called out after him, but her words were drowned out by the war cries up ahead.

The land fell away and he could make out the first signs of vegetation and a small pool of water. A handful of small tents clustered around the water, until a Tuareg rode through the middle of them swinging his sword left and right cutting guidelines and trampling the shelters under his camel's hooves. Screams of terror filled the air, and blue-robed warriors darted in and out of the date trees, most still mounted, some on foot. But their quarry were no soldiers. There were a few men, but the vast majority of the people running for their lives were women and children.

Foulques absorbed all of this in a split second. His heart seized in his chest and he forgot to breathe. He had spent his entire life fighting against the unadulterated evil of this very thing. He may no longer be a Hospitaller Knight but he would not stand by now and do nothing.

He kicked and whipped his camel until it descended into the chaos. He planted his foot in the back of the head of a blue-robed man as he careened past him. To his left, three sword-wielding Tuaregs had two men on their knees. Foulques yanked on his camel's reins but the beast only turned his head toward him and tried to bite him. Foulques cursed and pulled his leg away from its yellow teeth. He leapt off the back of the creature and hit the ground rolling. When he came up his sword was in his hand.

He sprinted at the Tuaregs and hit one of them in the center of his back with his shoulder, sending him sprawling to the ground. The other two turned with wide eyes. Foulques thrust at one of them to create space and then attacked the other with a flurry of side-to-side cuts.

The Tuareg was skilled at blocking and Foulques was unable to finish him before he had to turn his attention back to the first man and parry an attack. Movement out of the corner of his eye told him the man he had initially shouldered to the ground was back on his feet.

He was thinking how he would have given anything to be wearing his hauberk at that moment, when all three men shook at the same time. They shuddered again. The next thing Foulques knew his cheek was pressed against wet earth. Then, the midday sun simply disappeared and he was left alone in darkness.

✠

A RELIEVING COOLNESS ran from the back of Foulques's neck all the way down to his calves. If he could only shift his head a little, perhaps that relief could be shared with his throbbing head.

"He stirs," Zola said.

"Elvezio? Can you hear me?" It was Malouf.

Before he opened his eyes, Foulques took a moment to gather himself. He knew he had been unconscious, for he had experienced waking from that peaceful embrace on many occasions, but he had no idea how or why. He could tell he was on the ground, but he was no longer in the desert. The ground here was cool and damp, and the earth seemed to tug him into her embrace, refusing to give him up.

"Open your eyes. Slowly," Malouf said.

The oasis.

The memory hit him and he both opened his eyes and tried to sit upright in the same instant, but a hand planted firmly on his chest prevented him from doing so. Suspended above his head was a cloth set upon sticks thrust into the ground, providing shade for his head. Through the thin fabric he could make out a cluster of people leaning over, peering at him. Not all appeared friendly.

He focused on Malouf's face until he could keep it framed clearly within his vision.

"It is over, then," Foulques said. "They are dead?"

"No one is dead Foulques. The Tuaregs ran off some

Hausa tribes-people. That is all. Faraji wanted to put you in chains, but I explained some things about your past. They left you in my care. With a few more guards nearby, as you can imagine."

He leaned over and adjusted the sun shade. "Do you remember what happened?"

Foulques took in a deep breath and held it for a second or two. "More than I would like," he said.

✷

DESPITE THE DAY'S events, the necklace man did not shirk his duties. However, he did put them on hold for the few minutes it took to trade one of his more delicate neck chains for what Gruffydd attempted to convince him was the finest bodkin arrow point in this part of the world. Once the deal was struck, he sat amongst them and showed no sign of leaving. When Foulques rose, so did the little man, so Foulques took this as a sign that his lesson was still on.

Rashida's caravan tent was a smaller version of the one in the permanent camp, which was to be expected, but it came complete with the same guards standing outside its doorway and a high-strung uncle glowering nearby. Faraji was not working on his stick when Foulques and the necklace man arrived outside. He paced back and forth slowly near the entrance with his straight sword in hand. He also had his left sleeve rolled up and Foulques noticed a sheath strapped there that held a knife as long as his forearm. He followed Foulques's every move like a hawk watching a hole in the ground.

As the two men passed by one another, Foulques noticed the crossguard of Faraji's sword was wrapped in thick leather. It occurred to him that he had seen the same thing on many of the other warriors' swords as well. His head started throbbing again and he wondered if that was what he had been hit with. As Foulques looked at it, the flat of the crossguard seemed to match the size of the bump on the base of his skull suspiciously well. If so, that bit of leather on the sword's quillons could very well have preserved his life.

Rashida was waiting for him just inside the door. "Take my arm, Elvy."

She guided him to the small table by his elbow and settled him before she herself sat down. "How are you feeling?"

"Fine," he said. She sat back, perhaps to distance herself from the coldness in his voice.

"You had us all worried, Elvy. The warriors you attacked thought you had been possessed by djinn. But then your friend told us what happened to your parents when you were but an infant."

"What did he say exactly?"

"That your mother and father's caravan was attacked by Bedouin and they were both killed."

That was closer to the truth than Foulques had thought Malouf capable. "I do not know for a fact they were Bedouin."

"Do you think they were Tamasheq?" The question was direct, with no hint of offense at its implication.

"No," he finally said. "It happened far from your territory."

"We range farther than you might think."

"Why did you attack those people today? All they wanted was water."

She lifted the tea pot. "We all want water."

"And if they come back, will you kill them next time for drinking your water? For eating your dates? Standing in the shade of your trees?"

Rashida filled the two cups. She touched her cup to her lips and looked at Foulques over its brim and through her hanging braid. Without drinking, she set it back down to cool.

"We do not own the water, the dates, nor the shade. They all belong to the desert. Those people have been living at this oasis for over three weeks and it has already begun to retreat. Their animals eat the grass and expose bare soil, the people only drink the water at first. But then they begin to bathe in it, as well. Every day they gather wood for their fires, and strip the trees of their fruit. These people take and give nothing back. They anger the desert by abusing her gifts. At some point the desert simply stops giving. That is how it is done out here. Every year the desert takes away another oasis in just this way."

She tested her tea again and watched Foulques's face. This time it was ready and she sipped at it sparingly.

"We took no lives today, Elvy. But make no mistake. If we find them living here again, we will show no mercy. For we are Kel Tamasheq, and we will not be robbed of the desert's gifts."

CHAPTER SIXTEEN

WHEN THE SUN was high in the sky and the full heat of the day fell upon them, Rashida ordered the caravan to a stop. Everyone dismounted and made their camels lay down to conserve their energy. There was no shelter nearby, save for a few spiny shrub-like trees that had somehow carved out an existence in the hostile landscape. The men and women joined their camels, squatting or reclining in whatever small shade the beasts could provide. A few erected small tents to lie under while they napped.

Like many, Malouf and Vignolo rested with their camels. Vignolo sat leaning against his mount, his head hanging in a half slumber. He had fashioned a sun shade out of two sticks and his cloak. Malouf napped curled up on his side like he was on a thick, wool mattress rather than uneven earth and hard-packed stone. Gruffydd had abandoned his camel and set up some shade of his own against one of the few large piles of rocks within sight.

A clacking sound began to drown out Vignolo's snoring. Foulques recognized it immediately and he sought out its source, which he found only a short distance away. Zola and another warrior stood toe-to-toe with their training sticks in hand. They moved through a preordained series of strikes and blocks. It was not an energized effort on their part, for it was far too hot for that. It looked to be more of an exercise in rhythm. They kept their wrist and shoulder joints loose and flexible as they took turns attacking and defending. Neither man looked to be working hard. They were simply passing time.

Foulques watched for a few minutes as they repeated the sequence over and over. Strike to the left of the head, strike to the right, top, back to the left, left again, and right. Just when he thought he had the sequence committed to memory the attacker would add another strike. And occasionally, someone would perform a high leg lift followed by a forward hop, which led into an immediate strike. His curiosity piqued, Foulques pushed away from his camel and walked slowly over to the men.

When they noticed him standing there, watching, they both stopped the exercise and looked at him suspiciously. With more than a little embarrassment, Foulques recognized the patchy indigo robe of the man with Zola. He had been one of the men he had attacked at the oasis.

"Will you show me how to do that?" Foulques asked.

Zola squinted his eyes. "Why do you wish to learn? It is just a game."

Foulques knew it was no game. It was not all-out swordplay, but it was definitely not just a game. "We will be here for some time. What else is there to do?"

The other man shook his head. "It is a Tamasheq game.

You would not like it. Go sleep, like everyone else."

"I tell you what. You teach me the rules of this game and we will play for the right to ride my camel until our next stop."

This got the man's attention. Zola did not appear to like the idea, but after a few words Foulques could not understand, he relented and tossed Foulques his stick.

The stick was sword-length and surprisingly light. Foulques had no idea what kind of wood it was made from. Its one end, the handle presumably, was stained almost black from the natural oils present in a person's hand. Foulques curled his fingers around it and squeezed the smooth wood. It felt good, almost alive compared to everything else nature had to offer in the current landscape.

Zola told him where to stand and how to hold the stick. "Firstly, do not move your feet."

He led Foulques through the basic blocks as the other man attacked slowly. Next Zola showed him the strikes. Then, they went back to the beginning and repeated everything with the attacker gradually picking up speed.

"Good," Zola said. "Faster now."

As Foulques suspected, it was exactly like performing quick sword strikes in fluid combinations. But while his opponent's movements seemed effortless, Foulques was starting to breathe heavily and he could feel sweat building under his tagelmust and threatening to drip into his eyes.

"Stop," Zola said. He grabbed Foulques's wrist and forced it to bend. Then he shook the end of his arm. "Loose," he said. He started them up again and this time Foulques's partner began chanting in time to their strikes. Their tempo increased, faster and faster, and Foulques felt himself slipping out of rhythm. Then he missed a block and was rewarded with a rap on the side of his head.

"Good," Zola said. "Again?"

"Good," Foulques's opponent said. "Two more and you be walking." His eyes grinned at the prospect.

"Best of five touches it is," Foulques said, accepting the challenge.

The stick fighting made for a long afternoon, but he learned a lot. Not so much about Tuareg swordplay, but later, after dragging his feet through the sand and rock of the Sahara for three hours, he learned how much he truly loved his camel. His fellow man, in particular the one sitting on his camel, not so much.

✤

"THERE IS A man, a small man who wears many necklaces, who escorts me to your tent every night. Who is he?"

"Has he done something to you?" Rashida asked quickly.

"No, I only wonder who he is. I assume you did not ask him to be my escort."

"His name is Jomo. He is a blacksmith of the artisan caste, one of the *inedan* in my language. It is best if you ignore him and do not engage him in conversation."

"But why?"

"He is a blacksmith!"

Foulques waited for her to elaborate but apparently she felt her one word explanation contained everything he needed to know.

"Is he dangerous?" Foulques asked. "Should I be concerned that he seems to have attached himself to me?"

Rashida sighed. "His kind can be very dangerous, but I will see to it that he does no more harm."

Foulques recalled what happened to Zola when he had failed to protect his guests and he did not want to be responsible for anything like that happening to the little man. "He has done nothing to me, Rashida. I was only curious."

"Do you know who Gabriel is?" Rashida asked.

"If you mean the angel, yes, of course."

"And the woman, Eve?"

Foulques nodded, intrigued with where this would lead.

"Well, it is said, that one day Gabriel came to Eve and told her to show him her children so that he could bless them. She brought her children out and the angel graced them all with his blessing. Except one. She forgot one, or perhaps she did it on purpose. That child was the ancestor of all *inedan*."

"That is reason to pity them, not fear them," Foulques said.

Rashida shook her head vigorously. "No, for without the angel's blessing, demons and devils are willing to teach them many magical things. I know this because I can speak their language." She said this quietly, like she was letting Foulques in on the gravest of secrets.

"They have a special language?"

"Yes. My uncle can speak it too. You heard it on the first

day we met. We use it to speak together when we do not want anyone else to understand. We are not supposed to know it, but I like languages, so I learned. Of course, we are careful not to use it when any of the *inedan* are nearby."

Foulques had a hard time imagining the little man with the warm smile being a danger to anyone other than himself. "Why would you keep people like him in your camp, allow them free movement, if they are so dangerous?"

Rashida sighed. "They have their uses. They are our craftsmen, they can touch metal and shape it. They can do many things others cannot. We need them, but they are lazy, and loose-tongued. They lie and will cheat you if you let them, for that is their nature and you must always be on guard against it."

"Why not train some of your warriors how to use a forge and be rid of them, then?"

Rashida laughed. "Warriors belong to the same caste I do, the *imajeren*. None of us can touch metal, Elvy."

"Surely with a little guidance someone could learn how to work metal and—"

Rashida shook her head, setting off the charms on her headpiece. "No Elvy, you do not understand. If I were to touch anything made of iron, it would be the end of me. It would eat my spirit and cause me great pain. It would create a hole through which dark spirits could enter."

He waited for her eyes to widen and sparkle as they did when she made a jest, but they did nothing of the sort. She was quite serious.

"But your warriors use swords and the charms in your

hair, and your bracelets…"

She jingled her arm and touched a hand to the earrings in her one ear. "Of course silver is fine. It can protect you. And have you not noticed how our warriors' sword handles are wrapped in leather? Sometimes a skilled blacksmith can counteract the effects of iron through the use of secret symbols that only they know."

Foulques had forgotten about the leather-wrapped quillons on her uncle's sword, but it made sense now, in a pagan ritualistic way. He suddenly recalled a common theme woven throughout the tales Najya used to tell him when they were children, stories about magical beings who lived alongside humans in the desert.

"It is said that the djinn cannot touch iron either," Foulques said.

She put her hand over her mouth. "Do you think I am of the djinn, Elvy?"

She laughed and the movement set her earrings off like a wind chime. She had dismissed his comment so eagerly, it did lead Foulques to wonder.

CHAPTER SEVENTEEN

Najya wiped Grandison's face with a dry cloth since water had been tightly rationed. They had stopped for the night earlier than they had most days thus far. Dusk would soon be upon them and everyone would be sleeping under the stars once again. But this night promised to be colder than the previous ones for there was no firewood anywhere. Even the guards she could see encircling her and Grandison were eating a dinner of cold provisions. At least they had left them with their camel. She went to its saddle pile and pulled out the blanket that had been between the saddle and the camel's baggage, then dragged it over to Grandison and was able to cover his legs and some of his lower body almost up to his chest. He stirred and she gave him some water the Mamluk captain Safir had left for them before going somewhere with the Northman while the others set up camp.

"Thank you, Najya." Grandison dropped back onto his litter, like drinking water had just robbed him of his last reserve of strength. "Where are we?"

Najya shook her head. "I do not know, but I think we are

near a town, for some men came out and were looking over the people with us."

"You mean the slaves," Grandison said. "Call them what they are. What you too will be if you do not get away from here."

"I am working on something to get us both away," Najya said.

"The camel boy? You cannot trust him. If there is a town nearby I say you should take your chances alone. This may be your one opportunity."

"No! I will not leave you to die out here all by yourself like some animal wounded by a hunter's stray arrow."

"I told you, I am not at risk. My king will pay handsomely for my release. Who will pay for yours?"

"No."

Grandison grunted. "I hear your words but my mind sees Foulques saying them." He shook his head in frustration. "You are as stubborn as your lover."

It took a moment for Grandison's words to register with Najya. "He is not my lover! How dare you say that? I can see now you have no idea who he is. Foulques would never go back on his vows." She stood up, whirled around, and began walking away. She got two steps and shouted back at Grandison over her shoulder. "Never!"

She kept walking until a Mamluk intercepted her with his arms folded across his chest, stopping her in her tracks. She stood there trembling, trying to catch her breath. He lifted a hand and pointed back the way she had come. She trudged back to where Grandison lay and leaned against the camel for warmth, keeping the animal between herself and the knight.

She stared up at the starless, darkening sky, wondering where Foulques was at this very moment. She did not ask herself if he was still alive, for she knew he was. God would never be cruel enough to let her live in a world without him.

When Grandison spoke his voice was hardly a whisper. "I am sorry, Najya. I truly am. Lesser men have a need to bring all others down to their level."

Najya leaned back against the camel and closed her eyes.

✠

LIKE MANY NORTH African towns, Zuwila had no walls. Perhaps five hundred people called it their home, but being at one end of the trans-Saharan trade routes, it could have many times that number if the season was right. This was the case when Badru and Safir rode into the marketplace just before dusk.

There were very few stalls per se, as Zuwila was not that kind of town. But everywhere Badru looked, he saw traders with mountains of goods piled high, sometimes on carpets, but more often than not simply thrown haphazardly on the open ground. Often a camel in full tack, or two, waited nearby, for it was often necessary for merchants to pack up and leave just as quickly as they arrived. With all the caravans moving through, everyone was looking for one more thing to take to their destination where they could sell it at a profit.

"What is the name of the man we are looking for, Emir?"

"I do not know his real name, but he should be easy enough to find."

Badru told Safir to dismount and they led their camels through the maze of merchants, brushing away the advances of peddlers like black flies in the heat of summer. After they thinned out, a row of tents appeared and Badru stopped in front of the third one. A Turkmen, judging from the cut of his tunic and his fur-trimmed hat, sat outside a round tent, eating from a bowl with a wooden spoon. A small fire burned under a pot in front of him. He looked like he should be on the steppes five hundred miles away.

"God is great," Badru said.

The man nodded. "Peace be with you, big cousin." He took another spoonful of chunks of fatty meat in a gelatinous soup-like substance and eyed Badru over his bowl, which seemed to be held in just the right position to catch the drips running down his beard.

When Badru did not say anything further, and after an uncomfortable silence in which it became obvious he had no intention of doing so, the Turkmen put down his bowl and wiped his mouth on his sleeve.

"They say the first man to say a price has already lost the negotiation," the Turkmen said. "I know who you are. I sent some men out to your camp to look over your wares earlier today. They were not so impressed."

"If your price is fair, you will get a bargain here today. I am short on time," Badru said.

"How many and how old?"

"Twenty to twenty-five depending on the price. Half of

them are young enough to be molded to purpose."

"I can do a silver piece per head for those that have not yet seen their first blood. I want nothing of the older ones for they will eat more than I can sell them for these days."

"Five a head, or I might as well keep them with me until Bilma. There I can get ten per head easily."

"You will get nothing because these are your weak and your young you are trying to sell me. The desert's twenty percent, if you will."

Badru had forgotten how badly he hated this part of the slave trade. He was about to tell the Turkmen that he would rather watch his slaves drop dead one by one on the road to Timbuktu than see him make a single copper bit. On the other hand, the sooner he got rid of them all, the sooner he could be back in Cairo, or somewhere else hunting for his own bounties.

Just then a loud roar of cheers and whistles broke through the market's air. There was a gradual movement of people flowing out of the square ground toward the noise.

"What is happening?" Badru asked, still looking in the direction of the excitement.

"Butchers are in town for the slaughter," the Turkmen said.

"Dambe?"

The Turkmen nodded. "All week."

The brutal sport of dambe. Badru could hear the crowd calling to him. He started walking toward the noise.

"Hey! Do you want to sell them or not?"

Badru responded but did not look back. "Three silver a

piece for the young ones, one silver for the older. That or I feed them all to the desert and you will get nothing."

Safir fell into step with Badru. As they approached a ring of people in a wide-open area he asked what they were doing. Safir had been recruited from Georgia and did not know the local customs as well as Badru.

"Dambe. It is a Hausa game."

Badru saw the staging area he was looking for. A group of young men naked from the waist up, were stretching and doing their best to intimidate one another. They all had their right hand and arm wrapped tightly in white rope all the way to their elbow.

"Come Safir. It has been a long journey. Let us partake in some sport."

Badru found the game-master and told him he wanted to enter the contest.

"The fighters have been hardening their spears in the sun all day," the game-master said, pointing to a man who was even now plunging his arm into a cauldron full of salt. "There is no time for you to make a proper spear."

"I will wrap it now and fore-go the hardening treatment."

The game-master shook his head until Badru pressed a few coins into his hand. "Consider this the penalty for late admission."

"You must be of the butcher caste to enter." He held out his hand and Badru put one more coin into it.

"Very well. We have a late entrant!"

The crowd roared its approval but Badru got more than

a few dark looks from the other competitors. Especially once he took off his shirt to reveal his heavily muscled frame and the scars from an untold number of wounds.

"Safir, help me with my wrap."

Badru accepted a length of rope from the game-master before he was inundated with spectators wanting to change their bets.

Badru held one end of the rope in his palm and told Safir how to wrap his arm.

"Make it tight."

Safir did as he was told, but Badru could tell by his constant frown that he was not at all eager to be part of this.

"Emir, these men are butchers, untouchables. This is beneath you."

"Wrong, Safir. These people were pagans not so long ago, and even now they often revert to those ways. I am here to show them what a man can do when Allah is on his side."

Safir bowed his head and put his fist to his chest. "If God permits," he said.

"If God permits," Badru repeated back to him. "Tighter. I do not want it falling off when it gets wet."

Badru faced his first opponent: a short, barrel-chested member of the butcher caste with a face so criss-crossed in scars it looked like he had taken his knives to himself rather than his animal carcasses. It had been many years since Badru had played dambe, so he took his time to get to know the man and reacquaint himself with the sport. The hardened, salt-dipped right arm was the spear, the open left hand the shield, and each fight consisted of three rounds. A round ended when a man was knocked down. The fight was won when someone took two of the three rounds or his opponent could not continue.

The short butcher came on like a bull. Badru slapped his first thrusts aside with his open left palm. But then the man feinted and caught Badru with a hard forearm smash across his ribs. Badru glanced down and noticed a line of blood begin to appear where the rope had caused an abrasion. The butcher feinted low and reached to clip Badru across his face, then he followed up immediately low again to the cut ribs. This time the blow knocked the wind out of Badru and he fell to one knee.

"Round!" the game-master called and murmurs shot through the crowd.

Within seconds, Badru felt the salt begin to eat into his wounds. The constant pain of the salt, the struggle for air, the fear of being put down for good, that was what Badru remembered of dambe. That was what he had come for, what he craved.

The game-master called the men to him to begin round two. The butcher, sensing something that was not there, charged in and hit Badru again in the abdomen. People cheered, smelling the finish.

But dambe had more to offer than sweet pain.

Badru lashed out with his fist and caught the butcher square in the face. He deflected the shorter man's next attack and smashed his forearm across the butcher's nose, exploding it with a shower of red. As the man sputtered and choked on his blood, Badru attacked his body, roaring louder with each hit. Soon the screams rocked the man just as much as the blows. Another spear to the side of the butcher's head and he went down to all fours. Gore dripped from his mouth and nose like he was bleeding out, and Badru screamed at the sight as the game-master and two others tried to hold him back from the slaughter.

Dambe offered sweet pain. But it also offered an even sweeter release. After four more contests Badru's spirits were so high he returned to the Turkmen and sold him every single one of the slaves at a bargain. He kept only the English man and his woman. Badru was tired of crawling over the desert, dragging the Franks behind him. Now he would be able to travel at speed. The vice-sultan would be furious but he was not a true Mamluk and Badru decided he did not answer to him. If the sultan himself wished to punish Badru after he returned from Timbuktu, so be it. He would submit himself for punishment gladly, but not until he had meted out some of his own on a certain Hospitaller and a Genoan.

As he lay down to sleep that night he felt salt still burning in his wounds. He could have rinsed them out, for they were at an oasis and water was everywhere. He had purposely chosen not to. There was nothing quite like the simple world of dambe to clear one's mind and help set priorities. Once again, Badru ruminated on how much he had missed the desert.

CHAPTER EIGHTEEN

IT TOOK ONLY six sessions of the stick game before Foulques had become good enough to keep his camel most of the time, but he had no shortage of challengers even after that.

One morning, as he rode next to Malouf in the line, Najya's father said, "I should have stopped you earlier from joining in with the Tuaregs in their stick training."

"Why? It keeps my mind from dwelling on other things. What harm can come of it?"

"You bring attention to yourself. Word has spread through the warriors that one of the Venetians is sometimes possessed by a desert spirit. They line up for a chance to test their skill against one of the old ones."

"Or," Foulques said, "some just want to ride a camel for an afternoon."

"These men are many things," Malouf said, "but lazy is not one of them."

At the very front of the line, a camel ridden by an indigo-robed warrior broke formation and trotted toward Foulques and Malouf.

"The chieftain would like you to join her," he said.

"We would be happy to," Malouf said.

The indigo-robed man, who Foulques recognized as one of Rashida's tent guards, shook his head. "She said there is no room for the old man."

"There rarely is," Malouf said, touching his fingers to his forehead and bowing.

By the time Foulques arrived at the front of the caravan, the entire line had come to a stop. Rashida lounged on her camel, looking as fresh and relaxed as someone sitting on a marble bench in a bath house.

"Elvy! Please ride beside me for a spell. I thought we might as well conduct our lesson out here in the fresh air for a change."

There was nothing "fresh" about riding in a line of seventy camels, Foulques thought. But he kept it to himself. He was becoming quite adept at holding back the truth.

He guided his camel to a stop near hers and was quite pleased, and a little surprised, at how compliant he was.

"You become less civilized man and more nomad every day," Rashida said. "At least your camel thinks so."

"I have often wondered what my camel thinks of me," Foulques said.

She directed her eyes to his black head covering. "Are you getting sand down your neck? Come closer." She stood up on her saddle, and then put one foot on Foulques's camel and kept one on hers. Straddling the two beasts she deftly unwrapped Foulques's head wrap. Her indigo-robed guard shielded his eyes and turned his back toward Foulques.

"Who taught you to wear a tagelmust?"

"My uncle," Foulques said.

"Well, he did not know what he was doing."

Foulques could not hold back a dry laugh. "You do not know the half of it," he said.

She finished unwrapping it and held up one end, letting the other dangle between the camels until it almost touched the ground.

"No wonder! It is too short." She bunched it up into a ball and threw it to a woman on a camel behind her, one of her maidservants. The two of them exchanged a few words and the woman rummaged through a large pack tied behind her. She pulled out a carefully rolled up light blue tagelmust and Rashida shook her head. She put it back in the pack and retrieved one of a darker, much deeper blue. Rashida nodded and the woman tossed it to her. Again holding one end, Rashida let it unroll to its full length between her and Foulques. The color was the rich, deep blue of a pre-dawn desert sky, and evenly distributed, unlike some of the patchy garments Foulques had seen worn by some of the lower castes.

"It is a beautiful dye job," Foulques said, as Rashida held out one end to him, "but I cannot accept—"

She shrugged. "Then you will die." She smiled and brushed her braid from her eye. Even as she said it Foulques felt the strength of the sun on the top of his head, now that it was uncovered. She said it teasingly, but there was an element of truth in that simple statement. It was the hottest day of their journey so far and the landscape had become a true desert in all directions. Foulques had been born in the Levant, and was no stranger to its semi-deserts and the eastern steppes, but this was different.

"Are we in the Sahara now?"

"We are in the *Tinariwen*, which means 'deserts,' for what you call the Sahara is many different deserts to us."

She leaned over and pressed one end of the tagelmust against the side of his head. "Hold this end here."

He had learned not to argue with her, so he did as he was told and stared straight as she began to wrap his face in the light fabric.

"I helped dye this one myself," she said.

"How do you make the color?" Foulques asked.

"We acquire sea urchins by trade from the great sea in the north. Then grind them up and press the powder into the fabric by hand over many sessions. If we do not take our time and do it carefully, the cloth will not hold the color."

"That is why I sometimes see men whose faces have turned blue from the dye," Foulques said.

"Yes, but do not worry, Elvy. I promise this tagelmust will not leave its mark on you. Put your hand here." She had finished the face and neck portion and began to wind the remaining length in a tight coil on top of his head.

About thirty paces ahead, Rashida's uncle and two other men stood in conversation.

One was very old and used a walking stick to lean on. His robes were uncharacteristically white, only his tagelmust was blue. He was doing most of the talking and would raise his stick to point across the simmering landscape in one direction or another. Sand dunes dominated the landscape, but the caravan was on hard ground, like the remains of some ancient riverbed, though Foulques knew that was impossible for the shifting sands would have covered over any such riverbed within a few short years, or months even, of it drying up.

"Are we lost?" Foulques asked.

"Lost? There are times when we may not know where we are, but we are never lost," Rashida said.

"What are they doing then?"

"Deciding what to do next," Rashida said.

Her uncle and the other younger man nodded solemnly as they listened to the one with the stick. A young boy, seven or eight years of age, stood beside the younger man, shifting impatiently from leg to leg. Like his father, he was dressed head to ankle in a light blue robe. However, he wore a tight-fitting turban with no face covering.

"It looks like something is wrong," Foulques said.

She tucked in the last piece of the tagelmust and shrugged. "We are out of water. There! Look at me."

"Out of water?" Foulques turned his head and all he saw was sand, sun, camels, goats, and a hundred men and women. All who needed one thing above all else.

"Excellent! You look like a *mai* of a great empire, Elvy."

He touched his head and ran it over the tight-fitting cloth. He had to admit, if felt like he wore nothing at all.

"Pull up the face mask," she said. "Good. And this piece here," she grabbed a piece she had left long, "you can use as an eye shield if the sand is really blowing."

Holding it before his eyes, he was surprised he could still see through the gauzy cloth. But that thought soon brought him back to the need for water.

"What are they talking about then, if we are out of water? Is there an oasis nearby?"

"No. I do not think so." She waved her hand. "But that is the men's task. They will decide what to do."

"Not you?"

Rashida laughed. "I am no sand reader. No caravan master. I am a village girl!"

"I do not know what a sand reader is," Foulques said, "but I have known you long enough to tell you are no mere village girl."

Her eyes lit up. "Why thank you, Elvy." Her eyes drifted to where her uncle and his companions were walking back toward them. "And he," Rashida said, pointing at the man holding the hand of the boy, "is a sand reader."

Most of the Tamasheq were lighter skinned than their southern neighbors, but this man had a face the color of ox hide soaked in red wine. Though he was about the same age as Rashida's uncle, his skin had had an extra fifty years of sun added to it.

"Is he your navigator?"

Rashida shook her head. "No, only a reader. He tells us who, or what, has crossed our path. The older man beside him is our navigator."

As they came closer, Foulques realized something about the navigator as he held on to Faraji's elbow with one hand and steadied himself with his walking stick held in the other.

"Is he blind?" Foulques asked.

"In what way?" Rashida asked. "The desert has little respect for the senses of man or woman. The sands are forever shifting and the djinn are tricksters at heart. A road that was here yesterday can be gone tomorrow. Does it not make sense than, to have someone lead the way who has fewer senses to fool?"

Foulques shook his head as he watched the man stumble and lean on Faraji for support. "I will have to think on that one before I give you an answer," Foulques said. "I am not sure how I feel about wandering around the desert with no water and a blind man as a guide."

Rashida laughed and dismissed his concern with a wave of her hand, setting off a musical rattling of her many beaded and silver bracelets. "His line has traveled the deserts for centuries. And anyway, it is not his senses he relies on so much as his memories of past lives. So you need not worry."

The three men and the boy stopped before Rashida's camel. The boy pointed at Foulques and greeted him with an enthusiastic, "Ciao!" Rashida's uncle was at the other end of the spectrum. Faraji's dark eyes immediately settled on Foulques and did not stray as the blind man gave his chieftain a long-winded report which included a fair share of stick pointing and shaking. Watching the navigator, with his pale, milky eyes, brandish his stick so near the head of Rashida's camel made Foulques a little nervous. But not as nervous as the constant glare from Rashida's uncle.

After some time, Rashida began to translate bits and pieces of the dialogue.

"It is good news. There is water to the west, but too far for our caravan to reach without most of the goats dying and probably some of our slaves as well."

"That is good news?" Foulques asked.

"And we will have to endure a storm within the next few days."

Foulques was still waiting for the good news she had promised, but now her uncle chimed in on the conversation. Rashida and he spoke back and forth a few times.

"My uncle will go and fetch the water and bring enough back so the goats do not die."

"And the slaves?" Foulques could not help asking as he fixed Faraji with his own grim look.

Rashida laughed. "He is a warrior. He does not concern himself with slaves. Do not worry, Elvy. All my people are precious to me, but especially the slaves."

Her uncle rattled off another series of questions, looking many times at Foulques as he did so, and Rashida responded. Finally, she let out a breath and appeared to give in to whatever it was he wanted. A couple more less intense back-and-forths and Faraji turned away from them all and walked to his camel. Whatever had been said, Foulques had been the subject for a lot of it.

"What was that all about?"

"My uncle wants you to go with him to get the water."

"Me?"

"He says he cannot leave you alone with me. He does not trust you."

"It sounded like he said a lot more than that," Foulques

said.

"He also asked why I gave you one of his tagelmust."

"His? What did you say?"

"I told him it was not his tagelmust, for he owns nothing but the camel he sits upon. Then I said I liked the way its shade sets off the color in your eyes so nicely." She grinned and put a finger to one of her eye teeth, cocking her head slightly to one side. "I think, perhaps, he did not like to hear that so much."

CHAPTER NINETEEN

THE WATER PARTY consisted of Rashida's uncle, leading four camels with all manner of water-skins hanging off their backs, the sand reader and his boy, Foulques, and the ever-present Zola, who by this point Foulques considered his tribe-appointed wet nurse.

The sand reader led the way on one camel, with his boy sitting in front of him. The child was forever twisting in his father's arms, peering around one side of him or the other in a never ending quest to keep track of Foulques. Whenever Foulques strayed within range, the boy would pepper him with a series of "ciaos," so Foulques was more than happy enough to ride at the back of the line behind everyone.

After three hours of relentless travel in the hot sun, Foulques's mind began to drift and his eyes grew heavy. His new tagelmust was much cooler than his last one, but his mouth was dry and his body began to ache from lack of water. He had a pigskin with several mouthfuls of water left, but he refused to drink before anyone else. Riding at the back as he was, he could tell no one had yet raised a skin to his lips.

He wrapped the tail end of his tagelmust around his eyes, not to keep out the sand, but to cut down on the sun's glare. For some unexplainable reason, he was reminded of the cool, dark, moist cell he had shared with Hermes for all those days. What had become of him? he wondered. His thoughts then turned to his uncle Guillaume. How long would he have left him in that dank place? Another week? A month? For the rest of his life? Or only until he went mad and was no longer a threat to his uncle's plans? Foulques had no answer. Part of him still wanted to believe his uncle meant to come back for him, but the greater part was not so sure. Looking back on his childhood, he had very few memories of his uncle that did not include a training sword. It was as though he did not exist before he was seven or eight, and not only in his uncle's eyes but even in his own memories he could recall no sense of himself. In a way, he did not exist then, for that was before Najya.

He opened his eyes with a start and realized he had dropped into some sort of half-sleeping trance. His camel was still walking but there was no one in front of him. He looked left and right: nothing but sand. They had left him. His dry, swollen throat reminded Foulques that he had almost no water. He jerked his camel to a stop, to collect himself.

He sensed movement behind him and turned just as a camel pulled up alongside his. It was Zola. He walked his camel past Foulques and looked at him through the slit of his tagelmust. He said nothing but nodded his head to the east. Foulques put a hand to his chest to stop his heart from pounding and then urged his camel forward.

A short ride later, with Foulques following Zola closer than a peel to its fruit, they topped a low dune and there was the rest of the party, plodding along in orderly fashion. Zola kept to his original trajectory and did not once urge his camel on faster. Soon they merged with the path of the others and fell back in line like they had never left.

Faraji and the sand reader did not look back but Foulques could hear them exchange a few words. It was the first time Foulques had ever heard Rashida's uncle laugh.

Once the hottest part of the day had passed, they picked up their pace and Foulques witnessed first-hand the strength of the camel in these conditions. They trotted for miles, though he was not sure that was the best word to describe the loose-limbed gait of the gangly beasts. Then Faraji would let out a high-pitched yelp and they would break into a distance-eating run. They maintained that pace for a short period and then returned to the trot. After a few cycles they allowed the camels to walk for a mile or so and then the whole routine was repeated. By the time darkness arrived Foulques was exhausted from trying to stay in the saddle, unaccustomed as he was to the new gaits. He had no idea how much land they had covered, but he knew that in this heat, the journey would have killed several horses.

Shortly after sundown, the sand reader stopped his camel and Foulques almost ran his own into the pack animals.

They all dismounted and made their camels lay down.

"Why do we not travel in the coolness of the night?" Foulques asked Zola as they loosened the straps on their saddles.

"We are near to water," Zola said. He handed Foulques a water-skin.

"What about you?" Foulques asked. His words came out as dry as the landscape around them. He had long ago finished off his own skin.

"I drink soon. We are almost at water."

Foulques gratefully accepted the skin, which was still warm from the neck of Zola's camel. But the liquid inside was heaven sent. He took another long drink and passed it back to Zola, who stoppered it and hung it back on his camel.

"If we are so near to the spring, why have we stopped?"

Zola pointed at the sand reader, who was sitting on the ground leaning against his camel. Faraji was there as well and the two of them were smoking from a long tube.

"He cannot see our path until more stars come. Tomorrow, after the water, he will follow our…" he made a walking motion with his index and middle fingers.

"Tracks?"

"Yes. The desert moves but the reader can see our tracks and they will lead us back to the people."

The sand reader's boy, who was sleeping on a short carpet next to his father, suddenly sat up and rubbed his eyes. He saw Foulques looking at them. Foulques averted his gaze, but it was too late.

"Ciao!" the boy called, throwing out his arm with vigor.

Foulques returned his wave, but he was too tired to summon up even a fraction of the boy's enthusiasm.

"Come," Zola said. "It is good time for sticks."

"Now? It is dark," Foulques said, but what he really meant was that he was exhausted.

"It is a different game at night. And it is cool."

Foulques gave in and they played for a half hour while Faraji and the sand reader looked on. Faraji would occasionally say something to Zola and he would bow his head in acknowledgment. Whether the tips helped him, or Foulques was not used to blocking by starlight alone, Zola proved victorious taking three out of four contests. Afterward, when they all lay down to sleep, Foulques realized the sticks had loosened him up from the long day's ride and it took him a long time to fall asleep.

Five hours later, they were on the move once again. They stuck to a trot in the darkness but once the sun had revealed itself in its entirety, Faraji called out and the camels broke into their loping run.

Finally, shortly after dawn, Zola tapped Foulques on the shoulder with his riding crop. "We are arrived," he said, pointing straight ahead with the switch.

At first Foulques saw nothing but sand and a shimmering horizon that stretched on forever. But then he saw a rock and beside that rock was a tiny plant. As they got closer the plant turned into the top of a date tree set down in a natural rock-lined depression. When they finally arrived at the rim of the small oasis there turned out to be a half dozen trees and some grasses growing around a pond no wider than the length of a man.

Foulques crossed himself and mumbled his gratitude as

he followed the others down a rocky path that took them out of the desert and into Eden. At the bottom, it was all he could do to refrain from wading into the brownish-colored water and throwing his entire head under. But, despite what Faraji might think, he was no barbarian. He suspected there was an order to be observed, and he was right.

Faraji went first to the water's edge. He squatted and waved one hand through the pool a few times, watching how it responded to his touch. When he was satisfied that it met whatever conditions were required of it, he used the same hand to cup some up to his lips. He took it all into his mouth, held it there while he looked at the others, and then swallowed. He nodded.

The sand reader's son let out a whoop and dropped to his belly at the water's edge. He repeated Faraji's motions, with a great deal more haste mind you, and then drank four or five handfuls in rapid succession. His father joined in and Zola and Foulques followed. As Foulques went to dip his left hand into the water Zola grabbed his sleeve. He shook his head and wrinkled up the bridge of his nose. He pointed at Foulques's other hand and Foulques realized the situation with no further explanation necessary.

After everyone had sated themselves, they led the camels in and let them drink to their fill. As they did so, Zola and Foulques untied all the water-skins. The boy dragged them to the edge of the pool and Faraji and the sand reader began filling them.

They had filled about half the skins when Foulques thought he was going a little mad from the sun and the hard ride. Not a minute before, Faraji had handed him a double water-skin to carry up to one of the pack camels tethered a short distance away. When he got there he saw Faraji already at the camel searching for something in its pack. Struggling under the weight of the skins draped over his shoulders, he looked back at the pond and saw Faraji there, still kneeling at the edge of the water. He looked back at the camel and it dawned on him that the man there was not dressed in a deep shade of midnight blue, he was shrouded all in black.

Without thinking, Foulques shrugged out from under the skins and his hand flew to the pommel of his sword.

"Stop where you are!" he shouted. He called out Zola's name and scanned the area. No man would be alone out here. Sure enough, another black-robed man stood up from behind a rock and three more men appeared in tawny robes on the far side of the pond. They had their swords in hand. That was the last piece of the puzzle Foulques needed before he too released his sword from its scabbard.

The man closest to him could wait. He started to retrace his steps back to the water, where everyone else was, but the thief had seen him and ran at Foulques drawing his sword as he came. He made a downward cut aimed at Foulques's shoulder. Caught halfway through his turn back to the water, Foulques had just enough time to offer up a parry but could not get off a counterattack. Encouraged by his opponent's apparent lack of skill, the man let out a war cry followed by a powerful downward strike aimed at Foulques's head. It was a clumsy attack and the thief paid for it. Foulques slid to the side and out of danger, then he removed his attacker's sword arm at the elbow, and following through, removed his head. Before the man's head had hit the ground Foulques was running toward the pond. Faraji was knee deep in water, trading blows with a black-robed man, while Zola was a few steps away from the pond fighting with another. The sand reader stood nearest to Zola, his son wrapped in his arms. Movement caught his eye and Foulques saw three more men wearing sand-colored robes seemingly step out of the rocks behind Faraji. His choice of who to help was suddenly now clear.

In the time it took Foulques to put himself between Faraji and the three attackers, Faraji had driven his opponent out of the water and onto solid ground. Once away from the water, Faraji launched into a blinding side to side whirlwind of attacks that left his black-robed attacker on one knee and bleeding from three or four places. Faraji feinted and thrust completely through the man near his breastbone, the point of his straight sword popping six inches out of his back. Faraji retracted his weapon and as the man pitched forward face first, Faraji wiped both sides of his blade, one on either shoulder of his attacker, before he hit the ground. He tossed his sword over to his left hand, drew the dagger strapped to his forearm with his right, and turned to face the new threat.

The odds were now three to two, and after what Foulques had just witnessed, he liked those odds very much. He feinted at the first man, pivoted, and drove a straight lunge through the throat of his unsuspecting accomplice. He kept his blade in the man's throat, stepping forward and to the side so the dead man was between him and the nearest man. Only then did he withdraw his sword and assume a high guard as the next man closed in. He heard a yell to his right, one that eerily reminded him of camels charging through the night, followed by a squeal of pain and then instant silence. Knowing Faraji was in no need of help, he focused on the matter at hand and attacked. His opponent blocked and attempted to run down Foulques's blade. Foulques rolled his own over top of his and drew it across his forearms, slicing them both open. He followed with a deep cut to his inner thigh. Blood poured freely from his wounds and Foulques knew the man was dead. It was just a matter of time. He decided that time was now by piercing him through the liver.

As the thief folded to the ground, Foulques whirled, ready to help Zola. But Zola's opponent lay on the ground, a mess of sliced up cloth, blood, and bare skin. The sand reader sat on the ground holding his son and berating Zola for something. Zola had his sword sheathed and he stared at his feet.

Foulques could feel Faraji staring at him. He sheathed his sword before turning to him. "Who were they?"

"Hausa nomads."

"Brave, but foolish men," Foulques said.

"Foolish, yes. There are brave Hausa, but these were not them." Faraji was looking everywhere except at Foulques.

The sand reader and Faraji had their backs to one another and each scanned the low hills in front of him.

"What is wrong?" Foulques asked.

"These nomads are brave men only when they have an advantage in numbers."

"They had numbers. Little good it did them."

"Their greed convinced them they had numbers. They must have mistaken you for a rich Venetian trader with something of value on your camels." He stared at Foulques with his deep brown eyes, rimmed by those impressively long and thick eyelashes.

"I am certainly not rich," Foulques said, forcing himself to not look away from his stare.

Faraji waved his arm over the dead bodies around them. "And these are not numbers," he said.

A desert yelp came out of the sand reader's mouth, followed by a torrent of words.

Faraji sheathed his forearm dagger. "We must go."

"But we have only filled half our water-skins," Foulques said. The sand reader had already mounted his camel and Zola was frantically tying the pack camels together. Faraji grabbed Foulques by his shoulders and turned him to face due south.

"That is numbers," he said.

Foulques shielded his eyes and saw nothing but the horizon, until he realized the horizon was kicking up dust.

Faraji spoke as he pulled his camel down to its front knees. "These were scouts left to watch the water hole. One of their number most likely went back to the camp the moment we arrived."

"How many do you think they are?" Foulques asked, pulling his own camel down.

"Fifty more than a Venetian merchant and his poor Tamasheq guides can hope to stand against." He whipped his camel on its neck and was off, dragging the pack camels along with him. The sand reader and his boy followed close behind and then quickly took the lead as they climbed out of the oasis. Zola too was mounted, but he was not yet moving. He stared at Foulques impatiently and made shooing gestures with his hands like Foulques was some goat that had walked into his tent by mistake.

Foulques hunched over his camel as it picked up speed. He had no idea if Zola was still behind him or not, for he was too occupied with holding on to the camel's saddle as it raced faster than anything he had yet experienced. Foulques could see its legs kicking out to the sides underneath its belly at erratic intervals as it picked up even more speed and the sight seemed so unnatural he had to force himself to look away. His eyes were tearing over and he took a chance on removing one hand from his saddle to wrap them with his tagelmust.

They continued on at a dead run for fifteen full minutes and then Faraji brought them all to a trot. Foulques pulled his camel alongside Rashida's uncle.

"Are they still following us?" Foulques asked.

"They are. But I cannot run the camels any more until they have had a rest. We pushed them too hard yesterday."

Foulques turned in his saddle and caught a glimpse of their pursuers. They were much closer than he had thought.

"We can keep them at a distance for a time, but our only hope is that they decide we are not worth their trouble. Get ready. We run again."

They alternated between running and trotting for over three hours and still their pursuers would not give up the chase. Finally, Faraji ordered them all into a walk. The sand reader and his boy were at the front, following their tracks, Foulques assumed, for he spent a great deal of time focused on the ground. Faraji moved his camel up next to the sand reader and they exchanged words, heated words. The conversation ended with Faraji throwing the lead of the pack camels to them. The sand reader whipped his camel into a trot and led the pack camels ahead. Faraji came back to Foulques and Zola. His words were directed at Foulques.

"Follow them. Do not let them out of your sight."

Foulques checked over his shoulder. The dust clouds behind them had given birth to men and beasts. He looked ahead to where the sand reader and his boy were receding into the distance.

He turned back to Faraji. "No."

Faraji made a sucking intake of air sound and pulled the mask of his tagelmust down, exposing his full face. "You are a stubborn man," Faraji said.

"I am," Foulques said. "What do we do?"

"We die and the Hausa will take our camels." It sounded to Foulques like the second part of that statement was the part that really concerned Faraji.

"I am not giving up my camel without a fight," Foulques said.

For the second time in their journey, Foulques heard Faraji laugh.

"Very well. We know what you will do for your camel." He pulled his mask back up. "Now let us see what he will do for you."

The Hausa gained on them by inches, not feet, and as the sun got higher in the sky the pace was wearing on everyone, men and camels alike. Faraji called for yet another run and Foulques felt the great muscles beneath him spasm into action yet again. White foam trailed from either corner of his camel's mouth, streamed along its neck, and collected against Foulques's bent leg. They had held each run for a progressively shorter period each time. Faraji put an end to this one after not even a minute. He brought them all to a walk and looked at Foulques and Zola in turn.

"We will rest here," he said.

They stopped, eased their camels to the ground on their trembling legs, and walked several paces behind, putting the animals between themselves and the charging horde closing fast. Foulques recognized the tactic. Animals would do everything in their power to avoid trampling their own kind.

Zola drew his sword and adjusted his tagelmust. All three men had their eyes on the Hausa nomads thundering toward them. Foulques could clearly discern man from beast now, at least fifty of them. They would be on them in seconds, not minutes.

"How long do we rest here?" Foulques asked, drawing his own sword.

Faraji drew his sword, executed the same toss over to his left hand as before, and pulled his forearm dagger with his right. He looked at Foulques with his dark, soothing eyes and said, "A very long time, I expect." He took a few steps to his right, rested the flat of his sword on his shoulder and let his dagger hang from his right hand. He began tapping it against his leg in a rhythm only he could hear.

Foulques saw Zola swallow. He stretched out his sword and tapped Zola's blade. "See you tonight for the stick game."

Foulques was not sure, but he thought Zola may have smiled under his tagelmust. "If God permits," he said.

"If God permits," Foulques repeated.

Now not only could he hear the Hausa nomads coming, he could feel them. Hundreds of hooves chewed up the ground, their muffled thumps merging into one stomach-churning boom that repeated over and over, shaking them all where they stood. High-pitched desert dweller war cries broke out and quickly rose in volume, until Foulques thought his ears would burst. They drowned out the low booming of camel hooves entirely. The dust behind them obscured the sky, but Foulques could see each man clearly now for they were less than two hundred yards away. He watched a rider jostled by another fall off his camel. He bounced and was spit up and out, torn to pieces by the riders behind him. A camel may avoid stepping on another camel, but apparently it had no such qualms about stomping a man.

Foulques figured they would stream around their camel barricade and come at them from the rear. He looked behind him and a shape loomed on the horizon. At first, he thought it was the sand reader and his boy and his heart sank, for if they had only made it that far ahead, they had no hope of outrunning the Hausa. But then the figure moved in a manner Foulques knew well and in a split second his mind pieced together the entire narrative.

It was Gruffydd. And he was loosing arrows.

Foulques turned back to his attackers in time to see another nomad plucked from his saddle and spit out from under hooves. His riderless camel veered through the mass of man and beast causing confusion and making several riders slow up their pace. A heavy, yard-long shaft of ash penetrated deep into the forehead of one such man, the force so great it snapped his head back to bounce against his spine. It stayed in that position, and somehow the seemingly headless man remained seated as his camel, perhaps aware that something was not quite right with its master, broke away to the left in panic. And then suddenly, the entire charging mass pulled up and ceased all forward momentum. The camels milled around in confusion as their riders tried to keep them under control. The dust cloud chasing them finally caught up and contributed to the bedlam.

No one was more confused than Foulques. The complete disarray of the Hausa charge was not the work of a single bowman, no matter how skilled. Beside him the normally reserved Zola was jumping up and down, waving his sword at the enemy and screaming at the top of his lungs.

"Ay, yai, yai, yai!"

His high pitched cry was answered from behind Foulques. He turned and saw dozens of blue riders pass by on either side of Gruffydd, enveloping him in a cloud of dust.

The Hausa whipped their mounts, yanked on leads, collided with one another in their haste to turn around. As

Faraji had said earlier, these were not brave men. Nor did they lack intelligence, Foulques noted, looking at how eagerly the Tamasheq charged into battle. Their formation was tight and orderly. They had done this many times before.

The blue warriors divided and carried on past Foulques and his companions. One man jumped off his camel in front of Faraji. He interlocked his fingers and Faraji stepped into his hands, spring-boarding high up onto the camel's back. He shouted and his camel leapt forward, as eager as any warrior to get back with the main host.

Zola had regained his composure. He walked toward the man who had given up his camel and as he passed Foulques, he said, "Tonight, I beat you like a bad man."

Foulques could not help but laugh. He was still smiling when Gruffydd showed up bouncing on his camel. Faraji and his warriors had already given up the chase and were on their way back. When Gruffydd arrived, he did not bother dismounting, no doubt because he knew he would just have to get back on at some point. He tossed Foulques a waterskin.

"Ran into a man with a bunch of camels loaded down with these a ways back," Gruffydd said. "Anyone you know?"

"Was he with a boy that spoke fluent Italian?"

"That would be him. What is wrong with your camel?"

Foulques followed Gruffydd's eyes to see his camel laid flat out on his side. His chest was heaving and an awful lot of foam had built up around his mouth and nose.

"Sweet Mary, no..." Foulques muttered as he went to his

side. He finished unbuckling the straps of his saddle just as Faraji returned. He leapt off his own camel and knelt beside Foulques. He leaned over and put his ear on the camel's ribcage.

"Should we give him water?" Foulques asked, as he stroked the camel's neck.

"No." Faraji sat up and watched the camel's stomach area for a few long moments. Suddenly a ripple traveled up and down his side like two serpents fighting under his skin. The camel let out a howl of pain, raising his head off the ground. Foulques tried to offer comfort by stroking his neck and speaking softly.

"What is wrong? Is it colica?"

Faraji put his hands on his knees and sat up straight. He pulled his tagelmust down and looked at Foulques. His eyes, ordinarily hard and uncompromising, now glistened with moisture. "He has given everything. There is only pain left for him in this life."

Foulques looked into the camel's wide, fear-stricken eyes and kept stroking his neck.

Faraji started to draw his sword but Foulques caught his wrist with his free hand. "No," he said. "I will not let you do that."

"You are a stubborn man."

Foulques nodded as he kept his hand moving on the camel's great neck, quieting him as best he could. He slowly withdrew his sword with his other hand. *He has given everything.*

"I will do it, but you will have to show me where his heart is."

CHAPTER TWENTY

THE COOL NIGHT of the desert was beaten back by a large fire, its sparks rising toward the heavens to live amongst the stars for brief moments in time, before winking away to nothing. Slaves and warriors alike had collected wood and camel dung all day along their journey. While everyone else was setting up camp, a small group of women slaughtered a few goats. They spitted most of the meat and prepared fragrant stews with the rest of the trimmings on a series of small cooking fires. By the time the sun had retreated for the day and long before the large fire was lit, the smell of roasting meat was heavy in the air.

Foulques sat beside Gruffydd amongst the large inner ring of people closest to the fire. Though they were the nearest, there was still a large open area between them and the leaping flames. Unable to feel the heat of the crackling wood, he settled for pulling a blanket over his shoulders.

"The smell of that food has got me hungry enough to eat my own feet," Gruffydd said.

Foulques had grown fond of the Welshman, and that was not just because he had saved his life on two occasions now. Gruffydd Blood had an honest, easy way about him and the fact that he had come all this way to rescue his lord spoke volumes about his loyalty.

"You have a peculiar last name," Foulques said.

"What, Blood? I thought so too the first time I heard it, but it has grown on me."

"Is it not a birth name?"

"Nah," Gruffydd said. He picked up a handful of sand and let it slip through his fingers into the palm of his other hand. "My mates gave it to me when I joined Grandison's archers."

"You mean King Edward's archers," Foulques said.

"I suppose I do."

"What made them come up with that name?"

Gruffydd got a far off look in his eyes. "Aw, you know how these things happen. I was fighting against the English at that time and their infantry closed on us. Dropped my bow and did what I had to with whatever I could get my hands on. Cannot rightly remember everything. That is how it is when I get in the thick of it. You know how it is. Call it anger, fear, or just a black, devil-spawned nature."

Foulques nodded. He did not need to hear more, but Gruffydd continued regardless. "Anyways, I could not hold back and things got right bloody with the English. We won the day and the men started calling me 'Bloody' after that. Eventually, I became the Gruffydd Blood we have all come to love." He let out a dry, humorless chuckle and looked up at the night sky. He spoke his next words softly, directed at the sparks rising into the darkness more than at Foulques. "Not much of a child's tale full of dragons and princes now, is it?"

Gruffydd shrugged and grabbed a fresh handful of sand. "Life is strange. Longshanks killed my father and my grandfather, but I come here, halfway across the world, to fight in his army."

"You fought for all of Christendom at Acre, not Edward."

Gruffydd looked up and grinned at Foulques with that easy smile of his. "I fought because Grandison told me to, and because my mates were standing at my side. Do not need much more reason than that."

"Why are you here Gruffydd? Lord Grandison will most likely be ransomed back to King Edward eventually. He is not in need of rescue."

Gruffydd's eyes took on a steely glint as he looked at Foulques. "Do not get me wrong. Grandison is a good lord and a fair man, but I am not here for him."

"Oh?"

"I came for a crack at that big bastard that slit my mates' throats."

Foulques felt his guts twist. He was instantly reminded of Brother Connor, Marshal Clermont's young protégé who met Badru Hashim in single combat outside the walls of Acre. It ended badly for Connor that day and it was not anything Foulques wished to witness again.

"Gruffydd, that is not a path you want to follow."

Gruffydd lifted one shoulder and may have been about to say something, but Zola appeared out of nowhere and sat down, wedging himself between the two men.

"We will start," Zola said.

"Start dinner, I hope you mean," Gruffydd said.

Zola pointed to one side of the circle. Three men with drums stepped over and around people to get to the front where Rashida and several other women sat in a line on the ground. Perhaps they were not her maidservants after all, Foulques thought, for all of them were finely dressed and wore far more color in the form of jewelry and wraps than Foulques was used to seeing the Tamasheq women in. Rashida was especially resplendent in a red robe embroidered down the front and at the ends of the sleeves in intricate gold patterns. She wore no head covering save for a ring of elegant bangles that sat on top of her head and flashed in the firelight like a crown. Her hair was pulled back and rested on the nape of her neck, with the ever present braid falling across her forehead. She saw Foulques looking at her and raised her arm in greeting. Her eyes were big with excitement and anticipation as she chatted with the women sitting on either side of her.

One of the drummers shouted out into the night and began chanting. The other drummers followed soon after by putting their hands to the stretched skins of their instruments and began tapping out a slow rhythm. Rashida herself let out a loud cry and clapped her hands a single time above her head. The women seated beside her did the same and the drum rhythm changed. As one, the women, who were all seated cross-legged, began to sway side to side in time with the drums. One of the men began chanting again and the women's seated dance took a more energetic direction. Their shoulders bounced and twisted, they leaned over at the waists, and sat upright, all together in a preordained set of movements. Then from the crowd other women began to emerge and joined Rashida's group on the ground. They picked up the dance and now all the seated women, with smiles filling their faces, began chanting their own song. When the entire ring was complete, the drummers sped up their hypnotic rhythm.

Zola and many others behind the circle of women were bobbing along to the music as well. Then Foulques noticed a few blue-robed warriors appearing on the far side of the fire, their swords in hand. Foulques felt Zola grab his wrist. He looked down and in his other hand he held Gruffydd's arm.

"It is time," Zola said.

"Uh, time for what?" Gruffydd asked.

"The warriors must dance."

Gruffydd laughed nervously. "Have a good time," he said.

"We are not warriors," Foulques said.

"Tonight you are warriors. Tomorrow you will be nothing again."

He pulled them both to their feet and Gruffydd and Foulques looked at each other helplessly.

"I have never missed my ale so much," Gruffydd said.

They stepped gingerly over the swaying bodies of men and women and two members of Rashida's inner circle leaned in opposite directions to allow them passage. Soon warriors stood in front of the seated dancers, facing the fire. Zola drew his sword and he told Foulques and Gruffydd to do the same. The drums went eerily quiet and the crowd too fell silent.

"Do as I do," Zola whispered.

One drum started back up. The circle of men began to walk in careful, measured strides toward the fire. When Foulques could feel the heat reddening his face and threatening to singe his hair, the warriors all turned as one and let out a deep-throated grunt. Every one raised his sword high in the air and the other drummers joined in the beat. All the men began dancing in place, hopping from leg to leg while they waved their swords over their heads, while Foulques and Gruffydd did their best to follow along. The drummers picked up the pace and Zola snagged an arm each of Foulques and Gruffydd in the crook of his elbows. The warriors, still dancing in place, erupted into a chorus of war cries.

"Get ready," Zola shouted, tightening his grip on each man.

The drummers let out a unified shout and hammered madly on their skins. The warriors screamed at the top of their lungs and charged outward from the fire toward the ring of women who cried out in mock terror as their warriors came running at them. Foulques and Gruffydd were swept along with all the others.

When they reached the women, the drums changed rhythms once again. The warriors began moving in a circle, taking long strides and almost hopping as they lifted their swords into the air once with each long hop. By the time he fell into the rhythm of the warriors' dance, Foulques could no longer see Gruffydd, but every so often he would hear the unmistakable sound of a Welshman laughing.

✠

"DO YOU HAVE a woman, Elvy?"

"No," Foulques swallowed and shook his head. "I have never married."

Rashida smiled and looked at him from under her braid. "That is not what I asked. But you know that."

Foulques could feel his head heat up and his stomach clench, not with embarrassment but mild anger. Vignolo had warned Foulques the conversation would turn to this. How could he have known? Foulques decided the best course of action was to do what he always did when confronted with an uncomfortable situation. He would resort to the truth.

"There is someone," he said.

Rashida's eyes glowed and she leaned forward until her braid threatened to fall into her cup. "Tell me about her."

"What do you wish to know?"

"Everything your heart cannot keep inside."

He did not know what he would say, for at that moment he did not know if he could do justice to what he and Najya shared.

"She gave me life."

With those words he felt a wall in his soul give way, and he knew he was going to tell Rashida things that he could have never imagined telling another human being on this earth.

"I thought only God was capable of instilling life," Rashida said. "Tell me more."

"Then it was God who sent her to me."

Rashida was quiet, patient. She took a mouthful of tea from her cup and refilled Foulques's own.

"Her family suffered a terrible accident. A fire which killed her mother, burned up their house, and destroyed all their personal things. My uncle took her in for a time while her father got his feet back under himself."

"Tragic. How old were you?"

"Nine, perhaps. And she was nearly the same."

"When did you first know she was someone special?"

Foulques thought about that for a moment. "I suppose it was the very next day. When she stole my uncle's key."

Rashida clapped her hands as she always did when she was excited. "The key to what?"

"The... house we lived in. My uncle was a busy man and was often gone for long periods of time. He was unmarried, and had no wife of his own, so when he left he would always lock the door to keep me safe."

The light in Rashida's eyes died just a little.

"What else was he to do? He could not have a child dogging his every step as he went about his business," Foulques said.

"How did she get his key?"

"She stole it one night while he slept and passed it to someone who made a copy. The original was back on the hook before morning."

"Clever girl!"

"She was. She is."

"Now that she had the key, what did the two of you get up to?"

Now it was Foulques's turn to smile. "Every morning when my uncle left, she would put that key in its keyhole and open the world. I will never forget the first time she threw open that door. 'We can do anything,' she said, 'go anywhere.'"

Rashida squealed and sat back. "And where did you go?"

"To the markets, to the docks. She introduced me to her friends, we hid in warehouses and ran from the city guards. We stole dates from her cousin's stand and played games in the streets. We did anything and everything we wanted. As long as we returned home before my uncle, the city was ours."

"That must be such a wonderful memory," Rashida said.

"It is. But this memory is always followed by another. Two months later her father appeared at our door and took her away."

"Oh, Elvy. That is so very sad."

"I cried every day for a month," Foulques said, surprised his voice did not fail him.

Rashida reached out and covered his hand with her own. He kept his hand under hers and continued with the story.

"Then one day I was in the market with my uncle on one of his errands, and a boy I had never seen before pressed something into my hand and ran away."

"The key!" Rashida said. She leaned back and put her hands over her mouth, her soft brown eyes wide with excitement.

"The key," Foulques said. "We picked up right where we left off. Eventually, when I grew older, my uncle found a use for me in his business and I got my own key to the house."

"I think it is time," Rashida said.

"Time for what?"

"For you to give voice to her name."

It came out on its own, before he could give the matter even a second of thought. "Najya. Her name is Najya."

Rashida put her hand on his once again. "Thank you for telling me this wonderful story, Elvy. My people say that when you speak a person's name with love, wherever they may be in this world, no matter how far away, that person will hear you. This I believe."

Foulques looked down at her slender hand. "I pray you are right, Rashida. I truly do."

CHAPTER TWENTY-ONE

It was dark and Najya had to focus to make sure the knots would hold on Grandison's litter. Ever since Badru had left the other women and children behind, they had begun traveling at a rapid pace and Grandison was paying the price. His wound had started bleeding again and she was running out of honey. The last thing she wanted was for him to roll off somewhere in the desert when they were fleeing. He had been sleeping soundly, but was stirring now as she adjusted his blanket and bonds.

"I am sorry, Otto. You can rest again."

Grandison attempted to move his upper body. His eyes opened wide when he realized he was tied to his litter even though it was the middle of the night.

"Do not struggle," Najya whispered. "I had to make you ready to travel."

Grandison frowned, but he nodded. "It is tonight then? Your camel boy will come for us?"

"Yes. We must be ready when he does."

Akari had wanted to take them away every night since Najya had first met him, but she had been firm. They needed to prepare.

Every night after camp had been set, it was Akari's task to take the camels away and let them graze on any forage they could find. A fed camel was a fast camel and the more plants they could eat, the less they needed water. Camels were extremely efficient creatures and could replenish their fat stores with vegetation that appeared no more than brown twigs to human eyes.

The Mamluks had become accustomed to Akari coming and going as he tended the herd, bringing one camel back, taking a few others and returning them when they had eaten their fill. His routes were always varied, for one never knew how far a camel would have to range to find feed. So long as all the camels were back in place come morning the Mamluks left Akari to his work. It also helped that they considered him somewhat simple-minded.

And he was, Najya had to admit. Every time he saw her, he would ask for another bracelet for his mother. She told him he could get as many bracelets as he wanted once she and the white man were free.

Early that morning they had passed by a small community. Najya did not know its name but she had seen the huts to the north. During the afternoon rest stop, while most were napping under whatever sun shade they could piece together, Najya had caught Akari's eye and given him the signal that tonight was the night. He had sat up, excitement shining in his eyes, and she thought that he had understood. Perhaps she had been wrong, for it was difficult to read him at times.

Her plan was to steal away in the darkest part of the night and retrace their path back to the village. Once there, they could resupply and continue on, putting as much distance between her and the Mamluk slave caravan as possible in the shortest amount of time they could manage without jeopardizing Grandison's health.

The night wore on and she caught herself nodding off with her head resting on her knees and her back leaning into the pungent warmth of her camel. Just when she had given up on the boy, her camel stirred and looked into the night. A moment later she heard the soft plodding of a camel's hooves. She looked up and Akari emerged from the darkness as silent as one of the ifrit that he feared so much, born as they were of smoke and air. He greeted her with a smile and seemed in no hurry as he tipped the long poles of Grandison's litter up and over the front of his camel's saddle.

Najya stood and looked nervously about, the pounding of her heart the loudest thing for miles around. Needlessly, Akari put his fingers to his lips and pointed for her to walk on the camel's right side. They left Najya's camel there on the ground and set out in the direction from which Akari had come. With the soft sound of the legs of Grandison's litter plowing through the sand, it seemed to take an eternity-and-a-half for them to get anywhere. With every step, the tension in Najya's back grew, and her shoulders hunched up a little more toward her ears as she waited for a voice to cry out and sound the alarm. But it never came. Perhaps Akari's previous nights' meanderings in and out of the Mamluk perimeter had rendered them complacent. Or, perhaps they were merely the beneficiaries of the grace of Allah.

They walked for fifteen minutes before Najya began taking regular breaths. Another fifteen minutes and she could see the outline of two camels standing against the skyline. She glanced over her shoulder yet again, but there was nothing but stars above the horizon and no trace even of the Mamluk camp.

As they approached the two camels a man stepped out holding their reins.

"Akari! Who is that?"

"My cousin, Salim."

"I said to tell no one. Why did you bring him?"

Akari shrugged. "I showed him my bracelet and he began to ask questions. Why do you worry? He is my cousin."

Salim was a tall, thin man of middle years. Najya could see no familial resemblance between him and the much younger Akari. Salim's face covering was pulled down, revealing moist, bloodshot eyes set amongst dark crags and valleys deep enough to shelter permanent deposits of sand and grit.

He passed Akari a set of reins. "We must go," he said. "The sun will be up soon."

They rode for an hour, alternating the camels between a run and a trot. As the sun rose off the desert floor, so too did a low escarpment of yellow rock. As they got closer, Najya could make out the sway of palm trees.

There were only five or six small trees surrounding a cloudy pool of water, but Salim whooped with joy as they rode the camels into the oasis. They dismounted and left the beasts under the meager shade of the trees while they went to the pool. Najya wondered why she had not seen the oasis during the day's travel, but that thought was soon forgotten as she joined Salim and Akari at the water. The three of them laughed as they lay on their bellies, radiating out from the small grass-lined pool like the spokes of a wheel. Najya cupped a few mouthfuls to her face with one hand as she submerged a small goatskin container and waited for it to fill. She left Akari and his cousin there laughing and talking with one another in their strange language and brought the dripping goatskin to Grandison.

He was awake and lucid. She held the skin to his lips but he declined.

"Are we alone?" he asked in English.

She looked over her shoulder at the men still at the water.

"Yes," she said. "And we are free."

"Untie me, Najya. Give me a weapon. A knife, a rock, anything."

"Drink," she said, holding the goatskin up to his lips. "I cannot untie you for we have to keep moving. We are not yet safe."

His face was caked in dust from their recent flight and his eyes flitted about nervously, but he accepted the water this time. Najya let him drink his fill. As she stoppered the goatskin she noticed the men were unsaddling their camels.

She walked over to them and asked Akari, "What are you doing?"

"We will rest here," he said.

"Rest? We cannot stay here. We must put more distance between us and the camp."

Akari's cousin came over to stand so uncomfortably close to Najya, she could hear him breathe through his nose.

"Your princess worries much," he said to Akari but kept his eyes fixed on Najya.

Akari came to stand on the other side of Najya. "We are safe here. The ifrit will not come out during the day. We should rest."

"We cannot rest! The Mamluks will come for us," Najya said.

Salim chuckled. "They will not come. They have already been past here and the big man is in too much of a hurry. They will keep going."

Akari nodded. "Salim is right. They will not miss two slaves."

"We are not slaves," Najya said.

Salim said something in his tribe's language. Akari nodded and walked over to his camel. When he came back, he was holding a length of rope.

"Hold out your hands," Akari said.

"Akari? What are you doing?"

"We will rest here. Then I will give you to my mother."

"No…" Najya began walking backward but Salim encircled her with his arms from behind, pinning her own to her side. She heard him breathing through his nose again and felt his wet breath on her neck. She tried to throw him off, but he was strong and pulled her in even closer. "The boy's mother works hard. She needs a new slave. But since you are a gift, she will not mind if you come to her spoiled."

Najya heard Grandison thrashing around on his litter, his arms still tied in place. "Get away from her! Blood and ashes, if you touch her, I will pull your guts out through your arse."

Akari tied a loop in one end of his rope and came toward her. "Do not worry, Najya. My mother will like you."

"Akari, no. Do not do this."

He stopped moving toward her, his foot momentarily suspended in mid-air. He looked down to his stomach and saw gray feathers where there had not been any before. His eyes went wide as blood seeped through his black robe, making it even darker. He stumbled and went down on one knee.

"What are you doing boy? Get that…"

Akari fell to his side and the hard, rocky ground was instantly red. Both Najya and Salim stared in disbelief at the red stain creeping away from the boy.

Salim was the first to recover. He threw Najya to the ground and drew his sword.

"You will not need that where you are going," Badru Hashim said.

He sat on top of a camel forty paces away, a short bow with curved tips resting across the inner thigh of his bent leg.

"Unless you are more man than I believe, and you will put an end to the boy's suffering." He nudged his camel forward into a walk.

Salim looked at his cousin, who was groaning and twisting on the ground in an ever-growing pool of his own lifeblood. He looked back at the Northman. And then he began to run. After twenty paces he threw away his sword when he heard the thumping feet and the bellow of a camel bearing down on him.

Badru slapped the back of the man's head with the flat of his sword, sending him sprawling across loose rocks and sand. He bade his camel to kneel and took his time retrieving a brightly colored rope from his saddle. He tied it around the half-conscious Salim's neck and the other to his saddle. With his bow and two arrows held in one hand, he walked over to where Najya sat on the ground.

She could feel the tears building behind her eyes, whether from fear or frustration she could not be sure. Probably some of both, she thought. The Northman stood over her, his shadow covering both Najya and the boy still writhing in agony, his once beautiful face twisted and red like he had been possessed by one of his dreaded ifrit.

"Why do you resist so hard?" Badru asked Najya. "This is your life now. It is time to forget all that you once knew and walk the path God has laid bare."

Najya shook her head. "Let us go. We are nothing to you," she said.

"You are wrong. You and that old man are an obstacle put in the midst of my own path. One I must overcome to get the only thing I want in this life."

He drew his sword and before Najya could scream he brought it down across Akari's outstretched arm. The boy hardly let out a groan. Najya could no longer contain the tears. She felt them burst forth, streaking down through the dust on her face, leaving tracks of despair. Badru sheathed his sword, bent down and when he stood he held Akari's severed lower arm. Holding his bow and arrows under one armpit he wrestled with the boy's limb for a moment and then tossed something into Najya's lap. She recoiled even as she realized it was her own silver bracelet.

"You should scrub that blood off before you try giving it to another tribesman. Get on your camel. We have a full day of riding ahead."

A wind stirred the palms overhead, bringing with it a peal of laughter from where Grandison was still tied to his litter.

Akari had been wrong. Some demons do their best work in the daylight.

CHAPTER TWENTY-TWO

THE NEXT MORNING, while most in the caravan were busy breaking camp, Foulques and Zola decided they would partake in a session of sticks. They had been at it not even ten minutes when Faraji appeared out of nowhere carrying a few of the training weapons bundled under one arm. Zola stopped as soon as he approached. Faraji did not speak or greet them, he merely threw each one of them another stick. Foulques caught the stick with his left hand and immediately noticed it was half again as long as the current stick he was using.

Faraji too was armed with one long stick and one shorter one. He moved to stand across from Zola and nodded his head. The two men began to trade blows in a new pattern Foulques had not yet seen.

Faraji spoke as they fought. He held up his short stick. "Takouba, my sword," he said, launching a rapid combination at Zola's head. Then he held up his longer stick. "This is my spear." He demonstrated several thrusting techniques and a couple of curious swings from the side, which appeared to Foulques to be attempts to cut with the edges of the spear head, if there had been one.

"But the spear is also my shield," Faraji said.

He had held the spear couched under his arm, but now he spun it out to hold it in a vertical position. Another nod from Faraji brought on a series of different attacks from Zola. Foulques watched with interest as Faraji deflected blows with his spear and countered with his sword whenever Zola entered within range.

"Now you try," Faraji said to Foulques.

The morning became a lesson in co-ordination, for Foulques was unaccustomed to using the two weapons in conjunction with one another. He was no stranger to using a spear on its own, mind you a much longer one, but he had never seen it employed together with a sword. Faraji looked on, his arms crossed over his chest, as Zola taught Foulques the new sequences. It took some time for his hands to stop warring with one another and begin to work together. By the time the caravan was ready to pull out, the butt end of Zola's spear had left many an indent on Foulques's torso, and one round, angry welt right in the middle of his forehead.

"Enough," Faraji said. "You are both terrible." He walked away to the front of the caravan and mounted his camel.

"Is he always so positive?" Foulques, breathing hard, asked Zola.

The young Tamasheq warrior pulled down his tagelmust and also took in a few deep breaths. Foulques realized it was the first time he had seen his face. He had white, even teeth and a strong chin.

"Only in mornings," Zola said. "Later in the day, he becomes like an old bull camel."

CHAPTER TWENTY-THREE

THE SETTLEMENT OF Zuwila appeared on the horizon during the late morning hours, but it took another hour before the caravan stopped on its outskirts and began to set up camp. Even before they had finished unloading the camels, traders from the settlement appeared eager to see what opportunities this new caravan brought with it.

Foulques stood next to Malouf, waiting impatiently for him to finish removing unneeded baggage from his camel. To avoid attracting too much attention, they had decided that only the two of them would ride into the town, scout out the marketplace, and find a place where they could wait for Badru's caravan to show up. There was no need for all of them to go.

It was early afternoon when Foulques and Malouf rode past the first mud huts that marked the inner ring of Zuwila. They continued on through the town, past temporary tents set up in almost every open space, many of them hosting those who sought shelter from the heat of the day. It was obviously a busy time of year for the normally-small settlement. That thought pleased Foulques because it would make it easier for them to blend in and go unnoticed. They pressed on to the center of the town, where the wells and marketplace would be located.

Malouf suddenly stopped his camel in the road and it roared in protest.

"What are you doing?" Foulques asked.

"We are too late," Malouf said. His eyes were locked on a series of tattered tents directly ahead. As Foulques followed his gaze, a woman stood up from the mouth of one of the low, hastily-erected shelters. A chain around her ankles dragged through the dust. Her skin was pale overall, though crimson in spots. She was a Frank.

"Could Badru have beaten us here?" Foulques asked, the implications of which began to tear at his mind like rats trying to eat their way out of a wooden box. What if Najya had already been sold? Her new owner could have whisked her away to any corner of the continent and they would have no hope of ever finding her.

"Do not do anything rash," Malouf said. "This is a slave market. It is entirely possible that other Christians are here as well."

Foulques steeled his resolve and did everything he could to not whip his camel ahead recklessly. They walked on.

The tents were a ramshackle affair, patched together from odd bits of cloth and rope. None of them stood taller than waist-height, their sole purpose to keep the sun off their temporary inhabitants. There were thirty or forty shelters in total, clustered in groups of four or five, with each group surrounding a thick post driven into the ground. The weather-beaten women and children lying in and around the tents were chained to one another in groups and then they were tethered with one long chain to the nearest post.

Foulques could hold back no longer. He slid off the side of his camel and left his reins hanging in the sand. Malouf called out, but Foulques ignored him and walked swiftly to the first tent. He bent over and threw its flap aside. The stench of sun-baked sweat hit him full in the face. Two young women, their faces blistered from many days of travel exposed to the elements, sat up and squirmed away from the opening. They clutched at each other as they scurried away from him in fear. He cringed at the terror he had inadvertently instilled upon the women, realizing that his face was still covered with his tagelmust. He closed the flap and backed away quickly. He continued his search, going from tent to tent and inspecting the inhabitants of each one. He considered removing his face covering after the first tent, but decided against it. Seeing a fellow Frank at this moment would either give them hope or fill them with complete and utter dismay. Foulques did not want to be responsible for either.

He tried to maintain an air of calm to avoid startling the captives any more than necessary, but his search grew more frantic with every tent, with every face that was not Najya's. As much as Malouf had tried to counsel restraint, he too had dismounted and wandered amongst the captives. Foulques became aware of three armed men shadowing his footsteps, with another six or seven nearby. He did his best to ignore them and continued his methodical search.

The prisoners were all women and children, gaunt but fed and watered as well as any livestock. Foulques thought he recognized a face or two under the dirt and grime, but their eyes were vacant and paid him no heed. And why should they? No one had come here for them.

That realization ate at his stomach like acid as he strode toward Malouf.

The older man stepped in close. "Najya is not here," Malouf said.

"What are we to do with these people?" Foulques asked.

Malouf blinked. "Do? There is nothing we can do for them." He looked at something over Foulques's shoulder. "Do not lose sight of why we are here. I know it is difficult, but now is not the time to lose focus."

Foulques felt the armed men approach before he heard them. "Did you find what you were looking for?" came a voice from behind them. A Turkmen stepped around Foulques and eyed first Malouf and then Foulques.

"We are looking for a woman," Foulques said.

The Turkmen waved a hand toward the tents. "Then God has sent you to the right place. Though they are fresh from the road and I have not yet had a chance to clean them up, these are the finest Christians you will find anywhere. Many of them even have noble blood. I have a buyer coming in for them next week, but I think I can spare one or two if you are inclined."

"One woman is all we seek," Foulques said, his teeth gritting behind his face mask. "A young Muslim woman. She may have been kept with an older English man."

The Turkmen raised an eyebrow. "You are a Frank, though you do not speak like it."

Foulques stepped in close to the man. "Have you seen them?"

The slave trader's guards moved in, hands on weapons, but the Turkmen held up his hand.

"I may have," he said. "But I am a business man and I get the feeling that I am not going to make a sale here today. Even so, my time is valuable."

Malouf produced a coin and held it up in front of his face. The Turkmen reached for it, but Malouf pulled it away.

"Tell us what you know," he said. "That is all we want."

With the appearance of the coin, the half-dozen guards standing nearby seemed to relax a little, but they kept their hands on their weapons.

"They left sometime yesterday for Bilma under the care of a group of Mamluks. I tried to buy them both but the emir was not interested, at any price."

"What shape were they in?" Foulques asked.

The Turkmen smiled. "The girl was very healthy, by my standards. The man was not in such good condition. I did not see him stand even once. They dragged him everywhere on a stretcher."

Malouf tossed him the coin and Foulques felt a hand on his shoulder. "Come along Foulques. We do not have much time."

Foulques stared at the Turkmen and he stared right back. "Who is she, this woman, to you? Is she your wife? Sister?"

"What does it matter to a man like you?" Foulques said.

"Oh, it is no concern of mine. But I have known many in your situation over the years. If I were you, I would forget she ever existed. Find another, and in time, if God permits, her face will fade from your memory forever."

The hand on Foulques's shoulder restrained him. "We must go. Now," Malouf said.

Reluctantly Foulques backed away. As they turned to leave the Turkmen said, "Do not try too hard to find your woman. The man who owns her is consumed by a fire that looks to burn all in its path. That information I give to you for free."

The Northman may be holding her captive but no one could ever own Najya, Foulques wanted to shout at the slaver, but Malouf steered him away. They walked furiously for a few minutes before Foulques realized the camels were no longer where they had left them. However, Malouf was still walking.

"Where are they?"

Malouf pointed to a gap between a mud hut and a tall, weathered tent flapping in the breeze. Foulques saw a small, blue-robed man leading two camels between the structures. If he had been closer, he was sure he would have been able to hear an assortment of necklaces clinking against one another.

"What is he doing here?"

Malouf said nothing but raised his hands out to his sides and picked up his pace. Foulques followed suit, having to run for a few steps to catch up.

The camels had disappeared from sight when the two men rounded the mud hut. Malouf was the first to notice it was an ambush. He shouted a warning at Foulques as four black-robed men sprang at them. Two came from the doorway of the mud hut and another two came from around the side of the tent.

Malouf did not have time to draw his sword. He jumped against the corner of the hut and used it as shelter as one of the attackers swung at him, the sword clanging against the hard mud wall. Two of the men came for Foulques, but they did not have their swords in hand. One attempted to grab Foulques around his neck from behind but Foulques ducked under his arms and swung his forearm against his sternum. The blow lifted the man from his feet and slammed him flat on his back. Foulques had his dagger out by the time he spun to meet the other man. When he saw Foulques with weapon in hand, he took a step back and began to draw his own sword. But with the odds still three to one, Foulques could not allow that. He jumped forward, thrusting out with his dagger and at the same time pinning the man's arm against his body so he could not draw his weapon. The pyramidal shape of Foulques's rondel dagger was designed to pierce mail, so it popped through the man's robe and his chest with no more resistance than if he had dipped it into a still pond of water. And it came back out just as easily, although accompanied with a spraying arc of red.

Malouf had managed to draw his own sword and when the remaining two attackers saw Foulques appear at his side, armed with both sword and dagger now, they turned and ran. The first man Foulques had downed managed to work himself up to his hands and knees. Foulques reached down, hauled him to his feet, and slammed him against the mud hut wall.

"You work for the Turkmen?"

The man's swarthy face was uncovered and he was having difficulty breathing between clenched yellow teeth. He shook his head.

"The blue man told us of a price on your head."

"How much for killing him?" Malouf asked.

"Alive. We were to take you alive."

Malouf looked at Foulques. "Somehow the Tuareg must have learned that was why the men came that first night in the camp."

Foulques slammed the man against the wall again, eliciting a fresh grunt of pain. Spittle ran out between his yellowed teeth this time.

"You may have to take me alive to get your money, but I will not offer anyone who comes for me the same terms." He grabbed the man's chin and turned him to face the dead man at their feet. "That is the only reward I offer. Keep that in mind if you come looking for me again."

He threw the man on top of his accomplice. A few people walked by, gave them a quick look, and then moved on. A short distance away Foulques and Malouf found their camels standing near a market stall of overripe dates, swarming with flies, with no sign of the necklace man anywhere in sight.

CHAPTER TWENTY-FOUR

FOULQUES APPEARED EARLIER than usual at Rashida's tent that evening, and as he was about to enter, one of her maidservants was coming out. He stepped aside and she smiled at him with an impish look that brought color to his own cheeks. She ducked under his arm as he held the tent flap open and exited the tent, but not without looking back and giving Foulques another one of her mischievous smiles. Rashida stood just inside the entrance and the exchange between Foulques and her maidservant did not go unnoticed.

"Come in Elvy and do not mind her. Our nightly meetings have given the girls much to gossip about."

"Gossip?" Foulques allowed Rashida to lead him to his spot at the low table. "What exactly do they think is happening here?"

Rashida laughed at his discomfort. "Why, we are enjoying all the intimate pleasures a man and a woman enjoy when together and alone."

"And you would let them believe that?"

"I encourage it. It is rather exciting to listen to their

versions of what we have been up to."

Foulques had noticed many of the Tamasheq women looking at him with veiled glances and barely contained smiles hidden behind cupped hands. Now he knew why. Come to think of it, on more than one occasion he had suspected a man of hiding a smile behind his tagelmust, betrayed through his eyes. The heat Foulques had felt in his cheeks now spread over his entire head.

"Oh, I have embarrassed you. Did you not know that we are lovers in everyone's eyes but our own?"

"I... did not."

She looked at him from beneath her braid and he could tell that she enjoyed the subtle teasing, but he had come here to tell her something. Now was not the time for subtlety.

"Rashida, we must leave in the morning. I came to thank you for everything you have done for us, but we must be on our way."

She sat back and upright. The ever-present smile that always tinged her features faded away to a blank stare.

"Leave? Why? Did your business go badly in Zuwila?"

"Yes, you could say that," Foulques said. He closed his eyes and went over the lie that he was to tell her, but when he opened them and saw her concerned look he knew he was done with the lies and half-truths.

"My name is not Elvezio," he said in Arabic.

And then he told her everything. He told her how, until recently, he had been a knight of the Hospitaller Order of Saint John, he explained how Najya had been taken captive, and Malouf was her father. He even told her about his uncle.

By the end of it all, the words were coming out so fast he was certain he had repeated himself more than once. But he wanted her to know everything. It was a confession, of sorts, and though it felt good to unburden himself, it still pained him that he had not been honest with Rashida from the beginning. But one untruth begets another, and each new one comes easier than the last. He had always known this, but somehow he had deemed it all right this time around.

She sat upright, her face unreadable, looking every bit the chieftain that she was. When the words finished pouring from him, he looked at her and said, "I am sorry, Rashida. I truly am."

"What is your real name?"

"Foulques. Foulques de Villaret."

"You are French?"

"I am. But I was born in Acre."

"Then you have lost your home as well as your Najya." She shook her head sadly. "I knew you were not Italian, you know. That much was obvious."

"You knew?"

"I also suspected you were no textile merchant."

"How?"

Her smile came back ever so slowly. "Your clothing. No one who deals in textiles would ever dress so poorly. My uncle said you were a soldier, but I disagreed."

"Why did you never say anything?"

She shrugged. "I was too busy enjoying your company."

The mention of textiles and merchants made something occur to Foulques. "What exactly is it your own caravan is hauling for trade? I have not seen any specific goods on your camels."

"Me!" Rashida said. Her smile was back in all its splendor. "We are on our way to my wedding. And it will be wonderful. I wish you were coming with us. If you find Najya, will you come?"

"Your wedding?" Foulques could hardly get the words out.

"Perhaps you are not the only one who keeps a secret or two."

"But what of all the gossip your maidservants are spreading about us? Are you not concerned your future husband will hear?"

She pursed her lips and frowned. "It is to be expected. I am getting married. Some women take a different man to their tent every night in the month before they wed. What do Frankish women do?"

"Well, I do not know for sure, of course, but it is my understanding that a bride should be a virgin on her wedding night."

Rashida's laughter almost bent her in two and she had to push her hair out of her face when she came back up to a sitting position. "You have but one wedding night? I will have three. The first night my husband must consider me as his mother, the second as his sister, but the third, that is when we will become one." She shook her head and said, "I do not think I could ever live in your country. And I think I will keep calling you Elvy. Will that be all right?"

"I suppose so," Foulques said slowly, realizing as the last word was out of his mouth, that Rashida had just spoken to him in French.

CHAPTER TWENTY-FIVE

THE TAMASHEQ PROVIDED Foulques and his companions with six camels, and by two hours after dawn, the men had them almost loaded and ready for the road. Before Foulques tied his battered chest onto one of the pack camels, he rummaged through it and pulled out Najya's looking glass, tucking it safely away inside his robe. He had a feeling he would need it in the days to come and the irony that it would be used to find the very person who had given it to him was not lost on Foulques. For the thousandth time so far on this journey he dropped to his knees and prayed for Najya's safety.

He rose to find Zola and Faraji walking toward him. As usual, Faraji carried a long stick. Foulques did not have time for training this morning and he was thinking of a way to tell Faraji that, but he stopped ten feet short of Foulques with his stick in hand. Zola closed the remaining distance and said, "You must come with us."

"Zola, you know I would like to, but we have little time as it is." Foulques felt a hand on his shoulder.

"Go with them," Malouf said. "I will finish loading the

camels."

Foulques gave in and stepped in behind Zola. The three of them walked single file to a small, brightly-colored tent. Heat and very little smoke rose from a fire beside it. On his knees, holding a hammer and a pair of long blacksmithing pincers, was the necklace man.

Foulques stepped toward him with bad intentions, but Faraji thrust his stick out and stopped him. The little man did not look up, for he was focused on something in the small, blue flames.

"Do not disturb them," Faraji said.

Foulques was not sure who exactly he meant by "them". All he saw was a greedy, despicable man who had attempted to sell him and Malouf to bounty hunters. Faraji handed his stick to the necklace man. He took it, and with his pincers removed a hot piece of metal from the fire in the long, broad-leaved shape of a spear head.

He began chanting in the strange language of the artisans as he wedged the head down onto the wooden shaft. He squeezed it firmly with the pincers and pounded it with the hammer on a small anvil near the flames, their flickering light broken up by his dangling necklaces, casting strange patterns on his face. At that very moment he looked like some wizened elder. But once he finished, it proved to be just another form of desert mirage. The little man grinned and held up the spear, waving it in the direction of the men standing a safe distance away. The necklace man waved it again and said a few words, but neither Zola nor Faraji moved.

"Take it," Faraji said. "It is for you. He says he gave it special magic which only you can use. Take it."

Foulques reached out slowly and accepted the spear, being careful to keep his hand away from the still-smoldering collar connecting the deadly-looking head to the wooden shaft.

"Can I trust him?" Foulques asked, looking at the little man as he said the words.

Faraji stepped in and cuffed the man across the back of his head. "Of course not. He is a blacksmith." The little man grinned at Foulques and shrugged his shoulders. "But he makes fine things with powerful magic. That you can trust."

When Foulques returned to the camels with his new spear in hand, Rashida was there waiting for him. Malouf, Vignolo, and Gruffydd were already mounted and waiting to depart.

Rashida's face was graver than Foulques had ever seen it. "Travel due south for two days," she said. "Bilma is known for its salt fields and many caravans come from there. There is no road but there will be signs if you lose your way."

She took Foulques by the hand and led him to the rear of his camel. She pointed to a fresh pile of camel dung and then squatted down and grabbed a piece. She held it out in front of Foulques's face. To his surprise it gave off only the slightest hint of odor.

"This shows the size of your camel. A salt camel is much larger and will leave a good trail for you to follow, for they must eat a lot to bear their burdens." She grabbed the dung between two fingers and thrust it closer to Foulques's eyes.

"This is your road. Do not leave it."

She dropped the dung on the ground and wiped her fingers on her robe before taking Foulques's hands in hers. Her eyes glistened and tears welled around the edges.

"I will miss you, Elvy. And I will miss our many evenings spent together." She threw her arms around his neck.

"As will I," Foulques said. He returned her embrace without a thought given to who might be watching.

※

SEATED ON HER camel, Najya had to lean over to one side to catch a glimpse of Grandison. She could only see the lower part of his body and the poles of his litter as it dragged along the ground, leaving trails in the sand. Between the parallel set of lines, she could still see a long section of cut rope snaking its way along the ground. Until only a few hours ago, that rope had secured the torn corpses of Akari and his cousin. Badru had made a show of stopping the caravan and cutting the bodies loose in front of the Hausa mercenaries. By that point in time, the naked carcasses had been purged of all their gory fluids, along with most of their skin, but they had become so encrusted with sand and small rocks that the spectacle had lost much of its terrifying effect. So Badru had sliced the rope and they had carried on, the Hausa guiding their camels swiftly around the inanimate lumps in their path. But still the rope remained, bouncing and twisting as it chased Grandison's litter, a constant reminder that it was available should it be needed again.

"Are you all right, Otto?" Najya asked.

"Much better," he said. "Especially now that my view has improved."

His words were full of weariness, as they always were at this time of day. Najya had kept his wound clean and changed his bandage often. It looked to be improving, but she could not be sure.

Her camel suddenly stopped moving. Najya looked ahead and saw Badru had stopped the caravan. As Badru and Safir conferred with one another, Najya shielded her eyes and looked ahead. A short distance in front of them and to their left was a long line of camels. Each one was loaded with two thick slabs of salt, one tied to each of its sides. They must have been heavy because the camels carried nothing else. Their handlers, men dressed in robes as white as the salt they transported, had dismounted and knelt on the ground with their heads bowed. They were allowing Badru's caravan to pass by unhindered by their slow-moving beasts of burden.

Badru started the caravan moving again. As they passed in front of the kneeling merchants not a single one of their number looked up. It was as though they were trying to convince them all that they did not exist. They were about half way through the line of camels when Badru pivoted in his saddle and looked behind him. Najya flinched but quickly realized he was not looking at her. Four or five of the Hausa men had fallen back and dismounted in front of the first merchants. Najya saw one of the Hausa shove a merchant and kick him while he was on the ground.

Badru whirled his camel around and trotted back to

where it looked like the Hausa were intending to rob the merchants of anything of value, which, judging by their simple clothing and cargo, could not have been too worthwhile. Safir stayed where he was at the head of the caravan and brought it to a halt. Najya heard Badru shout a few choice words in his deep voice and the Hausa men stumbled over themselves to mount up and return to their places at the back of the caravan line, behind the Mamluk warriors.

"Who are they?" Najya asked Safir.

"Toubou traders."

Badru made his camel kneel and he climbed off. He helped up the man that the mercenaries had accosted.

"They do not look like they have anything worth stealing," Najya said.

"If a man looks long and hard enough at another, he will find something to covet," Safir said.

Badru was still talking to the man he had helped up off the ground. The white-robed man pulled his camel down to the ground, one that was not loaded with salt blocks, and rummaged through its packs. As the man continued to search, Badru produced a purse and began counting out coins into his meaty palm.

"Why do you follow him?" Najya asked.

"He is my emir," Safir said without hesitation.

"But I see you do not always agree with his methods."

"It is not my place to agree or disagree. Just as Badru must bend to the will of the sultan, I must follow my emir's lead in all things."

"He does not always follow the sultan's wishes though,

does he?"

"Silence," Safir said. There was a calm finality to that single word. Safir, like Badru, was used to being obeyed by those beneath him.

"There is a darkness growing in him, Safir. You have seen it, I know you have. Your men deserve better."

"Enough! One more word and I will gag you with a ball of your own hair."

Badru returned shortly after. He brought his camel alongside Najya's and threw her a bundle of white fabric.

"Put these on," Badru said.

Najya unrolled the cloth bundle to reveal a white robe like the Toubou were all wearing. Also tucked inside was a pale yellow turban and face scarf.

"Why do I need to wear these?"

"Because you have displayed an undesirable need to make friends with black-robed tribesmen. When we get to Bilma I want to be able to spot you easily." He looked straight ahead, as if trying to pick out the first signs of the oasis he spoke about. "Also, the man I will sell you to will pay more for a woman in white."

※

FOULQUES AND HIS companions rode hours into the night, but eventually they decided it was time to stop until daybreak. There was too little moonlight to guide them on their way and they could not take the risk that they might wander off course. They unsaddled their camels and both Vignolo and Gruffydd were asleep on the ground within seconds. Foulques and Malouf were also exhausted from the day's hard ride, but the thoughts haunting each man's mind overrode their need to sleep.

"Why do you think he did not sell her back at Zuwila with the others?" Foulques asked as he stared at the blanket of stars overhead. He sat on the ground, leaning against his camel. Malouf was in a similar position but faced the other way.

"He must need her for something," Malouf said. "Perhaps he has struck some bargain with Grandison."

"Do you think he means to take her all the way to Timbuktu?"

"It does not matter," Malouf said. He groaned as he shifted his position. "This is where we catch them."

"I will follow them all the way to Timbuktu if I must," Foulques said, quietly.

He sensed Malouf shaking his head in the dark. "No. It will end here. We must be prepared."

The men shared a silence for a few minutes and then Malouf asked, "Did she ever talk about me?"

Foulques folded his arms across his chest to keep in the heat. "A word here, a word there, but never in detail."

"She is right, you know. I killed her mother. It may not have been me who lit that fire, but I left alive the one who did."

Foulques had not lied. Najya had never told him everything about her relationship with her father and he had never pressed her on it.

"No one can know the consequences of his every action.

Only God can see that," Foulques said.

"I should have known. I was young but not foolish in the way many young people are. I left a boy alive after killing his father. He was only a boy, a child really. What could one so young do to me? It took ten years for that child to show me what he was capable of."

"Do you know what became of him?" Foulques had to ask.

"It took some time, but I finally did what I should have done in the first place."

"You showed mercy to a child. There should be no regrets in that," Foulques said.

Malouf let out a long breath. "So I thought at the time. I had been ordered to dispose of both father and son by my superiors, but I thought I knew better."

A chill went through Foulques and he leaned back into his camel. "Did my uncle know the reason for the fire?"

"He never said as much, but I suspect he did, for he did not bat an eye when I asked him to take in Najya for a time."

Foulques swallowed. His throat felt suddenly raw. "Why did he agree to help you? My uncle was never one to do something for free."

Malouf replied quickly, like the words burned his tongue and the only way to be rid of them was to spit them out. "He owed me a debt and he knew it. The man I killed was a Hospitaller knight and the contract was set by your uncle."

Foulques crossed himself in the darkness. It was far worse than he had suspected. "He... killed a brethren." Saying it aloud did not make it any less real.

"No," Malouf said, "I did that. And I showed mercy. If I had only resisted that virtue I would perhaps today have a wife, Najya would still have a mother, and I would have known a daughter. But who knows. God is great, Foulques. He will always have his way with us in the end."

CHAPTER TWENTY-SIX

NAJYA KNEW THEY were nearing the oasis of Bilma by the way the Hausa men kept trotting their camels ahead and talking excitedly among themselves. Badru had long given up trying to maintain their single line formation. As they came upon the oasis itself, Najya finally understood the men's anticipation. The Bilma oasis was indeed something special.

One moment they were in the heart of the Sahara and then suddenly the desert fell away to reveal a long rocky escarpment that wound through the landscape like some great serpent. The cliffs held back the sand and the wind, and in their shadows hundreds of trees and shrubs gathered along a meandering water way, with date palms nestled in every bend.

They stopped and partook of the clear, flowing water, and allowed the camels to eat for a few minutes under the shifting shadows of towering palms. Then they continued on south, past a farmer's field of cereal crops and a small cluster of mud houses. Ahead, more houses appeared to mark the beginnings of the village of Bilma itself. There, on the outskirts of the town, Badru had his men begin to set up camp. Then he told Najya to wash up at a nearby spring seeping from beneath tall grasses. When she was done he put her on a camel, took its lead in his hand, and walked her into the small village.

Judging by the number of mud houses and tents, the settlement was the permanent home of a little more than a thousand people. But the market square in its center, which proved to be less than a ten minute walk, was the size of a town ten times that number. This was a crucial way-point in the trans-Saharan trade route, a layover destination whether one was transporting gold from the west, salt to the north and south, or slaves in any and all directions. The people they passed were mostly Hausa, but Najya also saw a few white-robed Toubou men herding a dozen goats, and every so often a blue-robed Tuareg man or woman would walk by or try to sell them something.

Badru stopped and brought the camel to its knees. He helped Najya off and tied the beast to a skinny, young tree.

"Where are we going?" Najya asked.

"You said you needed honey."

Badru pointed twenty paces away at two small huts set next to each other. As they approached, Najya heard the bees before she saw them. There was definitely a hive nearby, perhaps several judging by the number of bees, but she could not see even one. As they got closer to the buildings, she realized why that was. The hives were inside the smaller of the two buildings. It was longer than it was wide and at the nearest end was a door made of heavy wooden slats, with generous spaces between them. The bees were flying in and out of the shelter through these slats. The mud shelter served to protect the bees both from the hot Sahara sun and the cold desert nights, either of which could decimate a hive.

The door of the other building, which Najya assumed to be the farmer's living quarters, opened and an old man with sharp eyes and hunched shoulders appeared. He leaned on a crooked staff and eyed the two of them with suspicion.

"Stay here," Badru said. "I think you know what will happen if you do not."

As Badru and the old man exchanged words, Najya took the opportunity to look inside the bee hut. She took a few steps sideways and could see through the slatted door. At the opposite end of the structure there was a large window made of the same wooden slats, which allowed the bees to choose their entry and exit. There were several hives inside, one of which looked ancient and was one of the biggest she had ever seen. The sturdy shelter protected a small fortune's worth of honey and beeswax inside its cool mud walls. With the amount of traffic that frequented the oasis combined with its remoteness, the bee farmer would have been able to name his price for both the honey and the wax. Najya was so busy calculating the potential profits the hives could produce that she did not hear Badru and the old man approach until they were right next to her.

Badru held out a small clay jar. "Fill this for the English."

Both Badru and the old man watched Najya closely as she unlatched the sturdy door and stepped into the bee's domain. Hundreds of them flew in and out of the doors and she marveled at the simple, yet ingenious design of the man-made bee cave. Not only did it save the hard-working insects from the elements, but it was also sturdy enough to keep out dangerous predators. Except for the most dangerous of them all, of course.

"There is a smoker there on the floor if you want to use it," the old man said.

"I think I will be all right," she said. It was only a small jar that she needed, so if she was careful and took her time, she could do without having to pacify the bees with smoke. And that is exactly what she did. She stood there in the doorway without moving for several minutes. Then she made her way to the nearest hive and lifted off its top. She slowly pulled out a section of honeycomb, shook off a few stubborn workers, and used her little finger to coax as much honey as she could get into her jar. When she was done, she just as carefully put the piece of honeycomb back in the hive and replaced the lid. She backed out of the hut and closed the door behind her.

"Congratulations," Badru said. "You passed his test."

Najya did not like the looks either of the men gave her. She moved to re-latch the door but Badru reached out and her hand disappeared beneath his. He pulled the door open once again and firmly pushed her back inside. He closed the door and Najya realized that after he swung the locking bar into place she was effectively trapped, for it was in a position that she could not reach from inside the hut.

"We have some business to discuss. Wait here," Badru said, and he followed the old man back to the other hut. She lost sight of them but heard a door open and close, and their voices grew muffled.

Najya turned and watched a bee's erratic journey as it flew the length of the hut and then claimed its freedom by disappearing between the wooden slats of the far window. No sooner had the bee disappeared then a figure dressed all in white stepped into her line of vision. She thought she was going mad.

"Hello Najya," her father said.

Perhaps she had been stung after all and was experiencing a fit of the type that sometimes killed people. She stood motionless in a storm of vibrating wings and tiny, velvety bodies. And then she was running. The wooden slats were sturdier than they looked and they repelled her assault with ease, but she thrust her arm out between two of them up to her shoulder. Her father wrapped her arm between both of his and begged her to be quiet. Tears filled his eyes.

"Please, Najya. You must listen to me."

"What are you doing here?" she asked.

"We have come for you and Grandison. It will be tonight and you must be ready."

"We?"

"Foulques is with me."

She closed her eyes and would have slid down to the ground if her father were not still holding her arm.

"Najya, I must go now," he said, looking to either side as he spoke.

"Father, take me with you."

A new round of tears dropped from his eyes as he shook

his head. "We must get you both at the same time. I am sorry, Najya, but we will only have one chance at this."

Najya wiped at her own eyes and took a deep breath. "Yes, yes of course. What must I do?"

"Tell Grandison to be ready. Foulques will come for you both after dark."

She nodded and he tried to let go of her arm but she grabbed his hand. This was the most she had spoken to her father in fifteen years. "Why did you come for me?"

He forced a smile. "There is nothing a father would not do for a daughter."

"Even if she would not do the same for him?"

"Especially then. For that would mean somewhere along the way he had lost her love. I will not ask you to forgive me, Najya, for that is something I cannot even grant myself."

Najya looked at her father and realized how much he had aged. She shook her head. They had lost so much time; time they would never get back. He disentangled her hands from his arm and walked slowly backwards, never taking his eyes from her own, until he disappeared around the corner of the hut.

Badru opened the door mere seconds later. Najya gave her eyes a last wipe and walked out of the hut.

"You have been crying," Badru said as she stepped into the daylight. It was a statement, nothing more.

"Of course I have!"

"You should be thankful," Badru said. "I have gone out of my way to find you a home and I have succeeded. This man has a son that is in need of a wife. But when he saw how good you were with the bees, he decided to keep you for himself."

"You sold me? What about Grandison? Who will tend to his wound?" She held up the small jar of honey.

"The farmer needs some time to get his denarii together, and I am not foolish enough to leave you here with nothing but his promise in hand. I suspect you will have another day or two to say your goodbyes to your English lord."

They headed back the way they had come, retracing their steps to the market square. Safir joined them there and Badru told him the good news about Najya's buyer. Badru spoke about her like he had just sold a stubborn goat that he was glad to be rid of.

The three of them continued on, and Najya noted it must be the busy time of day at the marketplace for the number of people in the area seemed to have easily doubled. Badru held her wrist and dragged her after him through the crowd of men and women until a foreign voice shouted at them from somewhere behind.

"There you are!" The language was English, and it was so out of place it cut through the noise of the crowd like the crack of a whip. The dialect was not so easy for Najya to understand. "I have been looking for you."

Badru stopped moving and Najya ran into his back. They both turned and focused on the speaker. Though his face was darker than the last time she had seen it, there was no mistaking the hooked nose and wide shoulders of the archer named Gruffydd. He had a sword in his hand. He saw her and recognition lit up his face, but he seemed to purposefully wipe it from his expression quickly.

Badru lifted Najya's wrist in the air and deposited her into Safir's care. "Take her back to the camp," Badru said. "I will deal with this."

"By Allah, I think he was the one who jumped off the English ship," Safir said.

"He was. Get back to camp. Wild dogs always travel in packs."

CHAPTER TWENTY-SEVEN

FOULQUES, VIGNOLO, AND Malouf stood next to a well in the middle of Bilma with their three newly-acquired horses. Two bay-colored mares and one white one.

"You saw her?" Foulques asked. He grabbed Malouf's sleeve. "How did she look? Was she injured at all?"

Malouf shook his head and stroked the neck of the white mare. "She was in her element, a house full of bees. She was beautiful. I almost did not have the strength to leave her there."

Vignolo looked up from filling a goatskin. "Has anyone seen Gruffydd?"

Foulques and Malouf looked at each other. "Where was Badru headed when you saw him last?" Foulques asked.

"Back to his camp. He had Najya with him." Malouf's eyes grew dark. "If that boy does anything to jeopardize my daughter's—"

"I will find him. You two focus on the preparations for tonight," Foulques said.

"You will need help," Malouf said. "I will come." He put the reins of his horse over her head, but Foulques grabbed the saddle and swung up onto her back before Malouf could protest.

"A good horse is all the help I will need. Help Vignolo and I will meet you back at our camp." He pulled the reins free of Malouf's hand and nudged the mare into a trot, leaving the men behind.

He ran the horse for a bit but soon there were too many people around for that kind of pace. He slowed her down and began to scan the crowd as he kept her moving north. He did not bother looking for the black-garbed Gruffydd for there were too many people in the marketplace. He checked that his tagelmust was pulled up to obscure his face.

There.

A man stood out above all others. For Foulques, it was never just the size of the man that distinguished Badru Hashim. There was something else there that never failed to draw his eye. Here he was in a crowd of at least a hundred people and it had taken only seconds to hone in on the Northman, as if God himself had grabbed the top of Foulques's head, twisted it in the Mamluk's direction, and commanded: "Look."

In that moment, Foulques knew they would never be free of one another.

And there was Gruffydd, his long measured strides propelling him unerringly toward his target. He drew his sword and shouted something at Badru's back. Gruffydd had given up his only advantage and now the Northman turned to look at the Welshman coming at him. With that small gesture, Gruffydd Blood proved what Foulques had suspected all along. He was no cold-blooded killer after all. Striking an unarmed man down while he had his back turned was not something "the Bloody" could ever do.

Two other figures caught Foulques's eye. One was a Mamluk and the other a woman dressed in white with a yellow turban. His mouth went dry and his heart froze in his chest. He could not see her face but he knew it was Najya. After all this time, all this distance, she was within grasp. The first thing that went through his mind was to charge the two Mamluks. If he got lucky he could kill one before the other dragged him from his horse. But then Gruffydd and Najya could take his horse and escape while he held back the Northman. It could work, he thought, as long as there were no other enemies nearby. But a quick scan of the crowd showed a half-dozen men who could have been mercenaries. The Mamluk grabbed Najya and started leading her away while Gruffydd closed the distance between him and Badru. He was out of time. Whatever he was going to do, it had to be now.

Badru Hashim rested his hand on his sword handle but kept it sheathed until Gruffydd was only two steps away and had committed himself to his attack. Badru drew and parried the Welshman's blade in a single motion, deflecting it into the ground and causing Gruffydd's momentum to carry him forward, making him stumble over his own feet. That was what the Northman did; he made even the most graceful men look like uncoordinated oafs. That was what he had done to Connor outside Acre and what he had done to Foulques himself years before. Foulques knew very well what would happen here today if he did not act.

He jammed his heels three times into his horse's side. "Hyah!"

The mob of people around the two combatants had dispersed to a safe distance. This was not a rare sight for this market. There were no screams, no women running with babes clutched tightly against their breasts. People backed swiftly away, and once at a safe distance, a few turned back to watch. But many simply walked away, intent on carrying out whatever it was that had brought them there in the first place.

Foulques weaved his way through the crowd, stopping and starting again, nudging some people out of the way with his horse's shoulders, causing a few others to leap aside as he closed in on the circle of onlookers.

Sitting high above the crowd as he was, he watched the fight unfold clearly before him like he was some winged creature. Gruffydd recovered and attacked again, with more tact this time. Badru blocked and countered with a series of side-to-side cuts, finishing with a hard overhead strike that drove Gruffydd back into the audience, scattering their ranks. The attack left Gruffydd's arm shaking and his face ashen. Foulques recognized then that he was already broken, for he knew firsthand how completely the Northman's strength could wither one's own. Foulques had no plan, no strategy. All he could think was that if he did not get to Gruffydd in the next few seconds the Northman would claim another soul.

The onlookers were five people deep and had their backs to Foulques. There would be no nudging his way through this time. Horse and man together found a short, open path, and they took it at full speed.

"Hyah!"

Foulques lifted his long-legged mare into the air and she responded, eager to be away from this forest of humans. They flew high over the first few rows of people, but on their way down the mare's back hooves clipped the shoulder of a man, knocking him to the ground, unhurt but bewildered.

Knowing it would be impossible to bring the mare to a halt, Foulques urged her on, directing her straight at the largest target he could find: the Northman's back. She was not a destrier, however, and so had not been trained to run a man into the ground. She veered away at the last moment but Foulques managed to extend his foot and lock his knee and hip in a straight line. The flat of his boot hit Badru in the center of his back, folding him in two as the combined weight of man and horse threw him flat, nearly tearing Foulques from his saddle in the process.

Foulques took a half-lap to regain his seat while Gruffydd looked on in awe at this latest development. The next time Foulques rode past the archer he extended his arm. Gruffydd threw away his sword and latched on, swinging up behind Foulques with a grunt as he landed on the horse's back.

The crowd broke apart and was in complete disarray when Foulques galloped through. One quick glance over his shoulder showed the Northman pushing himself to his hands and knees. Foulques gritted his teeth, wondering what he had done, as he gave the mare her reins and they raced through the town.

CHAPTER TWENTY-EIGHT

Badru sat before a small cooking fire sipping from a cup filled with warm camel's milk. He arched his back and could still feel where the English rider had struck him. He wondered again how many of Grandison's men had come with the intention of rescuing their lord. Was it only two? Was it fifty? He had no way of knowing for certain, but he doubted very much it was a great number, for Bilma was not a large town and the English would have stood out like the talking dogs they were. Someone would have noticed them.

After the encounter, Badru had sent his Mamluks scouring the oasis for further signs of them. They had searched many of the farmhouses and questioned the local inhabitants. No one knew anything and they were not lying. Of that he was sure. So he suspected there were only the two of them, and if they were wise they would have fled back into the desert by now.

But Badru was a careful man, and so he had locked Grandison in a small goat stable and positioned his Mamluks in four small groups in a square formation around it.

He put one of his best men at the stable's door and sent the woman to the bee farmer where she would be unable to assist with any escape attempt. The old farmer had not paid her price yet, but he would, one way or another. In the morning, they would pull up camp and continue on their journey.

Through the trees to his left he could make out the fire of the Hausa mercenaries and he could hear their laughter as it carried on the wind. He truly wished he could dismiss them from his service, for they were an unreliable lot in his eyes. But he needed the three guides, and they would not stay without the others. So he resigned himself to keeping his eye on them. He knew their kind were easily bought, so he put one group of his Mamluks nearby and warned them to be on the lookout for treachery.

A shadow emerged from behind a swaying date palm. It was Safir coming back from the beekeeper's farm. He joined Badru at the fire and Badru handed him his half-finished cup of milk, which he gratefully accepted.

"Was the old man accommodating?" Badru asked.

Safir nodded. "I told him if she is touched before we are paid, we will feed him to his own insects."

Badru heard raised voices and was glad he had put his own bedroll as far from the boisterous Hausa as possible. Safir looked toward the noise and both he and Badru realized at the same moment that the commotion was not coming from the Hausa but rather, their own men. They were both on their feet in an instant. Safir tossed his cup to the side and looked at his emir.

"Go see what is happening," Badru said. "I will check on the English."

Safir ran into the night before the last word was out of Badru's mouth. As Badru walked toward the goat stable, he could hear and see the Hausa were upset about something as well. Were they having a fight with his Mamluks? The thought brought a smile to his face. He could see black shapes darting in and around the trees, back-lit from the Hausa men's small fire and a couple of oil lamps. Badru picked up his pace.

He was still a hundred paces from the goat stable, but he could already see the guard he had stationed there was on the ground. His lamp stood nearby, clearly lighting the open door of the stable as it swayed on its hinges.

"Emir!"

Safir ran toward him, sword in hand. "It is the woman. She came back with a horse and has fled toward the cliffs with the English man."

"How? He cannot ride," Badru said.

"She has his litter strapped to her horse. They rode straight through the fire of the tribesmen, scattering them all. Many have already given chase."

"Where did she get a horse?"

Safir shook his head. "Some of our men are following her on foot but they will never catch her. I will saddle the camels."

They ran to where the camels were hobbled. Several Mamluks were already there working to tack out the beasts. Badru took the reins from one of the men and said, "Go find the guides. I will not follow anyone into the desert without them."

There was a frantic air about the men around him and it set Badru on edge. There was something strange about this situation that he could not quite catch the scent of.

Safir rose up on his camel, eager to be off. Badru pulled his animal down and climbed onto him slowly. Time and time again he had seen haste ruin the lives of men. Even now, he felt a voice whispering in his mind, telling him to hurry, to set off after his quarry before it was too late. They will get away, it warned.

A set of ice-blue eyes flashed in his mind. Who was the second man in the market square? There was no English archer alive who could handle an Egyptian horse the way he had.

Badru slowly turned his camel around.

"Emir? Where are you going?"

"To check on the woman."

"The Muslim woman? She is this way," Safir said.

"Perhaps. And if she is you and the others will not need my help to bring her back."

✠

FOULQUES AND GRUFFYDD crouched low in a thicket of palms and high grasses and watched as Vignolo, wearing the black robe of a Hausa tribesman, walked up silently behind the Mamluk standing near the stable door. The Genoan clamped a hand over the man's mouth and plunged his dagger up into the base of his skull. He left the body on the ground in the open and disappeared inside. He returned moments later with a lit lamp and placed it near the body and in front of the door. Its light clearly illuminated the dead body, but left the inside of the stable an impenetrable shadow.

"He has done this before," Gruffydd whispered.

Foulques put his finger to his lips, but it was so dark he was not sure Gruffydd had seen the gesture. He heard the two bay mares stir in the trees behind him and prayed they did not call out. It was up to Malouf now. All they could do was wait.

Long minutes later the Mamluk camp awakened in sections. After the furor reached its climax and the sounds of voices began to recede into the distance, Foulques grabbed Gruffydd by the arm.

"Wait here with the horses until you see me call you forward. Then you come in like the wind."

He stayed hunched over as he ran the fifty paces to the stable. He kept his eyes focused on the ground in front of him. The last thing he needed was to stumble in the night and break an ankle. He hopped over the dead Mamluk and plunged into the inky darkness of the stable.

"Vignoli?"

"Here," came the Genoan's voice from just inside the doorway, behind Foulques. "We have a problem," he said, coming forward.

Foulques followed Vignolo further into the building until the Genoan leaned over and threw aside a black cloak covering something on the ground.

Apparently, Grandison's eyes were more used to the

darkness than Foulques's own, for he said, "Nice to see you, Foulques. That is you, is it not?"

Foulques squatted down. "It is, Sir Grandison. We will have you out of here in a minute." He cast his eyes around the small room. He could see well enough now to know there were only the three of them. His heart dropped into his stomach.

"Where is Najya?" Foulques asked.

"Badru sold her to a honey farmer," Vignolo said.

"She is gone," Foulques whispered to no one in particular. It had all gone so well. He closed his eyes and shook his head.

"What do we do?" Vignolo asked. "Foulques?"

He felt a hand on his arm. "She knew where they were taking her," Grandison said. "It is the last farm before the town itself. Two small huts set next to one another." He tightened his grip in a manner that was meant to be firm and reassuring, but all it did was show Foulques how weak the knight really was. "Go to her, Foulques. You still have time, I will look after your friend here," Grandison said.

There was nothing left to think about. The time for well thought out plans was long gone. Foulques and Vignolo each took one end of Grandison's stretcher and carried him to the door. Just before Vignolo snuffed out the lamp, Foulques waved Gruffydd in. They picked Grandison up and moved out into the night.

✠

BADRU APPROACHED THE bee hut warily, uncertain of what

he would find. The feeling that there was something not right about this night had only grown stronger in the short ride here. He walked his camel once around the entire bee hut. It was dark and still within. The farmer's hut nearby was also quiet with no light coming from a lit taper. But it was late, and that was to be expected for someone of his age.

Badru dismounted and walked to the door of the bee hut, unlatched it, and stepped inside. An oil lamp hung on the wall and he took it down. He struck some sparks into its spout with his flint and it caught. Once he placed the lamp back into its holder on the wall, the small room erupted with light.

The woman was gone and the bees were silent. He had expected to find her cowering in a corner, trying to hide. But she was not. He looked at the spaces between the slats of the door and pushed his arm through them to see how far it would go. His eyes drifted to the large window at the far end of the room and he realized the slats there were spaced a little further apart. The gaps between them must have been just wide enough for her to slip out.

He slapped the side of the wall with the flat of his hand and bits of dried mud fell to the ground as the echo reverberated throughout the entire enclosure. He heard bees awaken in the hive nearest to him. He shook his head and left the hut. He had grown tired of this woman and her inability to accept her fate. He had been too lenient with her and vowed that he would not make that mistake again.

FOULQUES CREPT TOWARD the hut with the light and was shocked to see a glowering Badru Hashim standing in its doorway. He froze and crouched where he was, with nothing but the darkness for cover. His hand went to his sword handle and he waited breathlessly as Badru climbed onto his camel and trotted back toward the Mamluk camp.

Moving as silently as he could, Foulques approached the hut. Badru had left the door open and a lamp burning, and Foulques's mind started torturing him with images so evil he had to force himself to step into the doorway and look into the room. When he saw nothing but bee hives he let out a breath of gratitude. Badru had looked angry and distracted because, somehow, Najya had escaped.

Movement near the floor caught his eye and it settled on a bunch of bees swarming over a stack of honeycombs half-covered with an old blanket. He stepped forward and cautiously pulled the blanket aside. He jumped back as thousands of the creatures began to respond to the light and swarm over their honey receptacles.

Why would they be here on the ground when...

"Najya?" Foulques said, his voice hardly more than a whisper. "Najya? Are you here? It is me, Foulques."

The lamp sputtered and almost went out, but as it hissed back to life Foulques heard a muffled voice.

"Foulques?"

He turned to the sound, praying it was not the result of a demon tormenting his mind.

In the center of the room was a hive larger than the others and its top began to quiver. Ever so slowly, the top third of the hive raised itself up into the air and Najya stood there, tears streaming down her face and her arms shaking from the weight she held over her head.

Foulques ran to her and relieved her of the hive top before she dropped it. In one swift motion he lifted her out of the hive and squeezed her to him, thanking God over and over. Eventually, he let her feet touch the ground. She buried her face in his chest and let the sobs come. He held her there, breathing her in, knowing they should flee into the night, but the truth was, he did not care if his life should end at that very moment.

CHAPTER TWENTY-NINE

WITH NAJYA RIDING behind him, her arms wrapped around his waist and her head pressed into his back, Foulques allowed his horse to pick its own route through the darkness, as long as she kept on an overall northerly path. They had bought her in Bilma and he assumed the horse knew how best to avoid the marshy lands in the oasis better than Foulques did. It took some time, but they managed to reach the rendezvous point without incident, and more importantly, without being seen by any of Badru's men.

At the base of the rocky escarpment near the beginning of the oasis, Foulques found Vignolo and Gruffydd waiting nervously for his arrival. Standing in the trees nearby were all their camels, as well.

Gruffydd stepped forward and lifted Najya off the horse. "I am glad to see you unharmed," Najya said as he deposited her on the ground. "You are a man with many lives. That makes it twice now that I thought I had seen the last of you, but you keep coming back."

Gruffydd smiled. "Like a bad dream, my lady." A confused look crossed his face. "Forgive me for saying, but you smell really good for someone who has been dragged across the desert in chains. More like..." He stayed there for a moment, his hands on her hips, as he searched for the words to complete his thought.

"Like honey?" Najya offered. Her smile cut through the darkness.

"That would explain why your hands are still stuck to her," Foulques said.

Gruffydd dropped his arms and stepped back from Najya. "Oh, sorry I..."

"That reminds me," Najya said, "I better check on Sir Grandison's dressing." She hurried over to the older knight several paces away, taking with her a fresh jar of honey she had brought along.

"Where is Malouf?" Foulques asked Vignolo the moment Najya was out of earshot.

Vignolo shook his head. "He should have been here an hour ago. Something went wrong, I can feel it."

No sooner were the words out of his mouth, than a light flared up in the sky, winning out over the feeble competition offered by the sliver of moon. To the west, on a cliff edge overlooking the oasis, a fire burst out of the night.

Najya appeared beside the two men as they looked up at the far-off man-made beacon, for that was the only reason to build such a large fire in a desert where wood was precious.

"Does he have my father?" Najya asked.

Foulques tried to deflect her question by saying, "I will take Gruffydd and investigate it."

"You know what I am going to say to that, Foulques,"

Najya said, shaking her head. "I will not let you out of my sight for some time. Probably forever, so you better get used to it. And I will definitely not leave my father to die at the hands of Badru Hashim." She shivered as she said his name.

"And I suppose that leaves me with the old man and the camels," Vignolo said. "You better make it fast because come daybreak, there are very few places to hide in an oasis."

They decided to go on foot and scout it out from the cover of the trees below the cliffs. Gruffydd led the way, picking his path unerringly through the undergrowth toward the light. They were half way there when they heard the first scream.

Najya looked at Foulques. "What are they doing to him?"

"Gruffydd. We need to hurry," Foulques said.

It took only another ten minutes to get to a position directly below the flickering light source, but when every so often the stillness of the night was shattered by a new scream, ten minutes could seem like a lifetime. Especially when you knew that the one being tortured was your father. With every new shriek of pain Foulques watched helplessly as Najya's shoulders hunched and she cried out softly as though she herself was the one being put to the knife. But she did not stop moving. She pressed on, moving unwaveringly toward the sounds of her father's suffering.

The fire was not as large as Foulques had at first thought, for a lot of the light was supplied by a circle of lamps set atop spears driven into the ground. The fire was in the center of this circle, next to a thick pole dug into the ground or wedged between cracks in the rocky cliff itself. Tied to the pole, with his hands stretched high above his head, was the naked form of Malouf. They were too far away to identify him by features alone, but his cries of pain left no doubt in anyone's mind. The Northman stood next to him with a short blade in his hand. He reached out with the knife and sliced it across Malouf's back, eliciting a new piercing cry.

Najya turned to Foulques, her eyes red-rimmed and bloodshot from her recent trials. "What are they doing to him?" she asked once again.

Foulques did not think it was possible to feel so helpless. Or terrified. For he knew exactly what the Northman was doing to Najya's father. The scars on his own back twisted and burned every time the peace of the night was violated.

"Gruffydd. Is it possible?"

The Welshman glanced at Najya and then quickly looked away. He turned his face up to the night sky and let the faint wind tousle his hair. "At this distance I will need a range finder, but I can do it. I do not wish to, but if you order it, I will."

Another scream cut through the air from the cliff above. A confused expression flooded Najya's face and then she moved her head slowly from side to side.

"I wish I had the skill," Foulques said, reaching out for Najya. Her knees gave out and he caught her in his arms. "I am sorry," he said. She closed her eyes and began pounding Foulques's chest with one fist.

"Do it," Foulques said.

Gruffydd removed two arrows from his arrow bag, stuck

one in the ground in front of him and nocked the other on his string. He stood in place and breathed in and out twice, then leaned his body forward, pulled back on the great bow's string until his hand almost touched his ear, and let it slide off his fingers. He remained motionless as his arrow disappeared into the black sky. A spear holding a lamp ten feet to the right of Malouf swayed back and forth like someone had just kicked it. Another arrow appeared on Gruffydd's string and he repeated the same motions. Two seconds later, Malouf's head lolled to one side and did not move again.

Najya had opened her eyes and stopped crying while the first arrow was in mid-flight. She leaned into Foulques, continued pounding his chest over and over, but she was silent as she watched the second arrow arch into the stars.

CHAPTER THIRTY

THE FOUR OF them rode north out of the oasis with no more than a thin slice of moon as their guide. They had six well-rested camels loaded with water and two nervous horses, one dragging a litter bearing the half-conscious form of Sir Grandison. There had been talk of trying to be clever, of heading west or east for a distance before turning north toward their destination of Zuwila, but those thoughts died when Foulques reminded them all that they were in the Sahara. The desert never rewarded those who tried to outsmart her. In the end they decided that it would be more prudent to try and put as much distance between the Mamluks and themselves as they possibly could while it was still dark. To that end, Gruffydd and Vignolo each rode a horse until they were slick with sweat and then they stopped to change Grandison's litter over to a camel.

"We might as well set the horses free here," Foulques said. "They will find their way back to their stable before morning."

"And it will not hurt to have extra tracks around to confuse our pursuers," Vignolo said.

"Surely they will not follow us so far into the desert," Gruffydd said.

Foulques looked back the way they had come. The darkness was warm, comforting, but he could sense a threat at its outer edge.

"They are coming," Foulques said. "Never for a moment think they are not." They set the horses free and the darkness accepted them without question.

They pushed on with the camels for another hour and then Foulques brought them to a halt. "We will rest here until first light."

"Here?" Vignolo said looking around him. "Dawn is still three hours away. We could put a lot of distance between us and the Northman in that time."

"We could," Foulques said. "But we are exhausted and will need all our strength come morning. Tomorrow will come soon enough and it will be a long day. Get some rest."

Vignolo was unusually quiet as he eyed Foulques, but he did not press the matter. They loosened the camels' saddles but did not take them off. Najya and Foulques checked on Grandison, then Foulques went to one of the pack animals and pulled out his winter weight cloak from the bottom of his old faded and beaten trunk. He spread it on the ground next to Grandison for Najya and stayed by her side until her breathing evened out and he was sure she was asleep. It did not take long.

Foulques looked at the others and saw Gruffydd and Vignolo both asleep leaning against their camels.

He rose silently and went back to his trunk. He put Najya's looking glass back in, carefully tucking it deep under his belongings. He stripped himself naked and stood there in the darkness, letting the heat of the day's efforts rise off his bare skin like spray from the sea. When he was ready, he reached into his trunk and pulled out one of two sets of bries and breeches. He put them on slowly, balancing first on one leg and then the other. He then put on his padded gambeson, his fingers tying it closed over his chest in the darkness as though they had eyes of their own. Then he reached down with both hands and began to work them into his mail hauberk. Inch by inch, he worked the metal-linked garment up his forearms and then lifted it up over his head.

The stars above disappeared for a moment and then they were back in all their glory, along with a new but familiar weight hanging off his shoulders. He strapped on a belt, adjusted the hang of his hauberk, and then donned his black Hospitaller tunic. His hauberk had no mail coif attached so he wrapped his blue tagelmust around his head in the manner Rashida had shown him. When he was satisfied, he buckled on another belt from which hung his sword and dagger. Last of all, perhaps more out of reflex rather than need, he bent down and retrieved his hooded black mantle.

When he turned toward his camel, Vignolo stood there in front of him not two strides away. Vignolo said nothing, but in his hand he held a small flask. He tipped it to his lips and grimaced as he brought it back down. He held it out to Foulques with one hand as he wiped his mouth with the back of his other. Foulques accepted the flask and took a long draught. He stifled his cough as best he could but his throat was on fire. Vignolo gave him an approving nod.

"There is lots more where that came from," Vignolo said in a low voice. "You come find me when you are done." He reached out and gave Foulques's shoulder two firm pats and then walked back to his camel.

CHAPTER THIRTY-ONE

THE WIND DID not start until an hour before dawn. It came in short fits and then would die away to nothing. First light found Badru fully dressed, eager to be on the trail of the Hospitaller. He could smell the storm in the air. Soon their tracks would disappear in the shifting sands. He knew he had to hurry.

He threw open his tent flap and stepped out into the half-light of dawn. He looked to the east and considered unrolling a carpet, but time was of the essence. God could wait.

One of his men was already up and on his knees. It would be Safir, he thought. Good. He would have him assemble the others. As if to stress that they were in a race against the weather, a strong gust of wind pushed up against his back, whipped his robes against him, and showered his neck with sand. It was gone as quickly as it had come. He began walking toward Safir, picking up his pace with every step. He realized at that moment that Safir did not face east. He faced west. His bowed head came up, and then, as he raised himself to first one knee and then the other, Badru realized it was not the sun's shadow that gave the man's robe its blackness. When the man had risen to his full height and the cross on his chest shone across the fifty paces of desolate ground between them, Badru refused to believe what his senses told him. It had to be a trick of the desert, an image created by the longing in his mind.

When the black knight started to walk toward him, with his hood still up and a weapon in each hand, Badru dismissed the idea that it was a deception on the desert's part. However, he was not so sure it was not a trick of men. He scanned left and right for as far as he could see. There were no dips in the land that could conceal an ambush force. No boulders large enough to conceal an archer. Nothing but rock, scrub, and sand. Nothing moved. It was void of all life, godless even. It was beautiful.

Badru took the first step into a world he had seen only in his dreams. One where nothing existed except Foulques de Villaret and himself. When they were only ten feet apart, both men stopped.

"The desert can be merciless," Badru said. "But today it has delivered up a reward beyond measure."

His words shattered the silence of the land and the spectral image of the form before him. He was simply a man now. One who had taken the only thing from Badru that made him feel like he belonged in this world.

"Or have you come to negotiate? To sue for peace, as those who would control men like us do time and time again."

"There is a time and place for peace," the Hospitaller

said. "But it will never fill the space between you and me."

"You have not come to beg for your life?"

"I have not."

"Perhaps you wish to strike a bargain in which I do not execute the Genoan after I have finished with you?"

"That bargain would never be honored."

"That bargain," Badru said, "would never be made."

He heard shouts behind him, followed by more voices.

"Why did you come here, Hospitaller? Did you sin so badly that you think confronting me out here in the open will somehow prove your worth to God? That he will erase those sins of yours as though they were a bit of spilled wine? I have news for you. God does not care who lives and who dies. Offering up my life to your God will do nothing to tip the scales in your favor."

"I do not track my sins like some merchant's tally. I have come to rid the world of one man who thinks himself above all others. A man who haunts my dreams and those of people I care for. A man this world would be a better place without. I have come here to kill you, Badru Hashim. Let us not call it anything else."

The Hospitaller was armed with sword and spear, a Tuareg spear if Badru was not mistaken. Badru wore his armor, but he had left his sword in his tent. Of course he had his khanjar thrust into the sash at his waist, for he went nowhere without it. He considered meeting the Hospitaller with nothing but that short blade, and the potential glory of doing so brought a smile to his face. But no, he could not waste this opportunity.

His men had enclosed them in a circle by this time. Several had arrows nocked to their bowstrings.

"Safir," Badru called out, not taking his eyes from the Hospitaller.

"Yes, Emir."

"Fetch my sword. It is wrapped in lambskin beside my sleeping roll. Unless Brother Foulques intends to cut me down while I am unarmed."

"Admiral Foulques," the Hospitaller said.

The wind whipped dust up into a column a few paces behind Foulques de Villaret. It remained intact and drifted toward the Mamluks surrounding the two men. As it approached two Mamluks, they stepped aside and the plume pushed through the gap. The wind died and the column collapsed as soon as it was through.

God may not care about the outcome here today, but the desert does, Badru thought. The ifrit have come to watch.

"Come, Hospitaller. Let us give the Unseen Ones a show unlike any they have ever witnessed."

✠

FOULQUES COULD FEEL the arrows of more than one bow trained on him but he paid little heed to the circle of Mamluks or the world outside it. He knew every piece of himself, everything he had ever been and ever would be, was right here in front of him. He must not lose focus. But that is precisely what he did when Badru Hashim unrolled his sword from its lambskin covering.

"Do you recognize it?" the Northman asked. "It has been

so long since you have seen your old sword I thought you might have forgotten it."

"It is only a sword, a tool," Foulques said. "As you can see, I have managed to find another."

He refused to let his eyes settle on it by keeping them locked on the Northman's face. But his mind, that was another thing entirely. He stared at Badru's face, but the vision he saw was one of himself naked from the waist up, cringing in pain as the flat of the Northman's blade slapped across his back and drove him to his hands and knees. The deck planking was moist, and green slime had found a purchase within the cracks between boards.

No. That was a different life, one that he had revisited far too many times and overstayed his welcome. He forced the image from his mind and realized Badru was moving, circling, speaking as he did so. He was trying to steal the sun from Foulques's back. He probably did not even realize he was doing it.

The battle had begun.

Really, Badru had struck the first blow when he had shown Foulques his old sword, reminding him of his previous humiliation. A defeat of mind and spirit so complete, the thought of it still took Foulques's breath away eight years later.

The Northman may have won the first exchange today, but Foulques vowed that he would have to earn all others. And he would start by not surrendering the sun at his back.

It was a small thing, petty even, but Foulques stepped sideways as Badru tried to make him circle. Some of the

Mamluks had to back up and readjust their ring, but Foulques did not care. He knew no man of Badru's would dare slip a dagger between his shoulder blades.

Badru stopped moving when he realized what Foulques was doing. He smiled and shook his head. He held his sword, Foulques's sword, out and turned it over, letting the sun glint off its fine edge. He directed that concentration of light at Foulques's eyes and laughed as Foulques squinted. In his other hand he still held the lambskin, one end of it alternating between trailing in the dirt and flapping in the wind.

"This blade has not tasted anything but Hospitaller blood since the day I took it. How does that make you feel?"

"You should have killed me in Byblos," Foulques said.

"That was my intention," Badru said. He dropped the lambskin and the wind carried it a few feet before suddenly driving it into the ground in a crumpled heap. "As it is now."

Foulques couched the short Tamasheq spear under his left arm and assumed a high guard with the sword in his right. He focused on Badru and told his senses to ignore the sounds of men shifting nearby and the intermittent winds ruffling the tail of his tagelmust.

Without even assuming a starting guard, Badru slid into a fully extended thrust toward Foulques's face. It was a cavalier move meant to test his opponent's nerves, but Foulques had stared down too many lengths of steel to fall prey to Badru's feint. He also had the advantage of knowing Badru's weapon far better than its current wielder. So Foulques remained completely motionless as Badru's attack terminated far out of range. The Northman baited Foulques for a brief second, trying to lure him into initiating a bind, but Foulques did not adjust his guard, nor did he move back. He remained as motionless as granite. Badru was forced to withdraw.

"Are you used to fighting with a longer sword, perhaps?" Foulques said.

Badru cut the air twice with his weapon. "This one will suffice one more time. Then I will melt it down and have it made into something useful. A club, perhaps."

The words were not yet out of his mouth when Foulques launched his own attack. He stepped in with a thrust and diagonal slash combination with his sword aimed at Badru's chest, leaving him no option but to step back and defend. He was caught off guard but Badru's parries were effortless, graceful even. For a big man, he moved like a dancer.

But Foulques was counting on his keen reflexes taking control. He lulled him into a false sense of security with the sword and then struck out at his face with his couched, almost invisible spear. Not only did the strike come from an unexpected place, but it also had an extra foot and a half of reach over Foulques's sword.

Badru's next action possessed none of his usual grace. He jumped back and twisted his head at an odd angle, his eyes wide. He avoided the spear splitting his skull by the width of a hair, but as Foulques retracted his weapon he was able to put enough sideways pressure on it to lay one sharp edge of the head across Badru's cheek. It sliced open with no sound but a grunt from the Mamluk.

Foulques had drawn first blood.

Badru backed away and cut the air with his sword again. He started circling to his left and Foulques could tell he wanted so much to put a hand to his cheek but he would never give Foulques the satisfaction. The bleeding had already stopped, but the damage had been done. Badru kept circling and Foulques relinquished the sun. He did not need it anymore.

Badru came at Foulques in careful, measured attacks now, using his strengths to feel out the Hospitaller. He had the advantages of both size and reach. But Foulques knew he could counter Badru's reach advantage with his spear. He needed to keep Badru far enough away that he was not able to attempt a grapple. Locked in a hand-to-hand struggle with a man the size of the Northman was the last thing Foulques wanted.

Badru caught Foulques's spear in a bind and slid down it to slash at Foulques's face. But Foulques brought his own sword around, parried the blow, and countered, forcing Badru to back away as fast as his feet could slide. Foulques thrust at him as he retreated, and Badru had to beat down the point of the spear, inadvertently driving its point into his thigh. He pulled his leg back before it could penetrate deeply, but an uneven patch of blood began to spread against the cotton of his breeches.

Foulques kept his spear couched under his arm, and every time Badru came at him he used it to threaten his advance. Again and again Badru would knock the spear aside, only to be met with Foulques's sword.

Finally, he backed off and threw his sword point first into the dirt. It quivered there like the legs of a horse that had been ridden too far and too hard.

"You have picked up a few tricks from the blue men, I see," Badru said. "But tricks will not win the day. Safir! Give me a real blade. And your buckler."

Badru waited with his arms stretched out, his massive chest rising and falling as he brought his breathing under control, while the wind, which had grown into a steady gust, tore at any bits of his clothing it could get under.

The curved length of a kilij appeared in Badru's right hand and a Mamluk slipped the loop of a small buckler shield over his left.

"The Tuaregs are good fighters," Badru continued. "That is why when I was with the Cairo Tabaqa we would organize blue warrior hunts. Today is not the first time I have felt the prick of a Tuareg spear."

He banged his kilij on his small shield. "Now. Let me show you a few Mamluk tricks I picked up over those years."

He moved forward in a crouch, with a slight limp Foulques noted with satisfaction. But even with the limp, he seemed much more balanced and at ease with the curved sword in his hand rather than Foulques's straight hand-and-a-half blade.

Foulques stuck to his tried and true strategy of thrusting out with his spear as soon as Badru put weight on his front foot. Of course, he quickly found out that was exactly what Badru wanted him to do. He took the point of the spear on his buckler and deflected it to one side. Then he delivered a blinding six, or possibly seven, cuts to either side of Foulques's head. Somehow, Foulques managed to catch them with his own blade, but when Badru finished his attack sequence with a downward diagonal cut, Foulques used the opportunity to parry it and back away as quickly as he could out of danger. He realized then he could never hope to stand toe to toe with Badru and match the speed with which he wielded his kilij.

The two men circled, feinting at one another, and Foulques became conscious of his breathing and the sound of blood pumping in his ears.

"You know what we did with the blue people after a successful hunt?" Badru used his kilij to point at Foulques's spear. "We left their corpses in the desert, with their heads mounted on the ends of their own spears. And we would unravel their tagelmust a ways. On a windy morning, like today, you could see that blue streamer from miles away."

"I do not remember you talking so much," Foulques said.

"It is only right that you know what your future holds," Badru said.

The Northman dropped down into that crouch that Foulques was beginning to despise. It served to elongate his already long reach and reduced the total target area Foulques had to attack. He changed strategies and lunged forward with his sword this time. The two men clashed, and once again Badru's blinding speed and fluidity proved too much for Foulques. His buckler turned aside both sword and spear thrusts and Foulques was forced to improvise on a whim. He uncouched his spear from under his arm and held it vertical. It became his shield, as Faraji had taught him, and he used it to deflect Badru's next attack. Then, instead of thrusting with it, he swung the spear, attempting to slice with its heavy head. But Badru was too quick with his more agile blade. He parried the spear and deflected it down into the ground. Pinning it there, he brought his knee up high and stomped down on the shaft. It splintered, the head burrowing into the ground, and thin pieces of wood flew away on the wind.

Foulques tried a desperate backhand strike with his sword that Badru parried with his buckler and then brought his shield smashing across Foulques's face. Foulques spun in place and went down to one knee. Close to the ground, sand stung his eyes and he thrust his blade upward in the direction he would have attacked if he had had the fortune to be in Badru's position. He was rewarded with a vibration that shook his arm and he turned his blade and body to redirect some of the force. He blinked the sand away and steeled himself for another attack, but Badru had stepped back.

Foulques pushed himself to his feet in time to see Badru pull off his buckler and toss it aside.

"No more tricks." He spun his kilij and continued the momentum into a series of strikes that left Foulques's every limb shaking. He flexed his sword hand to work feeling back into his forearm muscles.

Badru Hashim was too strong. Too fast.

And he came again.

Foulques was aware of the Mamluks behind him, but

there was nowhere else he could go to escape the fury of the Northman. His cuts broke through his defenses and two hard hits smashed his ribs, tearing a gash in both his mail and gambeson. If he had not been wearing his hauberk he would be dead. As it was, the second hit knocked the breath out of him and sent him stumbling backward, through the circle of Mamluks and sprawling onto the hard ground beyond. He put his hand to his side and it came away slick. He groaned and looked at it as the ever increasing wind deposited specks of sand on his bloody palm.

"Get up!"

Rough hands were on him and he was lifted to his feet and thrown back into the middle of the circle. Badru attacked immediately and Foulques put up a block, but Badru kicked him hard in the chest, sending him sprawling once again. Foulques coughed as he hit the ground this time, but had the presence of mind to pull his tagelmust up over his mouth and nose. He was not sure if the roaring he heard was the wind or the Northman yelling at him. He groped around him for his weapon but could not find it. He lifted his head and saw not the sword he sought, but another. His uncle's sword was there, standing upright, impaling the earth. Foulques almost laughed at the iconic image of it. Like he was some kind of hero in one of the King Arthur fantasies the puppeteers were so fond of.

He crawled to the sword on hands and knees. He was no mythical king. He was no hero. But he was a Hospitaller Knight of Saint John, and he would not die on his knees.

He grabbed the quillons of the crossguard and used

them like ladder rungs to pull himself to his feet. Then, setting both hands on the handle, he pulled the sword out of the dirt, and this time, he did laugh. The sword had long ago been abandoned by his uncle, given to Foulques almost as an afterthought. He had been little more than a boy when he was presented with the sword on the day of his knighting, but the long-forgotten thrill of that moment came to him once again. He flexed his fingers around the handle and the sword melted into his hands like hot wax.

Badru was several steps away, nodding his head appreciatively. He recognized the poetry of the moment but he also smelled the blood. He came on like an enraged lion.

The Northman wanted his head, so Foulques decided he would give it to him. He stood with his right leg forward with more than half of his weight leaning on it, with his left heel raised slightly and ready to spring. He held his sword with both hands, its point just inches off the ground and in front of his rear foot. He leaned his head forward, presenting it as the only target. A target that was not really there. It was a baited trap that would never work on someone as experienced as Badru, but Foulques was done running. From this moment on, he promised himself he would move forward or he would never move again.

Badru came roaring in and feinted at his exposed head, but changed his angle of attack and tried to take Foulques again in the torso, where his armor was torn and bloodied. Foulques parried by lifting his blade the short distance needed to intercept Badru's blade and then he sent a controlled thrust at Badru's face. His sword had become his new spear, and Badru had to backpedal to safety.

Badru wasted no time. He stepped in for the attack and again Foulques lifted his blade to knock the curved sword away and then quickly pulled it down onto Badru's hand, slicing the back of his arm. Foulques stepped forward to thrust at his face, forcing Badru back. Four more times Badru came at Foulques and each time Foulques swatted his weapon away and stabbed viciously at his face, or his leg, then at his hands, pushing the giant Mamluk backward gradually step by step, until it was Badru the Mamluks had to open the circle for. Badru tried to come at him from the side but Foulques would have none of it. He pivoted, refusing to draw his front foot back even an inch. His movements were efficient and straight, while Badru's became wilder with every effort. His breathing was heavy now. Foulques had neutralized his speed. Now he would take his strength.

Foulques resumed his low, outside guard and presented his head once again. Badru did not feint this time. He went for the head and stayed on course. Foulques again parried by lifting his blade and stepped forward with his thrust. Badru parried it, of course, but Foulques rolled around his parry and began a two-handed strike to the right side of Badru's head. Badru read the attack and was already in position to block before Foulques had passed the point of no return. Foulques kept his sword moving but let go with his right hand, slid it up the blade, and grabbed it near the last third of its cutting edge. He spun it over his own head and down. His left hand joined his right in an upside-down sword grip on the blade, holding it like the club Badru had called it, and he brought it down hard, smashing the quillon into the side of Badru's knee. A sharp crack and crunching of bone won out over the howls of the wind for one split second. His knee wobbled sideways at a strange angle and Badru screamed, his face twisting in agony.

Foulques let his sword drop out of his hands as he slid forward once again, drawing his rondel dagger and burying it deep under Badru's right armpit. He withdrew the dagger, its entire length saturated with blood, and kept moving past the Northman. Foulques looked over his shoulder in time to see the Northman crumple, joint by joint, to the ground.

Badru hugged his right arm tightly against his body in an attempt to stem the flow of blood, but Foulques knew it was a futile effort. He had pierced the Northman's lung and he was filling up with blood on the inside. Foulques leaned over, retrieved his sword, and took yet another step forward, leveling his blade at the Mamluk called Safir.

The wind was so strong now the men on either side of Safir had one hand on their turbans and one on their swords. One of them shouted something at Safir but Foulques could not make out what he said. Safir ignored the Mamluk, for his attention was fixed solely on Foulques. Safir drew his sword. Foulques spared a hand to tighten the veil over his eyes and began to walk toward him.

Foulques slowed as he closed with the Mamluk. Keeping eye contact, Safir slowly stepped to one side, breaking a hole in the circle of men. He pointed at the opening with his sword. Bent against the wind, Foulques kept walking forward, ever forward, out of the circle of men and into the swirling madness of sand and wind.

Several camels lay on the ground hunkered together, determined to wait out the storm. Foulques climbed onto the nearest one and she protested loudly. She had no saddle, but was bridled, so Foulques was able to coax her into a standing position and point her into the wind. He urged her into a trot.

He did not know what direction he was going, nor did he care, so long as it was forward. He had to fight the camel constantly, for unlike him, she had the good sense to not want to be out in a sand storm. Breathing was difficult and he had to keep cleaning off the front of his tagelmust as it clogged with sand. Eventually, he realized it was not just the sand that hampered his breath, it was also the injury at his side. The blood had not stopped flowing and it had begun to burn. Every breath was accompanied with a hitching pain that forced him to clench his eyes. He began to settle for taking smaller breaths and leaned his head over onto his camel to relieve the pressure in his chest. He found a comfortable position and closed his eyes.

Foulques either fell asleep or blacked out. When he came to, he panicked and sat up in a frenzy not knowing where he was. The sudden movement made him groan and jerk and the camel responded by jumping sideways. Foulques was too weak to hold on and he toppled to the ground, crying out as he hit. Finally free of its uncooperative burden, the camel bolted away. She could have stopped only steps away but Foulques could not see far enough through the blowing sand to tell, and it did not matter, for he did not have the strength to climb back on.

He lay there, unmoving, and tried to catch his breath. Although he could see the air dancing around him mercilessly, throwing clouds of sand all about, he could get none of it into his lungs. Faces began to emerge out of the storm. First he saw his uncle, then Vignolo and Grandmaster Villiers. Then he saw Najya.

"The fight is over," she said.

The pain in his chest and side dissipated with her words like water sinking into parched earth. Her face threatened to break up in the wind, but he held onto it until all became dark.

✯

BADRU FELT HANDS under his arm and heard a voice cry out, a human voice, fighting against the elements to be heard. The hands were strong, and they hauled him to his feet, supporting him there against the desert's best efforts to carry him away. Badru looked through squinting eyes battered by flying debris and saw the faithful face of Safir, his shoulders hunched against the wind, the lashes of his own eyes thick with sand. His mouth opened but Badru could not hear his words. He tried to pull Badru along with him but Badru's feet were planted firmly now that he was standing. Safir pulled harder and his expression grew desperate when Badru shook his head. Safir was strong, but he was no match for the strength of the Unseen Ones.

Faithful Safir. Badru knew he should not think of him

that way, for only masters and gods deserved to have the faithful as followers. Struggling with the effort, Badru pulled Safir's hands, one by one, from around his arm. The Hospitaller had stolen his breath, the desert would claim the rest. Safir resisted at first and Badru thought how much easier this would be if he were his master. He could simply tell Safir to leave, to go find another to serve. But no matter how much Badru wanted to dismiss him, to send him to someone who deserved his loyalty, he knew he could not. One slave cannot be released by another.

Safir must have understood at least some of what Badru was trying to communicate, for his hands dropped to his sides. He took a step back. And with that, all Badru's remaining ties to this world were severed. He could feel the current of the netherworld tugging at him, exerting more force with every second even as his resistance faded. Columns of sand leapt around him as he turned away from Safir and began a painful, leg-dragging walk toward the calls of the Unseen Ones.

CHAPTER THIRTY-TWO

THE SERPENT BEGAN to swallow Foulques whole. It slithered out of the darkness, unhinged its great maw, and inch by agonizing inch pulled his feet and then his lower legs deeper within its gyrating body. At first, he kicked at it, pushed away with his feet and arched his back onto his shoulders in a desperate attempt to keep it at bay. But the serpent continued its relentless climb up his lower body, its fangs raking against the bare skin of his legs. Eventually, paralyzed by its poison and the massive weight of it, Foulques was unable to resist any further. It was not a steady, gradual procession, but rather a series of stops and starts. He screamed as its fangs passed over his stomach and stopped at his chest. Foulques stared into its emotionless, uncaring eyes and steeled himself for its next inevitable advance. Even if he was not paralyzed, he knew there was no escape now, for the slant of the serpent's teeth allowed movement in only one direction.

Forward. Only forward.

The poison had not yet spread to his upper body, for he could feel something beginning to nibble at his left hand. He jerked it away and light flooded his senses as granules of sand stung his eyes. The nibbling of his arm began anew, but this time it was accompanied by a voice.

"Ciao! Ciao!"

Foulques laughed out loud as the serpent unhinged its jaw once again and retreated into the darkness, away from the voice of the sand reader's boy.

"Ciao," Foulques heard himself say.

CHAPTER THIRTY-THREE

"Are you ready?" Foulques asked Najya. She finished adjusting her head scarf and smoothed down the front of the new robe the Tamasheq had given her.

"Oh Foulques. Look at me. I am hardly in a state to meet royalty. I am not sure this is such a good idea."

Foulques laughed. "Rashida is a chieftain, not a queen. And no matter what you think she is going to be like, I guarantee that you are wrong." He laughed again as she fretted some more over her head covering.

"Do you think I should wear a veil?"

He grabbed her by the shoulders and gave her a good-natured shake. "Najya. You are beautiful as you are at this very moment. I would meet a thousand queens with you at my side. Now come. We will be late."

He threw open the tent flaps and stepped out into the early evening air. Standing ten feet away was the necklace man, pretending to be minding his own affairs. Foulques gave him what he hoped was a dark, uninviting look. The little man looked away, but as soon as Foulques and Najya started walking he scurried a few paces ahead and led them all the way to the chieftain's tent, greeting everyone they passed whether they wanted him to or not.

Faraji was sitting on his chair outside the tent whittling on a stick and the same two guards flanked the opening. Foulques shook his head. Nothing ever changed in the desert.

"Tell the blacksmith his spear broke. The magic did not work," Foulques said.

Faraji relayed the message to the necklace man, who said something back to him.

"What did he say?"

"You are here. The magic worked," Faraji said.

The guards relieved Foulques of his sword and they held open the entrance flaps. As Foulques went to step through, a long stick appeared in front of him and barred his way.

"Let me guess," Foulques said.

Faraji shrugged his shoulders.

Foulques pulled out his tiny eating knife and surrendered it to the guards, fighting to keep a smile at bay. They ducked inside the softly-lit tent and Foulques was surprised to see no table in its center. Rashida walked forward from the side room, her personal quarters.

"Najya!" She came forward and grabbed the stunned woman in a tight embrace, squeezing her new robes into a mass of wrinkles as Foulques looked on.

It was not the greeting he had expected, but like he had said, Rashida never failed to surprise. Rashida let Najya up for air, but still held on to both her hands as she gushed about how happy she was that Najya had finally come to visit. Najya was tongue-tied and hardly managed to get a word in.

Finally, Rashida turned to Foulques. Her eyes sparkled and the lamps reflected off the charms in her hair. "So nice to finally meet you as well, Brother Foulques. Please come inside."

She motioned for them to follow her into the curtained-off section of her tent. A pile of carpets and blankets had been pushed into a tidy pile in one corner and cushions were spread around the small table Foulques had come to know very well. Next to it, on a bare piece of earth, was a cooking fire with an iron pan set atop glowing coals. They sat down and Najya gradually found her voice. It took only minutes for the two women to settle into the easy conversation of friends.

"Are you happy, Foulques?" Rashida asked him suddenly.

He nodded. "Yes," he said, and meant it.

"Good!" She wrapped a cloth around the long handle of the pan in front of her and poured what looked like the old, faded-green pits of some forgotten fruit into it. She kept the dry pits moving with a wooden spoon as she spoke to Najya.

"What will you do now?"

Najya looked at Foulques. "We will go to Zuwila and pick up some slaves."

"Slaves? If you need only a few, perhaps I could give you some of mine?"

"Thank you, Rashida," Najya said, "but these are our

people the Mamluks captured in Acre. If they are still there when we arrive, we intend to free them all."

"I see," Rashida said, though Foulques could tell by her voice that she was having difficulty seeing the sense in Najya's plan. After a few moments of thoughtful seed stirring, she looked up. "You mean to set all those slaves free? Where will they go? Who will look after them?"

"We will," Najya said. "At least until we can get them to Cyprus. After that, I am not sure what any of us will do."

"Cyprus? Then you must cross the great sea." She shook her head at the enormity of it all. The pits had begun to crackle. She poured them out of the pan into a stone cup and began crushing them into a powder with a blunt stick.

"Do not worry. Foulques has a plan."

Rashida pursed her lips. "Be careful, Najya. Sometimes his plans are not so well thought out."

Najya laughed. "Did I say plan? Perhaps I should have said direction."

Apparently, Foulques had missed his cue, for Najya drove a not so subtle elbow into his side.

"Yes," Foulques said. He cleared his throat, not exactly sure how to make his request. "I am confident there is a Mamluk ship in Barqa large enough to accommodate us all. If you can spare him Rashida, I would like to ask Zola to guide us there."

She stopped grinding the seeds and looked up in surprise. "Zola? Nonsense." She dumped the powder into a piece of cloth suspended over a large clay mug. "I will take you to Barqa." She lifted a kettle and began to pour hot water over the powdered seeds. "We will all go. Barqa is lovely and I will get some sea urchins."

Foulques could feel Najya looking at him in shock. He was more than a little surprised himself, but he had the advantage of being somewhat used to Rashida's nature.

"But what about your wedding arrangements?" Foulques asked.

Rashida brushed his question aside with one hand. "I am too young to be married. Perhaps next year, when I am wiser." She tossed her head to remove her braid from her line of vision, lifted up the mug, and divided the resulting liquid into three tiny cups. "It will be an exciting trip and Najya and I can get to know each other much better." She passed a cup each to Foulques and Najya.

"I am at a loss for words," Najya said.

Rashida held her cup in the air. "Then let us drink. To a monk," she said, holding her cup toward Foulques, "and his strange harem," she said, laughing.

Najya's eyebrows furrowed and a half-smile played across her face. "Foulques? Is there something you want to tell me?"

"Many things," Foulques said. "But right now all I want to do is drink this tea." He took a sip and the thick, bitter liquid was not what he expected. He clamped his teeth together to refrain from spitting it out. Judging from Najya's face she underwent a similar experience, but they both did their best to finish.

"Would you like another?"

Both Foulques and Najya politely declined and Rashida

put the pan off to the side. Foulques noted with a smile that even though it was now cold to the touch, for it had been out of the fire for some time, she still handled it carefully by the cloth-wrapped handle.

Tamasheq or djinn? Possibly a little of both? Foulques was sure he would never know. But he had a lot of time to think about it that night as he tossed and turned in his blankets. For whatever reason, sleep had a hard time finding him.

CHAPTER THIRTY-FOUR

"Are you sure this is what you want?" King Henry of Cyprus, formerly King Henry of the Kingdom of Jerusalem asked. He stood at his desk, hands clasped behind his back.

Foulques and Vignolo did not even glance at one another. "It is what needs to be done," Foulques said. "There is a difference."

"For some people, perhaps," Henry said. He gave Foulques a moment to reconsider, then gave him a curt nod. "Very well." He reached out and pulled the long cord hanging from the ceiling next to his desk, then he settled into his chair.

Besides Foulques, Vignolo, and the king, there were four other men in the room. Two, like Foulques, were garbed in the battle reds of the Hospitallers. Another man wore a black mantle bearing the cross of the Brotherhood, and another was clothed in the simple linen breeches and tunic of the common man, albeit one with a modicum of means at his disposal. Even though they were in the presence of the king, all of the Hospitallers were fully armed.

The man in the black Hospitaller robe was none other than Jimmy the Neckless. He had shown up at the docks shortly after Foulques and his companions had come to shore from their newly acquired warship, the Wyvern. With the help of the Tamasheq, Foulques had rescued the slaves in Zuwila and then taken the most direct route they could to Barqa. From there it had been a simple matter to overpower the three men Badru had left on his ship. Foulques did not know how Jimmy found out Foulques and Vignolo had arrived on Cyprus, and he did not care. He was simply happy to see the man.

Jimmy took up a position on one side of the door. He was not in red because they did not have time to find a red tunic large enough to slip over his frame. There was only one tunic in all of Christendom that may have sufficed, but it would have encased him like a sausage. And anyway, the owner of that tunic, Pirmin Schnidrig of Tasch, flanked the other side of the door.

Brother Alain, as always, stood beside Foulques. As one, the two of them turned and waited for the door to open.

Guillaume de Villaret, the current grandmaster of the Order of Saint John stepped through with a brother close on his heels. The brother's hood was up, putting his face in shadows, but Foulques recognized him instantly. For the last time he had seen that flattened nose, it had been darker than it was now. Much darker.

Guillaume, excited with his ability to gain an audience with the king in these trying times, was three full strides into the room before his keen mind registered the identity of its occupants. His eyes took in the room, touched on the red tunics, and when they spotted Foulques, they did not move again.

"Thank you for escorting me, Brother Reynald," Guillaume said. "You may leave us now."

Reynald, who had almost run his flat nose into the back of his master's head, was not so quick to assess his environment. But then he saw Foulques and the situation became clear as a full sun winter's day. He whirled on his heel to exit the room.

But Pirmin stepped forward, ducked his head to avoid banging it on the stone lintel, and slowly eased the door shut. He turned and faced Reynald, stopping him in mid stride, for when Pirmin stood in front of a door, that door ceased to exist.

"Hello, Uncle," Foulques said.

Guillaume saw he had but one direction to go so he continued on into the room until he stood before King Henry's desk. He bowed to the king and then turned to Foulques.

"Welcome home, nephew. I see God has answered my prayers and brought you back to us unharmed."

"The journey was longer than I had hoped," Foulques said, holding his uncle's gaze.

"Any news from the Mongols?"

"Nothing you want to hear, I am afraid."

"Master Guillaume," Henry said, not even attempting to leave his chair. "There have been some serious accusations leveled. I have called you here so we can get to the bottom of them together."

"Of course, Your Majesty. What can I do to help?" Outwardly, his uncle was calm, but Foulques could sense the turmoil roiling just below the surface where no one could see.

"Bring forth the witness," Henry said.

Stephanos the Greek stepped forward, hat in hand. His unruly eagle's nest of gray hair looking like it could be hiding a handful of unhatched eggs in it at that very moment. He leveled a thick finger at Reynald.

"Aye, that is the man, Your Grace. I would not forget his face if the devil himself told me to do it."

"Your Majesty? What is going on here?" Guillaume asked.

"If you will," Henry said to Stephanos, "please repeat your testimony."

The Greek let out a high-pitched sigh and looked at his feet. "If I have to, Your Grace. Though it chills me to the bone to think on it even in the light of day." He did not start speaking again until Henry waved him on.

"After I fled the unholy wrath of the Mamluks at Acre, I had nowhere to sleep here on Cyprus. So I would sneak into the waterfront stables at night. That is when I saw it."

"Saw what, exactly?" Guillaume asked.

"That man. Him and two others dressed like him. They had a goat."

"A goat?" Reynald said, unable to contain himself.

"And what were they doing with this animal?" King Henry coaxed him on impatiently.

"Well, his two friends flipped that goat on its back and held it tight. Then, this here man went down on all fours and he... he..."

"I know this is not easy, but continue," Foulques said.

"That man, before my very eyes, well, he began to suckle that goat."

"This is ridiculous!" Reynald shouted.

"Be quiet," Guillaume said.

"Now, Your Grace, understand I am no country man, or farmer, or any such thing," Stephanos wrung his hat in his hands, "but I am fair certain that was a boy goat."

Vignolo gasped. "I missed that part from your earlier testimony."

"He lies! I have never been to the waterfront stables and I have never seen this man before in my life! What are you trying to do here?"

"Did anyone besides yourself witness these heinous acts?" Foulques asked.

"Aye, my lord. About a dozen of my closest friends."

"Brother Alain. In our charter, what is the punishment for such a transgression?"

"Complete loss of habit, Admiral Foulques."

Foulques looked at his uncle, who did not so much as twitch. "Sergeants. Defrock this man."

Pirmin and Jimmy stepped forward and grabbed Reynald, who suddenly was as game as a cornered rat. He threw a punch that bounced off Pirmin's chest like it was an ale barrel. Pirmin grabbed him by the throat and pinned him up against the wall. Reynald managed to call Guillaume's name once before Pirmin clamped down, but after that he was only capable of making hisses and grunts. As Pirmin held him, Jimmy twisted his big fists around Reynald's black robe and jerked downward with a series of vicious yanks and tugs. The robe came away in pieces leaving only the hood portion still on Reynald's head. Jimmy grabbed his hood and ripped it off with a flourish. Then he wound his fist in Reynald's hair and forced him to the ground.

"On your knees, goat-licker! Repent in the name of God!" He cuffed him about the head and kept shouting, "Repent, goat-licker!"

"Brother Jimmy," Foulques said.

Reynald was a sobbing mess on the ground, but Jimmy kept at him. "Repent, I say!" He slapped him again.

"Brother Jimmy! That will be enough."

Jimmy stood up straight, breathing heavily. "Sorry Admiral. Some sins just bother me more than others."

"I can appreciate how you feel," Foulques said. "Now remove this man from our presence and round up his fellow conspirators."

"Can we de-frock them, Admiral?"

"Absolutely," Foulques said. "Brother Alain, go with the sergeants to make sure the experience is not unnecessarily traumatic. For anyone."

Once they dragged the half-naked Reynald out of the room, Guillaume spoke for the first time since the ordeal had begun. "You may not believe it, Foulques. But I have never been prouder of you than at this very moment. You have come a long way."

"You are right, uncle. As I said, the journey was long. But it gave me time to think."

"Oh?"

"I decided I was premature in my decision to resign as Admiral of the Order."

"I see," Guillaume said.

"So immediately upon arriving in Cyprus, I came to the king to inform him that I would be keeping my rank and position."

Guillaume smiled. He risked a glance at the king, no doubt trying to determine where his place was in all this. "But an admiral is nothing without ships and men. Both of which the Order does not have the means to support at this time."

"Precisely," Foulques said. "Hence my decision to come see the king first before the grandmaster of my order. I came to ask him if he would not consider returning my men to my command. And he told me something absolutely shocking. Something you could never imagine."

"Which was?"

"We have a usurper in our midst. A snake of the lowest form."

Guillaume's eyes narrowed. He turned to the king. "Your Majesty. Whatever Brother Foulques has told you—"

"*Admiral* Foulques," King Henry corrected him. In that moment Guillaume knew precisely where the king stood.

"You see," Foulques continued. "It seems Prince Amalric has set his covetous eyes upon King Henry's throne. He is at this very moment organizing to overthrow his own brother.

As you can well imagine, I was dismayed to hear this and immediately offered to help. I am pleased to report the king has accepted my offer and we have come to a formal agreement."

Foulques stepped over to the desk and lifted up a long piece of parchment covered in flowing script. He blew on the ink to make sure it was dry.

"You will recognize the king's seal, here." He pointed to a red blob of wax at the bottom of the page. "And next to it is my own clumsy signature as Admiral of the Order." He looked at his uncle. "I seem to have misplaced my own seal."

Guillaume cleared his throat. "And what exactly did you agree to?"

"King Henry has returned the Schwyzers to my command and will provide for their upkeep as long as they, and I, remain in Cyprus. In return, I will use all my resources as Admiral of the Order and acting Knight Marshal of the Order, to defend his throne from any and all pretenders."

"Well done, Brother Foulques," Guillaume said, but his face was not at all congratulatory.

Foulques held up his finger. "Admiral, Uncle. Or if you prefer, Marshal."

"You cannot simply assume the title of commander of all our military forces on a whim. Not without a meeting of the Grand Cross."

"That would be redundant, for I already command the only fighting force we have left. A force I have been training for years, I might add, and one I would readily match against any soldiers Christendom could patch together in these desperate times. Prince Amalric, or anyone else, will rue the day they try and test our mettle."

"Do you threaten a member of the royal family?" Guillaume asked.

"Yes. And anyone else that dares to stand between us and our divine calling to defend the citizens of Christendom. We are at war, Uncle. Do not think for a moment we are not."

Guillaume once again looked to the king. Foulques could see his mind working, grasping at alternatives. He sought an avenue of escape, a ledge he could leap for. "And Your Majesty agrees to all this? That is beyond generous to pay for all these men, all this equipment, for as long as we need? I confess, I did not know the treasury was so robust."

"The terms are there," Henry said, nodding to the agreement still in Foulques's hand. "I am to pay until the Hospitallers leave Cyprus."

Guillaume laughed out loud. He had spotted his ledge and so he leapt. "Leave, Your Majesty? Where in this world can we go?"

Vignolo answered for the king. "The Dodecanese Islands. Rhodes, to be exact."

"Rhodes? What is Rhodes?"

It was Vignolo's turn to produce a document. He handed Guillaume a tube. "It was sure good timing you stopping by here. I was just on my way to see your treasurer. But, as I always say, why give a bill of lading to a clerk when you can press it into the fat, fleshy palm of the man who actually holds the purse?"

"What is this?"

"Sales agreement," Foulques said. "On behalf of the Order, I have purchased an island to serve as our future naval base."

"You did not purchase anything from this pirate," Guillaume said. "I will not allow it."

"Too late," Vignolo said. "Even witnessed by none other than the king."

"Unfortunately, you are right," Foulques said. "This man is an unscrupulous business man and he sold me property with some… encumbrances. It turns out our island has been annexed by the Byzantine Emperor."

Vignolo shrugged. "I thought you knew. Honest omission on my part."

Guillaume shook his head. He clutched at that ledge and managed a tentative finger-hold. "And what do you intend to do about that? Go to war with the Byzantines? They are Christian, for God's sake! The pope would never allow it."

"Oh, he will allow it," Foulques said. "Someone will have to petition him, and it will take time. But the pope has no love for the Archbishop of the orthodox church or the Byzantine emperor. And now that we are the rightful owners of that property he will have just cause. He will not be able to resist this opportunity to butt heads with Constantinople and not come away bloody for a change."

"How far will you go? Will you use that sword of yours on your fellow Christians?" Guillaume pointed to the blade strapped around Foulques's waist and his eyes widened. He recognized the hilt, for it was the family heirloom he himself had given Foulques on the day he was knighted. A sword that Foulques had lost over eight years ago. It was at that exact moment that his tenuous grasp on the ledge failed him, sending him plummeting into an abyss from which there would be no climbing out.

"The people of Rhodes are fishermen, farmers, and sailors. All they want is a fair lord who will guarantee them protection. Who can offer that better than the Knights of Saint John?"

The fight was gone from Guillaume's eyes and his spine had begun to wither into a crescent. "I suppose you will run for grandmaster at some point."

"I will," Foulques said. "But my work as admiral is not yet done. I will strongly suggest to the council, however, that we send our current grandmaster back to France to recruit new members and secure more backing for the future of the Order."

"I meant what I said," Guillaume said. "I am proud of you."

He turned his back on them all and walked slowly toward the door.

EPILOGUE

1309 A.D.
The island of Rhodes in the Aegean Sea

Q UEENS ARE NOT born, they are made. Through some mysterious selection process, slave bees choose a few amongst thousands and begin to feed them royal jelly. Over time, this enriched diet transforms them into much larger, enhanced versions of what they had once been. When they are ready, they grow wings and go out into the world searching for a place to settle and fill with new life. The path they take is difficult, fraught with danger and seemingly insurmountable obstacles. Very few survive.

These thoughts flitted through Najya's mind as her eyes traveled over the land from one end of the lush valley to where she now stood. Olive, carob, and a dizzying assortment of other fruit trees swayed in a gentle breeze on a perfect day. The fresh scent of pine filled the air, along with myrtle and thyme, but from where she stood, the sweet smell of rock roses won out over all others. As it should, Najya thought, for it was from these hardy flowers that the Greeks had given the island its name. She imagined the valley singing with the sound of a million pollinators and it made her heart swell.

There, on her little hill, she turned from the valley and looked out over the Hospitaller army, resplendent in their red tunics and white crosses, standing in formation before the city gates. She spotted Dimitri, her son, and her heart filled again, but with pride this time. Even though he wore a red tunic just like all the other sergeants, the boy was easy to pick out for he stood between the giant Pirmin and Captain Thomas. Foulques had promised to keep him safe. Dimitri was only fourteen but this was an important day, one the boy would remember forever, Foulques had said. He needed to be here.

Further along the road, Najya watched as two figures marched toward one another. When they met, the one who had come from the city bent to one knee and held up his sword. Foulques de Villaret, Grandmaster of the Hospitaller Order of Saint John accepted the sword with both hands and bowed his head. He then placed a placating hand on the city commander's shoulder and raised him up to his feet. Together they walked toward the open gates of the city of Rhodes.

Strong arms encircled her waist and Najya leaned back against her husband's chest. Gruffydd's heart beat as quickly as her own, for it was not just their son's future they saw, it was theirs as well. Rhodes was the home they had all been searching for. This moment had been made possible by the will of one man, though he would deny it to his grave. It was all part of God's great plan, he would say. But Najya knew better. Without Foulques de Villaret none of them would be standing here today, of that she had no doubt.

But nature connects us all and Najya knew that she had played no small part in the making of the man. God may have provided the direction, but she was the one with the key, the one who had opened the door and released him out into the world.

AUTHOR'S NOTE

Rhodes is a lush, fertile island in the Aegean Sea that is forty-five miles long and twenty miles wide at some points. It is next to a series of smaller islands known collectively as the Dodecanese. Eventually, the Hospitallers would control most of these and use them as a concentric line of defenses, much like the outer walls of a castle.

The Hospitaller Order of Saint John and its Genoese allies landed on the shores of Rhodes in 1307. It would take two full years before the Rhodians would surrender their city, and thereby, their island. But surprisingly, very little blood was spilled over the entire campaign. The knights took a series of outposts by trickery or bribery, with one local legend even saying they used Ulysses's trick of sneaking inside the walls of one fort under the cover of sheepskins.

The Rhodians were orthodox Greeks and made their living by farming, fishing, and at least some pirating of the nearby Muslim trade routes. This was, of course, not a one-sided relationship. The seaside hamlets of Rhodes, as well as many of the other nearby islands, were themselves often the victims of frequent raids by Muslim pirates, for the islands had much to offer. Rhodes had been known since classical times for its fine wine. Another island was famed for its beautiful women and was often seen by the Muslims as a good source of slaves. So, in the end, the Rhodians were probably not too unhappy to have the Hospitallers as their lords and protectors. The renowned shipbuilders would have plenty of work, the seaside villages their protectors, and the entire economy would benefit from the constant stream of funds sent to the islands by the Hospitaller estates in countries such as France, Spain, and England.

No one knows for sure what the Rhodians thought of their new masters, for history is always written by the victors, but at least the knights were Christians and keen to rid the waters of their Muslim enemies, pirate or not. In fact, to Muslim eyes, the Hospitallers were the new pirates operating in the Aegean. To a Muslim merchant, the sight of a ship flying a flag with a white cross on a field of black, appearing out of nowhere from behind one of the many Dodecanese islands, would have been terrifying. It was the skull and crossbones of the day.

In the same year the Hospitallers were landing on the beaches of Rhodes, a different war was underway in France. On Friday, the 13th of October, 1307, King Phillip IV ordered the arrests of dozens of Templar Knights, including their grandmaster, Jacques de Molay. Some people like to claim this is where our modern fears of Friday the 13th come from, but I have not found any reliable source documents to support this.

It seems that King Phillip had borrowed a lot of funds from the Templars and he decided to file his own version of medieval bankruptcy, one in which the borrower not only refuses to pay his debts, but also throws the lender in a dungeon to keep the torturers gainfully employed. Phillip no doubt also had his eyes set on the many rich estates owned by the "Poor Fellow-Soldiers of Christ" throughout France. Of course, the Templars also owned estates in Spain, England, and Germany, but Phillip could do little about those.

The Templar Grandmaster Jacques de Molay would remain in a dungeon in France for years, until he was eventually burned at the stake in 1314, along with two of his subordinates. Where was the pope in all this, you might ask? Well, he wrote a couple of letters asking Phillip to calm down, but other than that he did nothing until 1312 when he officially dissolved the Templar Order.

Enough has been written about the fall of the Templars that it hardly needs repeating here. But there are a couple of points that bear emphasizing. Firstly, the bulk of their wealth, the fabled Templar treasure, was never found. Secondly, for all his efforts, King Phillip of France never did officially gain control of the Templar estates in France. Through some mysterious machinations, the pope decreed that all Templar properties in all countries, and all the associated earnings that went with them, were to be given to the Hospitaller Order of Saint John.

So if only the Templar grandmaster and a few of his brethren were burned at the stake, what happened to the thousands of other knights in the Templar order? Many gave up the cross, went back to their noble families, and resumed their knightly duties. A few joined the ranks of the German Teutonic Knights and went on crusade in eastern Europe. Many of the sergeants became men-at-arms for lords and kings, and a few joined the ranks of the Hospitallers.

When Acre fell in 1291, Europe had already turned its eyes away from Jerusalem. The crusading will was gone, the Christians had lost their hold upon the Holy Land and been cast back into the sea. But a small force of Christians, beaten and ravaged by their enemies, would crawl up onto a rock in the Aegean and continue the fight to reclaim their lost lands from the Infidel. They would be "the bone caught in the throat of Islam" for many generations to come.

ABOUT THE AUTHOR

J. K. Swift lives in a log house deep in the forests of central British Columbia, Canada. When he is not busy cutting wood to survive the winter, he spends his free time feeding his chickens, shoveling horse manure, making mead, shooting longbows, roasting coffee, and writing historical fiction and fantasy.

website:

jkswift.com

...a message from the author:

Thank you very much for reading my work. Reviews and

personal recommendations from readers like you are the most important way for relatively unknown authors to attract more readers, so I truly am grateful to anyone who takes the time to rate my work and leave a review. You leaving a review or telling a friend about one of my stories is the best way you can help me write more books. To see what I'm working on next, please visit me at jkswift.com.

Thanks very much!

All the best,
JK.

Sign up for the **New Releases Mailing List** (http://eepurl.com/hTAFA). Your information will never be shared and you will **only** receive notifications when J. K. Swift publishes something new.

Printed in Great Britain
by Amazon